Out of Focus

Center Point
Large Print

Also by Nancy Naigle and available from
Center Point Large Print:

The Adams Grove Series
  Sweet Tea and Secrets

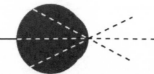

**This Large Print Book carries the
Seal of Approval of N.A.V.H.**

Out of Focus

An Adams Grove Novel

NANCY NAIGLE

CENTER POINT LARGE PRINT
THORNDIKE, MAINE

This Center Point Large Print edition
is published in the year 2015 by arrangement with
Amazon Publishing, www.apub.com.

Originally published in the United States
by Amazon Publishing, 2011.

The text of this Large Print edition is unabridged.
In other aspects, this book may vary
from the original edition.
Printed in the United States of America
on permanent paper.
Set in 16-point Times New Roman type.

ISBN: 978-1-62899-765-1

Library of Congress Cataloging-in-Publication Data

Naigle, Nancy.
  Out of focus : an Adams Grove novel / Nancy Naigle. — Center Point
Large Print edition.
    pages cm
  ISBN 978-1-62899-765-1 (hardcover : alk. paper)
  1. Photographers—Fiction. 2. Missing children—Fiction.
    3. Large type books. I. Title.
PS3614.A545O95 2015
813'.6—dc23
                                                    2015033509

This book is for anyone whose life
has taken an unexpected turn.
Always trust your heart and have faith.

Chapter One

Kasey Phillips snapped off three more pictures of the country singer straddling seven hundred pounds of sleek American-made motorcycle. Cody Tuggle looked more rugged than the Virginia Blue Ridge Mountains that swelled in the background.

At her command, Tuggle leaned forward across the wide chrome handlebars. Even with the bandanna tied around his head like a do-rag, a look she'd never found appealing, there was no denying this guy was sizzling hot and all man.

Kasey's eyes narrowed as she leaned to get a unique angle. The estate was the perfect setting for this magazine shoot. It belonged to Cody's agent, Arty Max. From the looks of the place, Tuggle's fame had paid off big for everyone.

Band members and roadies lined the perimeter, but she stayed focused on her subject. Curious onlookers were one of the biggest obstacles at an outdoor shoot, but it was easy to tune them out when the subject was someone with such star quality.

Working with the light and shadows, she repositioned to find the right interplay to intensify the image. The camera clicked at a fast clip, and then not at all, as she considered the next best opportunity.

Click. Click. Click-click-click.

"I thought this was supposed to be hard work," Cody said, pulling her out of her zone. "Those bikini models are always complaining about it on TV." Laughter laced his voice. "Y'know, that fanny duster job, dusting the sand off those cuties' hind ends. Now that looks like a right sweet gig. Got any connections?"

Kasey lowered her camera. "You mean, in case the singing thing doesn't work out for you?" She gave him a scolding look. As the mom of a three-year-old, she'd pretty much perfected it. "If you keep talking I'll catch you with your mouth wide open, and you'll look dopey. Shhhsh."

"That must be why I always look drunk in those tabloids." Cody flashed a devilish smile. "Anybody ever tell you, you're kinda bossy?"

"I got both of those shots," she warned. "Those weekly gossip rags pay big bucks for celeb uglies. The uglier they are, the more they pay. They'd pay top dollar for those last two pictures."

"You wouldn't."

"You're right." She raised her hand in front of her like a traffic cop. "Stay still. Yeah. Right there." A perfect shot. The candy-apple red Harley was only feet away from the black fence that surrounded the estate. Light swept through a stand of birch trees in the distance, their thin white-barked trunks making the colors appear more vibrant and crisp. The forest displayed a myriad of green shades now. Those leaves would boast orange, yellow, reds and purples in the fall as the chlorophyll faded and autumn arrived—an awesome display to capture on film.

Cody spoke to someone just behind her.

She shot him *the look*.

"What? It's hard to sit still this long and not say a word." Cody rewarded her with a natural smile. She took advantage of it, snapping the image.

Kasey enjoyed the gentle sparring. "What's the problem? You got ants in your pants? You said this modeling stuff was so easy, but all I've heard for the past thirty minutes is a bunch of girly complaining."

"Hey now, be nice. Girly? Me? You're gonna hurt my feelin's."

The roadies and band members nudged one another.

"Somehow I doubt that." Kasey watched the star's smile fade into an exaggerated pout. He might be used to women falling at his feet, but she wasn't one of his groupies. "Did I bruise your frail ego?" *What a ham.* "Maybe it's that silly rag on your head makin' you all girly."

She couldn't help herself. The man in front of her was huge, at least six foot four, with shoulders so broad the wide-set handlebars on the motor-cycle didn't look nearly as impressive. This guy could wear a pink tutu and look masculine.

The band members and roadies seemed to enjoy the banter, but she wasn't sure whom they were rooting for—Cody or her.

Cody sat up straight on the bike, his smile gone. He pulled the bandanna off and ran his fingers through his flattened mass of blond hair.

She took in a quick breath. *Maybe that last comment* had *crossed a line.* She knew the do-rag was symbolic to the band, but then if her jab got him to quit mugging around, it would be worth it. She'd get the best shots of the day.

His hair bounced back into its usual tangle of waves, softening his chiseled look. He stuffed the slip of fabric into his back pocket with a half grin, maybe just short of a smirk.

Kasey clicked like mad. "Now we're talking."

Cody tugged open the snaps of his western shirt.

She switched cameras and gave him a nod of encouragement. Tuggle's PR guys had left last night. She called the shots now. Just the way she liked it. This was all Cody.

His tan accentuated his chest. Flawless. He didn't have a soft, white-collar body. This was the body of a guy who enjoyed getting physical.

"Looking right manly now, Mr. Tuggle." Her heart and soul belonged to Nick, but staring at Cody Tuggle for hours at a time was no punishment.

"Mr. Tuggle? Why is it the less I'm wearin'

the more business you get?" He stepped off the motorcycle in one easy movement and took a step in her direction.

"Quit it, you big flirt." She took another picture. "I'm married." She wiggled her ring finger in his direction.

Kasey glanced at her watch. It was almost nine. "Let's take five." She walked to a table nearby, pulled her phone from her hip and dialed home. Every day on the road, at nine o'clock sharp each morning, there was nothing more important than checking in with Nick and Jake. She loved her work, but they were the light of each day, and three days in a row of not being with them was torture.

With her back to Cody and the others, she talked to Nick. He caught her up on their plan for the day. She checked her watch again, then forced herself to wrap up the call. "Love, love, love you boys."

"I love you ten and five, Mom." Jake's tiny voice made her heart bubble. Ten and five was the biggest number in the world to him.

"Love you, babe. See you at the other end of the day," Nick said and hung up.

A familiar surge of happiness consumed her. She couldn't wait to be home with them. She and Nick had wed just a few months after they'd met. It was a marriage made in heaven, and Jake was the icing on the wedding cake. That little angel was the best thing she'd ever done in her life.

She snapped her phone shut and headed back to the shoot. "Let's go, guys."

Tuggle turned his attention back to her. "Call home to check in with Mr. Phillips?"

"Not exactly. Phillips is my maiden name." She switched to her digital camera for the final run. "But yes. I was checking in at home."

"That dude's one lucky guy."

"Two, actually."

Cody leaned forward and lowered his voice. "Two? I bet number one doesn't think much of that."

"Funny." She wrinkled her nose. "Husband and son."

"You had me worried there for a minute."

She lowered the camera. "Nick and Jake. Jake's three, and the most adorable child. Not that I'm biased."

"Got his momma's good looks, did he?" Cody smiled a perfect smile, the kind he wasn't good at performing on demand. "You know I'm just playing around, right?"

Kasey captured one last shot, ignoring the remark. "You're done." She lifted the camera strap over her head and wiped her palms on her jeans. "I've got what I need."

"I was just getting into it." He struck an Egyptian pose. Everyone howled and cheered.

"You're too much." She tucked the cameras

into her case. "Give me a couple of hours and I'll let you and Arty take a look."

"Great. We'll be down at my guesthouse."

Over the past two days, she'd walked every path that wound through the estate. There were eight guesthouses in all. Each one named after a different star Arty Max represented. Over the years, he'd done quite well spotting raw talent and nurturing it to the ultimate reward.

Kasey made short work of processing the morning shots. She'd driven her RV to this shoot. It was the best investment she'd ever made. Not only could she develop film the old-fashioned way when it was called for, but she had a computer system to edit and crop the digital shots on site, and high-quality print capabilities.

She gathered the proofs and went to meet with Cody and Arty. On her way, perfect orange and yellow rose blossoms caught her eye. Roses always made her think of her wedding day. One of her best memories ever, second only to the day she'd had Jake.

A light breeze pushed her hair across her shoulders. She lifted her chin to enjoy the warm sun on her face. The low eighties here in the mountains was a relief compared to the blazing heat at home on the Virginia coast in August.

Cody and Arty sat at a wrought iron table on the front porch of the guesthouse. Arty's wiry arms moved in wide, exaggerated movements. Cody sat back in his chair, twisting a cloth napkin between thick fingers, looking a little bored.

Kasey flipped the folder against her thigh as she walked within earshot. "Am I interrupting?"

Arty stopped mid-sentence.

Kasey's glance connected with Cody's just long enough to make her breathing stutter.

Cody jumped up and pulled a chair out for her. "Naw. Join us."

Kasey sat, hooking her feet around the legs of the chair, and placed the proofs on the table. "The extra morning shoot produced the best pictures."

Cody flipped through them. "Damn, you make me look pretty good."

"It was a *really* tough job." Kasey tried to look serious.

Arty made approving sounds as he looked through the pictures. When he finished, he tapped the folder on the table and leaned toward her. "These are incredible. No one has ever caught Cody on film like this."

"I'm glad you're pleased, Mr. Max. I enjoyed it." Kasey extended her hand and stood to her full height of five foot three. Standing, she was barely taller than Cody, and he was still sitting. "I'm heading home. I promised my boys I'd be there this afternoon."

"Wait." Arty bounced to his feet. "You have to

shoot Cody's tour. I've been after him for two years to do a tour picture book."

Cody turned from Arty to face Kasey. "It's true. He's relentless."

"It would sell millions." Arty shook a proof under Cody's nose. "Pictures like these could bring your tour to life in a book. You have to agree."

Cody looked at the proof for a moment. "Yeah. You know, you might be on to something there, man." He looked to Kasey and lowered his voice. "Help me out here, girl. Get him off my case. If you can do that, I'll owe you big." He pretended to beg.

"You're too funny." Kasey waved and turned to leave. "Thanks again."

Cody's chair screeched. "No, seriously. Wait. We want *you*." He stepped off the veranda to the walkway. "Come out on the road with us. I never liked the idea of some stranger hanging out with us, but you fit right in."

She froze, then turned back to face them. "You're serious?" The two of them looked like bobble-head dolls the way they nodded in unison.

This could be big. Huge. It could also mean fewer jobs on the road next year so she could spend more time with Jake and Nick. And it would keep her name out there, which was getting harder now that she'd cut back on the number of shoots she accepted. It was a tricky trade-off.

Her heart skipped a beat, but she managed to keep it in perspective. "No. I can't. I'm married and have a young son at home. I'm very selective about what I do these days. I'd be happy to refer someone."

"Naw, that wouldn't work." Cody shook his head.

Arty slumped and ran his hand through his hair.

"Tell ya what." Cody took a card from his wallet. "Call me if you change your mind. The tour doesn't gear up for a few weeks. You wouldn't have to be gone long. We'll email you the schedule. You can even pick the city dates you want to shoot."

"Cody, there are a hundred photographers who could do this gig." She laughed. "And a million single women who'd kill for it."

"This isn't a come-on, if that's what you think. I'm not the horn-dog the gossip rags make me out to be."

She knew better than to believe everything in the tabloids, but it was hard not to believe some of it. Eyeing him cautiously, she said, "I don't like to be away from Nick and Jake for that long. This kind of commitment takes time."

"Bring them with you. I'll cover their expenses, too." He looked flustered. "I'm serious. I respect you. I'm comfortable with you, so are the guys, and you're hell with a camera. I'll do that project with you, but no one else."

She took the card and rubbed her thumb across the raised letters. Four years ago she would've packed up and hit the road, but her life was different now.

"Thank you. I'll think about it, but changing my mind would be a first, because I never do." She waved as she left.

"Never say never," he called after her.

Kasey knew her best friend, Riley, would be giving her the same speech right about now if she'd been there.

Never say never, and never tempt fate.

Chapter Two

Usually the ride home seemed longer than the ride to a location shoot, but today, as Kasey sang to the radio, the time passed as fast as the trees in her rearview mirror. It was hard to keep from speeding when she was anxious to get home. She eased up on the accelerator, coasting back to the speed limit.

Her mind drifted back to the idea of photographing Cody Tuggle's tour. The exposure would be good. Experience told her that she could probably get all the shots she needed in a few dates in key cities if she planned it right. She and Nick had talked about taking Jake to Sea World this year. *Maybe we could turn this opportunity into a work vacation combo.* It was worthy of a discussion.

"Making memories." Just saying Nick's favorite words made her smile, and she loved making them with him.

On autopilot, she turned down the lane that led home. The road to the Rocking R Farm ran parallel to their property. With road frontage of over a mile, she couldn't see their farmhouse until she got past the second curve.

Nick's truck wasn't there. Disappointment swept over her as she pulled into the driveway.

She grabbed her bags and headed for the house. On a bright note, maybe she had time to whip up a quick surprise for them now. It wouldn't take but a minute to throw some of those pre-formed chocolate chip cookies on a tray and get them in the oven. Even *she* could pull off that level of baking.

Dutch, their black lab, greeted her with a yawn but didn't bother to get up from the living room rug. She dropped her bags right in the middle of the hall and tossed her purse on the couch. She dashed to the kitchen to get started on the treats, patting Dutch on the head as she zipped by.

Just as she slid the cookie sheet into the oven, she heard a vehicle pull into the driveway.

"Perfect timing." She set the timer to reduce the chance she'd ruin the cookies. Not that it was any guarantee. She'd burned so many meals Jake

18

thought the smoke alarm was the dinner bell. He and Nick never let her live that down, but it hadn't improved her cooking any.

Dutch barked.

"C'mon boy. I'm excited, too." She hurdled the suitcase she'd left in the middle of the foyer and opened the door.

"Oh!" Kasey halted, nose to nose with a stranger in her doorway. "Excuse me." She took a step back.

A man in a suit stared at her with his hand still in the air, mid-knock. "Mrs. Rolly?"

"Kasey Phillips, but yes, I'm Mrs. Rolly." She looked over the man's shoulder. Only a blue sedan. No sign of Nick's truck. "I was expecting . . . Never mind. Can I help you?"

Dutch pushed his nose between the door and the jamb, imposing himself between the stranger and Kasey.

"I'm Officer Thomas with the Virginia Beach Police Department." The man handed her his business card, then flashed a police badge. "May I come in?"

"It's okay, boy. Dutch, go lie down." Kasey read the card. "Of course. What can I do for you?" She glanced at the card again. "Officer Thomas." She motioned him into the living room.

He stepped inside, but remained standing.

Kasey gripped the arm of a chair and lowered herself into it. "Is something wrong?"

"Are you the wife of Nicholas Rolly?"

Anxiety bit at Kasey's nerves. She couldn't even nod. "Yes," she answered, but it sounded more like a question.

"I'm sorry, ma'am." He paused, his eyes avoiding hers. "There's been an accident."

"An accident?" She leaned forward. Icy fear prickled her skin. *This only happens in the movies.*

"Yes ma'am." Officer Thomas shifted his weight from one leg to the other. "At about 11:15 this morning we received an accident report of a truck going off the road into the river, and a separate report of gunshots on Route 58. We aren't certain if the two are connected."

The words replayed in her mind. Slowly, like translating a foreign language, then a wave of concern consumed her.

"I'm sorry to deliver this news."

Kasey grabbed the arm of the chair. The room swirled around her. "He's going to be okay, right?"

"I'm sorry, Mrs. Rolly. Your husband didn't survive the crash."

"No. It can't . . . Nick?" Her heart pounded too fast, and her brain buffered everything around her.

"His body is at Southeastern Virginia Medical Center. Investigations are still underway to determine the cause of the accident."

She swallowed with difficulty, then found her voice. "What about Jake?"

His brows flickered a little. He looked uncertain

as he tapped the keys on an electronic device for information. "There were no other passengers—"

From that point, the officer's lips moved, but his words didn't register. "No. My Nick wasn't alone. You've made a mistake." She raised her hand to quiet him. "Where's my son? This doesn't make sense. Where did you say they were?"

"Traveling east on Route 58, not far from I-95 and Emporia. The vehicle, the registration and ID all match."

She rubbed her palms against her jeans and let out a long breath.

"My husband was on the Eastern Shore this morning, and he had Jake with him. It can't be him." She twisted her wedding rings, letting them glide up and down her finger. "Thank God," she whispered into folded hands.

His tone was apologetic. "We're careful with this information."

"No." She hugged her arms to her. "It can't be. Not on Route 58. That's too far out of the way." She pushed her shaking hands into her lap and took a deep breath. "I'm telling you there's been a mistake. Nick's an excellent driver. He's very careful. And he'd never leave without Jake. They're fine." Kasey moved to the edge of the seat. "I just spoke to him this morning."

"When did you expect him back?"

Stress lined the man's face. She forced herself to look away.

"We just talked at nine this morning. I was on a photo shoot." She chewed on her bottom lip. "I expected they'd be here when I got home."

"I'm sorry. I'll connect you with the officer in charge of the case for details. Meanwhile, I can offer you a ride to identify the body."

She recoiled. "Identify? No, I'm not going anywhere with you."

He paused. "Is there someone I can call for you?"

She glared at the officer. "Nick. You can call Nick, because this is a mistake. He's fine. Do you hear me?" Kasey snapped her head up, meeting the officer eye to eye. She gathered her composure and stood. "I don't need comforting. They are just fine." She went to the front window and pushed the curtains to the side. The country lane was empty. "Officer Thomas, I think you should leave."

"Ma'am?" He called after her as she stepped from the front window toward the hall.

She spun around. "I know you're doing your job, but this time you're wrong. Nick wouldn't have been on Route 58, and he wouldn't have been alone. I'm telling you there is a mistake. Why aren't you listening to me?" Kasey grabbed her cell phone from her handbag, punched speed dial to Nick's cell and waited for him to answer. "I'm calling him." She redirected her stare at the officer as the first ring sounded on the other end.

Officer Thomas held her gaze.

The phone rang a third time—no answer.

The room shrank around her. A loud hum filtered the sound from the phone. Her heart beat so hard it constricted her breathing. Nick always answered his cell phone. Even when he was on the tractor he put it on vibrate. There had never been a time she'd dialed his number since the day they'd met that he hadn't answered.

Pick up.

Ring.

Please, answer.

"Voice mail." She mouthed the words, and her jaw went slack.

Officer Thomas must have predicted the next move because he was already at her side, to steady her, as her knees gave way. He reached for the phone as she shouted into it.

"Nick. Nick, it's me. Where are you, honey? Why aren't you answering? Please?" She knelt or fell. She wasn't sure which. "Oh. God. No."

Officer Thomas caught the phone mid-air as it fell from her hand.

"Who can I contact? A family member? A friend?" He released her as she settled back into the chair. He closed the phone and placed it on the table. "I'm sorry, Mrs. Rolly."

"How can this be happening? Where's Jake?" Kasey pulled her hands to her chest. She opened and closed her fists, as if to pump her lungs to make herself breathe. "Why is this happening to me?" She glanced at the clock on the wall. It showed 4:11, like 4-1-1 for information. This was information she wished she wasn't getting. She slumped forward as reality struck, clutching her heart, tears streaming down her cheeks.

The buzz of the oven timer broke the silence in the room.

The cookies.

Thankful for a reason to flee the room, Kasey shot straight up in her chair, then to her feet to escape this man and his message.

She punched the buzzer on the oven to silence it. The smell of the warm chocolate chip cookies only made her cry more as she slid the metal baking sheet on top of the stove. She leaned forward on the kitchen counter, breathing in the smell of better memories, hoping to push the terror out of her mind. If she had come home yesterday as originally planned, would this be happening right now?

Kasey edged toward the doorway to the living room praying it would be empty, and that she'd imagined all of it. If Nick and Jake were gone, she prayed God would take her, too. She pulled her shirt tight across the front of her, suddenly chilled despite the hot August temperatures.

"Mrs. Rolly, who do you want me to contact?" Officer Thomas opened her cell phone and clicked through the directory. "You have numbers for

Grandma Emily, Riley Randals, Dean Zander . . ."

He didn't mention Nick, though she knew there were entries for him at home, at the barn and for his cell. Her chest burned. A moan escaped as she choked while trying to gulp air. Tears streamed along her cheeks and settled in her fists. Kasey opened her hands and rubbed her fingers across her eyes.

"Riley." Her voice strained. "Call Riley."

Officer Thomas punched keys on the phone and headed to the hallway. Kasey heard him ask for Riley, overheard him explain the situation, and then the phone snapped closed.

"She's on her way, Mrs. Rolly. I'll stay with you until she arrives."

"Thank you. She's just up the street." Why was she being polite? *Thank you?* She wasn't thankful for him at all. This man had just unraveled her world. She lowered her head to avoid looking at him. She couldn't bear it. "Jake. Where are you, baby?"

The front door burst open without a knock. Kasey jumped to her feet, wishing for Nick to saunter through the front door with Jake on his hip to set everything right again. The spark of hope vanished.

"Kasey?" Riley raced to Kasey's side and held her. "I'm here. What happened?"

Kasey's voice trembled. "I don't know. I can't really . . . He was shot in a car crash?" She ran her

25

hand across her nose and tear-stained cheeks. "I don't know. It's some kind of mistake. You've got to help me." She turned into Riley's arms.

"Shot in a car crash? Which was it? He was shot, or in a car crash?" Riley asked Kasey, and looked to the officer for help.

"I . . . I don't . . ." She slumped forward, releasing control into Riley's capable hands.

Riley wrapped her arms around Kasey, and then directed her gaze to the officer. "Thank you for calling me. What exactly happened?"

"When police arrived on the scene, Mr. Rolly's vehicle was in the river. Witnesses heard a loud series of shots just before the vehicle swerved off the road, making impact with several trees. The truck flipped, then careened into the river below. It was clear the driver . . ." Officer Thomas took a deep breath. "He didn't survive. Investigations are underway to determine the chain of events."

"Shots fired?" Riley pressed her hand over her heart. "And Jake? What about Jake?"

"No one else was in the truck, ma'am."

Kasey's tears flowed, but her voice was strong and steady. "We have to find him." She grabbed for Riley's arm, her eyes pleading for one shred of hope.

"Jake's her son. He's three." Riley pointed to the picture on the table of Nick and Jake.

"There was no sign of a car seat to suggest a child was in the vehicle at the time of impact.

Could he be at a sitter's, or with a family member?"

"Oh, my God, my baby. Where is he?" Kasey cried into her fists. "This can't be happening."

"We'll find him." Riley turned to face the officer. "Nick never leaves Jake behind."

"I'll call it in to the investigating team right now." He turned his back and made a call.

The room fell silent except for the sound of the policeman talking to the investigating unit.

The loss hung heavy.

Officer Thomas approached them. "They have the information. They're stepping up a search for your son."

"My husband is an investigator," Riley explained. "You might know him. Perry Von? Who can he call to get all the details?"

The officer took a business card from his chest pocket and scribbled some information on the back. "I'll be happy to assist in any way. We're going to need someone to identify the body." He extended the card to Riley. "This is the name of the lead officer. I'm really sorry for your loss."

"Me too." Riley's voice quivered. "Me too." She licked her dry lips. "My husband will identify the body for her." Riley turned to the officer. "I heard something on the news about some shots on that stretch of road a few weeks back."

He nodded and said, "An older couple from

here in Virginia Beach. They were shaken up, but no injuries."

"That's the one. Was this in that same area? Do you think there's a connection?" asked Riley.

"It's early in the investigation. I'd hate to speculate."

"I understand. I guess living with an investigator rubs off on you." Riley flipped the card in her hands.

She showed the officer to the door.

Kasey rocked, hands to chest, eyes closed—praying.

Her words came out just above a whisper. "Please, please, Lord, don't do this. I need Nick." Her breath caught, choked by the tears. "Where's my Jake?" She swept the tears away with trembling fingers.

Riley knelt beside her. "I'm calling your grand-mother. I bet Nick left Jake with her." She stroked Kasey's back. "Breathe, honey. I'm right here," she said as she dialed. On the fifth ring, the old woman picked up the phone. "Hi, Grandma Emily. It's me, Riley. I expected Jeremy to answer."

"He's got the day off. Again," Grandma Emily complained. "Good to hear from you. When are you coming to visit? It's been too long, dear."

"I know. I need to get over there. It's overdue, I know. By the way, is Jake spending the day with you? I have something for him."

"No? Why would you think that?"

"Oh, you know me. I must've gotten the dates confused. Sorry to bother you," Riley said as she disconnected the call and rushed back to Kasey's side. "Where else could Jake be? He's not with your grandmother. I didn't tell her about Nick. I figured that could wait."

Kasey shook her head and stared off. "I don't know. Nick never leaves Jake behind. You know that."

"I know, but he has to be somewhere."

"Jake was with Nick when I talked to them at nine. Nick would never lie to me. He wouldn't. There is no other explanation."

"But there was no car seat." Riley moved in closer to Kasey. "You know how cautious Nick is. He'd never have Jake in the truck without the car seat."

"Maybe it came loose. I don't know, but what I do know is that Jake needs me. I can't explain it, but I can feel it. We've got to get out there."

"Do you think that's a good idea? Detectives are working the scene. I'll have Von get in the loop and make sure they're doing everything possible to find Jake in case he's out there."

Kasey drew on inner strength. "I need to be there. I have an eye for detail. I might see something they didn't. I have to find Jake." She ran her sleeve across her face to dry her eyes, then grabbed the keys out of her purse.

"What are you doing?"

"I'm *not* going to just sit here." Kasey stood, her chin held high. "I'm going to find my son."

Riley got her phone out of her purse. "You're in no shape to drive. Neither am I. I'm calling Von. He'll take us."

Perry Von jumped in his truck and headed to Nick and Kasey's house, less than a mile away. Riley had given him the information she had, and he'd called the lead officer on the case as he drove. They didn't have much more to share at this point.

The news echoed in his thoughts. He and Nick had been childhood friends. Losing him was like losing a brother, and it tore at his gut. He knew what Kasey was getting ready to face. Deidre's murder was ten years in the past, and his life had moved on, but the blow of that loss still held power. His focus needed to be on Kasey.

Before he could remove the key from the ignition, Riley and Kasey took the porch steps two at a time toward him. Riley jumped in the front seat and leaned in to give him a kiss as Kasey climbed into the back.

"Kasey. I can't believe it. I'm so sorry." He reached over the seat and gave her hand a squeeze.

"Me, either." Kasey slapped the back of his seat. "Don't worry about me. Just drive. Quick. Jake needs us. This can't be happening." She secured her seatbelt. "Hurry!"

Chapter Three

They rode in silence to the scene of the accident nearly eighty miles away. With just ten miles to go, traffic came to a complete stop on Route 58.

Kasey clutched the seatbelt in anticipation. "Can we walk?"

"I'll get off here and take the side road," Von said as he whipped the SUV onto the grass to get to the next exit. He sped down the single lane road and then got back on the interstate closer to their destination, then drove on the shoulder the rest of the way to the scene. He parked his red Yukon behind the row of police and rescue vehicles.

Blue lights bounced across the lanes, bright against the dimming day. Flares kept the small trickle of traffic from the local roads off to the far lane. Officers waved on the rubberneckers in an attempt to keep the traffic moving past the yellow tape that marked off the section of road before the overpass that spanned the Nottoway River.

Kasey jumped from the backseat and ran for the railing with her camera in hand. A police officer caught her by the arm. Her body swung past him, then recoiled like a bungee. She tugged hard, trying to free herself from his grip. Von ran up behind her. He wrapped his arms around her to calm her.

Von said to the officer, "She's the victim's wife."

The officer took a step back. "I'm sorry. I can't let you get any closer than this for now. You'll have to stay behind the marked area, and I'll need some identification." He waved to another officer, who hustled over to his side carrying a clipboard.

Von gave the man their identification.

Kasey stepped toward the whipping tape. She clutched her hands near her heart and peered over the guardrail. The water rushed and sloshed against the truck in the middle of the rocky bed.

Her heart seized when she caught sight of the one-of-a-kind farm sticker on the back window. It was definitely Nick's truck.

She lifted her camera and clicked off several pictures. Through the camera's lens, she'd see things later that she couldn't absorb now. She snapped another picture then let the camera swing from the strap around her neck. *Is this camera all I have left? Nick, Jake, what more could I lose? This can't be happening. It wouldn't be fair.*

Von reached for her hand and gave it a squeeze.

She noticed something dipping in and out of the water near the truck. She lifted her camera to snap a picture, then turned back into Von's arms, pointing to Nick's ball cap bobbing in the water.

Riley ran to them and wrapped her arms around Kasey, too.

The truck was in bad shape. It was little wonder anyone could have survived that crash. The big truck sat twisted, cocked to one side, half-covered by the rushing current. Several trees were injured witnesses. Oaks and pines, with fresh wounds that shredded their bark, recorded the path the truck had taken off the road and into the water.

The smell of fresh pine burned Kasey's nose. She dropped to her knees and snapped more pictures. The lights of the emergency vehicles bounced around the terrain.

It looked like Officer Thomas's call had expanded the team to find Jake. Kasey leveled her camera on two divers as they marked off a grid in the water. A land and water grid search ensued to find her son. Men and women, some in uniforms, others in jeans, combed the edges of the waterway. *Please find him on land. In the water, that would be . . . no, that can't be an option.*

Officers and volunteer firefighters fanned out into the woods.

Had the car seat been thrown from the truck? Swept away by the current? Did Jake crawl to safety? He could. He's a tough little boy.

So many questions. So much to process. So much going on.

She clung to her camera, not sure what to pray for first.

Kasey watched as almost fifty volunteers gave up their Saturday night to search for Jake, walking, step-by-step in unison, through the thick swampy underbrush and vines.

Please let him be safe.

Men erected huge generator-run work lights to enable the team to continue the investigation in the dark, if needed. A tropical storm was supposed to push through on Monday. With Saturday nearly gone, they were running out of time and time was precious in these first few hours.

They wouldn't let Kasey into the woods. It was numbing to stand by. Helpless. Clinging to the camera brought comfort, but she only took a few pictures. She lowered herself to the curb praying for news—whispering promises to God, and anyone else who might matter, that she'd do anything in exchange for Jake's safe return. Nick was gone. She couldn't process that now. Not with Jake missing.

Please don't take Jake, too.

Voices rose and people gathered near the bright yellow tape at the tree line.

Kasey grabbed Riley's arm. "Please let it be good news."

Von sprinted toward the commotion.

Kasey and Riley clung to one another in hope.

Von joined the small group of men.

The minutes ticked by as they waited.

Kasey and Riley jumped to their feet when they saw Von heading in their direction.

"Anything?" Kasey pleaded.

"It's all hands on deck. Even the neighboring counties have sent in their best to help," Von said, trying to reassure her. "They found shell casings. They could be connected to the accident. There were also marks in the mud on the bank but it's hard to know what made them." He grabbed for his hat as a gust of wind lifted the bill. "The wind is picking up." He tugged it lower on his head.

Kasey spun away.

Von put his hand on her shoulder. "It takes time, and with the storm coming, they don't have much of it. They're collecting everything in the grid to insure no evidence is overlooked."

"Jake!" Kasey screamed into the woods. "It's okay. Where are you?" Her whole body trembled as she choked on the words.

Von stepped behind her. "It's getting late. Let's get you home. They'll call us if something turns up."

"I'm not leaving." Kasey folded her arms across her chest. "He's out there. He needs me."

Von and Riley exchanged a glance. Von moved closer to Kasey. "Things are going to go even slower as it gets darker. You need your rest to keep up your strength."

"Jake!" She shouted over the rail. "Jake, where are you? It's Mommy." Tears blinded her and choked her voice. "Jake. I'm here." The plea carried across the riverbank.

Men paused and heads turned in her direction.

Riley wrapped her arms around Kasey. "Come on, honey."

"I can't leave him." Her voice faded to a hushed stillness.

"We'll come back first thing in the morning."

Von guided Kasey and Riley to the truck. "Once they finish collecting the evidence you'll be able to get closer. They've put an Amber alert out, too. He'll turn up."

Kasey followed blindly a few steps, and then stopped. "No. I can't. You go. I'll be fine."

Von stepped closer. "Kasey, it would help if we knew what Jake's wearing. If I take you home, do you think you can sort through his clothes and figure it out?"

She nodded.

"And a picture. They'd like to put a report in the paper and on the news to see if anyone has seen him."

"He's alive. I know he is," she said again.

Riley held Kasey's hands. "This could help us find him faster."

Kasey tucked her hair behind her ear as she looked back over her shoulder. Von and Riley led her to the Yukon to head back home.

"Don't be afraid, baby," Kasey whispered into the dark as they drove away.

Kasey froze in the doorway to Jake's bedroom. The familiar smell of his favorite fruit loop cereal overwhelmed her. The room was in disarray from the random attention that only a three-year-old could give to so many interests. On the floor, trucks and tractors corralled a herd of plastic horses and longhorn cattle alongside blocks and a superhero.

Jake's Spider-Man shirt was on top of the dresser. She reached for it and held the worn cotton to her cheek. Nick probably had to scrape it off him to get him into something clean for their road trip this morning. The short-sleeve camouflage t-shirt, his second favorite, wasn't there. She sat in the middle of the toys with the Spider-Man shirt in her lap. This was the world at Jake's level. It had to be so scary in the dark, in the woods. Her heart ached. She closed her eyes tight, hoping that when she opened them she'd see Jake sitting amongst the chaos with his tiny fingers curled around one of the action figures.

She dragged herself to her feet and walked back into the harsh reality with Jake's shirt clutched to her chest. The late night show echoed in the room around her. The shutters slammed against the house as Von secured the old home for the storm.

"The wind is really kicking up out there," Von said as he stepped back inside and pushed the front door closed behind him.

Kasey told Von what she thought Jake was wearing and gave him a picture they could use. He gave her a hug for reassurance, kissed Riley goodbye, then left to take the information and picture back to the police and identify the body.

Riley walked Von to the door. "Are you going to be okay?"

He pulled her close and whispered into her hair. "It's Nick's truck. It's just protocol, but I couldn't let Kasey go through that. It'll be bad enough for me. He was like my brother."

"I know. I love you, Von. Thanks for being here through all of this," Riley said.

He hugged her close. "I'll call after I check in up there."

"Be careful with the storm."

"I will. I'll stay up there if I have to. I know you girls will be safe here together." He squeezed her hand and left.

Riley waved one last time from the door as Von pulled away.

Kasey curled up on the couch next to Riley and cried into the sweet smell of Jake's shirt.

Riley held Kasey's hand. "We'll get through this. Somehow."

A stiff-haired news anchor leaned into the camera to make his point about how serious the weather had become. School closings crawled across the screen in preparation for the dangerous storm.

Graphics from prior storms popped in time to the ominous music in the background. A swirling icon exploded across the television screen.

"The National Hurricane Center has upgraded Tropical Storm Ernesto to a hurricane. This storm is slogging north along the I-95 corridor dropping inches of rain in its wake. Flooding is the biggest concern. Meteorologist Wendy Raines will have an update after the next commercial break. Stay with us for up-to-the-minute coverage."

These newsy folks loved a good storm.

The storm headlined all three local channels along with the Rolly accident. Kasey hated that the weather might shift attention away from finding her son.

She sat forward and turned up the volume as Jake's picture filled the right side of the screen. That was fast. The local newscasters recounted the accident. A list describing Jake, right down to the camouflage t-shirt and his trigger thumb on his left hand, preceded requests for information that might give them a lead. Jake's wide smile and laughing blue eyes broke her heart again.

Kasey flipped from channel to channel, reliving the moment when that officer had shown up and given her the news for what seemed like the hundredth time. She wanted to be at the accident site—to at least do something besides wait.

I have the right to be there, don't I? It's my family—my tragedy, for God's sake.

An Amber alert had been broadcast, and she'd been ordered to sit tight until the FBI arrived in the morning.

. . .

Overnight Ernesto picked up significant wind speed. A dangerous category three, sustained winds were expected to increase with gusts over 130 miles per hour by later in the day.

Kasey watched the investigation unfold on the television between storm warnings. Von had gone back to the crash site. He called to give Kasey and Riley updates every couple of hours through the night—but minutes slinked by. They hadn't heard anything in a while.

Ernesto was relentless in his path of destruction. Once the full brunt of the storm hit, there'd be no way anyone could search for Jake. Precious evidence would wash away under Ernesto's powerful force.

Kasey drifted in and out of a restless sleep, arousing to the familiar sound of her son's name. She'd slept but hadn't rested. She sat up to listen again to what she'd already memorized. No changes, but then she expected that. Loneliness consumed her. *How can I face this without Nick by my side?*

Riley came from the kitchen with juice. "Here, girl. You need to keep your strength up."

Kasey took a sip from the glass and placed it on the table. "I hoped I'd wake up to find this was all a bad dream. Nothing new?"

"Afraid not. The Child Abduction Rapid Deployment team will be here soon."

"I know." Kasey dropped her head into her hands, then pushed herself to her feet. She forced herself to get up and go out to the front porch. She sat on the steps. The rain pounded on the metal roof. A toy car lay abandoned nearby. Kasey picked it up and pushed it back and forth. The wooden deck was scarred from the many hours Jake had raced his cars along these planks.

Two dark nondescript sedans filed into the driveway. She squeezed the tiny car into her palm. Her nails pinched into her skin as she pushed against the handrail to stand.

Riley burst through the screen door and stood behind Kasey, one arm wrapped around her friend's shoulders.

"Please, Lord, give me the strength." Kasey grabbed Riley's hand. "This is too much."

"It's okay. They'll help us. That's why they're here."

The southeast region specialists from the Child Abduction Rapid Deployment team, better known as CARD, blew in with as much gusto as Ernesto. They gathered their information with an eager-ness that left Kasey dazed and exhausted. The questions from the team were so in-depth that she began to doubt her ability to answer the easiest of them about her own family. Now the big guns were involved. Their special work-force had been successful in a high percentage of cases similar to this.

Riley escorted the last of the federal agents out the door less than an hour after they'd arrived.

"Lord." Riley leaned back against the closed door. "That's way more difficult than they make it look on television."

"You're telling me." Kasey tucked her feet underneath her on the couch.

The phone rang again, and it felt like each ring sucked a little more life out of her.

"I've got it. Don't move." Riley ran to the kitchen to answer the phone. She'd been fielding calls all morning. There were twice as many from concerned friends and media than updates from Von and the police.

Kasey sprawled out on the couch and pulled a pillow over her head. Thank goodness Riley was there to field the calls. Kasey couldn't bear to give any more reality to this situation. If she kept it to herself, maybe it would all go away and Nick and Jake would be back.

Dutch pushed the pillow off her face, nudged his wet nose into the crook of her neck, then licked away her tears.

"Kasey!" Riley lunged into the room with the phone in her hand. "It's Von. They've found the car seat."

Kasey jumped to her feet and ran to Riley's side. "Jake? Did they find him?" She wrapped her hands around Riley's arm and tipped her head toward the phone, struggling to hear the conversation.

Riley took down the details then hung up the phone. "They recovered a car seat downstream. It's Jake's. That State Fair belt buckle of Nick's is still hanging from the bracket."

"He has to be nearby. Come on. We've got to be there when they find him."

"Not so fast. They don't know anything more yet. Von will keep us posted." Riley led Kasey back to the couch and sat down next to her. "The best thing we can do right now is remain calm and let them do their jobs."

Kasey buried her trembling fingers in her hair. Her heart ached for Nick and worried for Jake. "I'll never make it through this."

Chapter Four

Sheriff Scott Calvin took the information from the lead officer at the accident site and ran to his car. He'd worked in this county before he became Sheriff of nearby Adams Grove, so when he'd heard about the accident he'd wasted no time volunteering to help.

The tip was from Penny's Candy and Soda Shoppe. The popular stop for folks traveling this stretch of highway was located just down the road from the scene of the accident.

Bells tinkled when he opened the door. He crossed the shiny black-and-white tiled floor and slid onto the stool at the end of the counter.

Penny smiled when she saw him. "Hey, stranger." She grabbed a glass and filled it with root beer. "On the house."

"You remembered." He raised the glass and took an exaggerated sip.

"Of course. How've you been? You haven't been down here in a while."

"I'm here about the accident," he said.

Penny leaned on the counter. "Heartbreaking," she said shaking her head. "I still can't believe it. They were in here, just before . . ." She pressed her lips together, and closed her eyes for a moment. "That poor woman."

"I know. They told me you have the security tape." He scrubbed the back of his neck. "If it proves that boy was with his dad, it's like he's vanished. There's not a sign of him out there yet."

Penny reached under the counter. "I remember the truck. Handsome guy. Cute little boy. I wouldn't forget them. Here it is." She handed Scott the tape. "If there's anything else I can do, let me know. Posters, whatever."

He took another sip of his soda, then picked up the tape and stood. "I will." He tossed a couple of dollars on the counter. "Thanks, Penny."

When Sheriff Calvin arrived back at the accident site, the swampy terrain had become slippery and dangerous. One of the rescue volunteers was on his way to the hospital with a possible broken leg. The river rose against the shoreline as the trees leaned over, slapping its surface with their branches. Blinding bands of rain from Hurricane Ernesto increased the risk and finally forced them to halt the search.

"I don't have a choice," the lead officer said to Sheriff Calvin.

Scott shook his head. "You don't. You can't risk any more lives." He knew this was a hard decision to make, but the risk of more loss of life was too high to ignore.

He watched as the lead officer went out and made the announcement. Soaked men and women reluctantly filed out of the woods. There was nothing more they could do until Ernesto finished his punishment, but it was hard for anyone to leave knowing there was a child unaccounted for.

The team was thinking two steps ahead. Thank goodness, because there wouldn't be much evidence left at the crash site except battered trees, and their story had already been told.

Scott helped pull together volunteers to work through the night in the safety of the precinct logging each piece of potential evidence from the bags of debris collected at the accident site. Even the smallest item could be critical in locating Jake Rolly. It was a slow and tedious process.

Ernesto pounded southeastern Virginia through

the night, dumping over five inches of rain and toppling trees. Tens of thousands of residents lost power.

Damaging winds were a problem, but because Ernesto parked himself over the region, flooding had become the top concern. Rivers were expected to crest at new heights, and flash flood warnings crawled across the television screens of those who still had electricity.

By the end of the day on Monday, the lead detective gave a public statement.

"We are continuing to examine the evidence and are determined to find Jake Rolly," he said on camera from the police department in Southampton County. "We've partnered with neighboring counties, but we need your help. Anyone who has information should contact their local authorities."

Assumptions and evidence nipped away at the corners. They would get to the root of what happened eventually. Tomorrow, as soon as the waters subsided, they'd canvass the neighboring shops and residents along Route 58. A small team would search the area one last time, but any evidence was lost to Ernesto.

Back in Pungo, Von worked his way out from Nick and Kasey's house, trying to reconstruct Nick's activities on the morning of the accident.

The clerk at the corner store nodded and bowed his head. "Yeah, I heard about the accident. Nick came in on Saturday. He's in here every Saturday."

Von knew that. Nick was a creature of habit. Always had been. "Was Jake with him?"

The clerk rubbed his moustache. "I can't be sure if the little guy was with him or not. It was so busy. I've got the security tapes though. Give me a minute and I'll get them for you."

The clerk disappeared behind a security door and came out with a tape.

"It's a start," Von said. "I appreciate it."

"Hey, anything I can do. Let me know."

Von hurried out of the store. He needed to leave now if he was going to make it on time. He'd offered to take care of all the arrangements for Kasey. Nick had pre-paid and planned his funeral years ago, so it was just a matter of following that plan. Von had an appointment in thirty minutes with the funeral home. It was the least he could do for her. Burying a spouse was a torture he wished on no one.

He remembered only too well how unpredictable grief was. How it swept in and took you right off your feet with no warning. Everyone gave him unsolicited advice on how to navigate it; they'd do the same to Kasey. She'd have to find her own way—in her own time. A lesson he'd learned the hard way.

The funeral director was helpful, and a lot smoother than when he'd had to go through it for Deidre. Of course, he'd been in a fog then.

With all the details finalized, Von headed home. Losing Nick brought on a familiar grief that burned in his chest like a raw, gaping wound. It was like reliving losing Deidre all over again. But if Jake was out there, the most important thing he could do for Nick was find his boy. That was all he could think about the whole ride home.

He walked into the house feeling tired and impatient. His specialized skills weren't getting him anywhere with this case. Maybe it was true that you shouldn't work on cases you were too close to. The video tape tucked in his pocket was the only glimmer of hope he had. He tossed his hat on his desk, and inserted the video surveillance into the player. The date stamp was blank. The clerk had warned him that the power had gone off that week and he hadn't reset the recorder yet. Von wasn't sure why he even bothered looking at the tape, except that any hope was better than none, and there were no other leads to follow.

Von rubbed his hand across his chin as he pressed the buttons on the remote, fast-forwarding, then rewinding, then pausing to analyze the less than perfect images as people came and went. The process was slow.

After numerous stops and starts, a familiar image caught his eye. He pressed the Pause button and moved closer to the screen.

Frame by frame, he watched his best friend push open the glass door. Nick was dressed in a camo t-shirt and a ball cap, with a junior version of himself clinging to his hand.

Jake.

Von settled on the edge of his desk, rewound the tape, watched it again, and let it play out. He watched Nick and Jake walk to the counter and then leave the store together. He rewound the tape and played the scene again, and then again.

"This is too much."

It was bad enough Nick was gone, but no man could bear to think of a young boy like Jake in danger or hurt . . . or worse.

He bowed his head. The loss was like a steel weight, empty and cold in his gut.

"Damn it, Nick," Von said to the screen. "This isn't enough to go on." He pounded his fist on the desk. "Help me find him, man. Point me to a clue. Where is he?"

Von pitched the remote against the wall, then headed to his truck.

Chapter Five

Over the past few days, Kasey's life had moved on without her having a say. She couldn't manage to make even the simplest decisions. Nick was gone. Jake had disappeared. She replayed the news and the chain of events that followed in her mind a thousand times, wishing for an answer.

None of it made sense. Her faith in God wavered in the wake of the unimaginable string of events.

The morning of Nick's funeral, Kasey rode to the church in the limo, then sat in the chapel with Riley and Von and a hundred other people who had loved Nick. The names of people she knew escaped her, which was just as well, because she couldn't seem to get any words out. It was nearly too much to breathe, much less talk. She wasn't sure if she could speak even if she tried.

She could barely take a breath at the sight of the rose-colored wooden casket. Masses of colorful wreaths and sprays filled the front of the large chapel. It made the heavy casket appear to hover above a meadow of flowers. An enlarged copy of the black-and-white portrait of Nick, with Jake on his hip, was propped on an easel—the same picture she kept on her mantel. Her favorite.

The preacher stood at the front, speaking— saying something. It didn't matter what. She wasn't ready to listen to him.

God, you took Nick and left me behind. But why, if not to take care of our son? How could our sweet Jake disappear without a trace? How could you let this happen? Help me. Please, help me.

Sorrow hung heavy in the packed chapel.

How long had the preacher been talking? His words were meant to comfort, but they didn't. Each word felt like a knife cutting into her heart. If she could move her legs, she'd run right up the aisle and out the door. Away. As far away from the pain as she could get. But her legs weren't moving. She felt paralyzed, glued to the pew, wondering why she bothered to breathe. The alternative seemed more appealing right now, except she knew Jake needed her.

She'd find him.

She had to.

One by one, people came to the front of the chapel, stepping up to share their stories about Nick. It gnawed at her gut to share the moment, afraid her own precious memories would be lost in their voices. She looked in their direction, but through them, avoiding their memories—concentrating on anything but their words.

She nodded in an attempt to look appreciative. That was the best she could do.

The organist played *The Wind Beneath My Wings*. The first three notes took Kasey's breath away. There was no wind, no air. Her own wings had been clipped.

She'd been blessed to share a true love with Nick, a love that had come without effort. But now she felt cursed to have known that love. Alfred Lord Tennyson was a fool. It was not better to have loved and lost, than never to have loved at all. If she hadn't loved Nick with every part of her being, she wouldn't be so devastated now.

"You okay?" Riley rubbed Kasey's arm.

"Numb," Kasey whispered.

There were so many people. Nick had been well-known, well-liked, for his many contributions to the community. She knew that, but the number of people here today overwhelmed her. She didn't want to share this private moment between her and Nick and God.

Kasey clutched a handkerchief between trembling fingers. No lace, no embroidery, just one of Nick's that she'd pulled out from a load of laundry he'd left in the dryer. A point they'd often debated. Nick would leave clothes in the dryer so long that the wrinkles baked in. She'd have to iron or rewash them, and she wasn't a fan of ironing. The hanky she held had been a wrinkled mess even before she'd balled it in her hand.

The funeral ended, and Riley wrapped her arm around Kasey. "It's time to move outside."

Kasey's hands shook. She grabbed Riley's arm and they left the church.

The sky was bright and the air warm. They rode in the black funeral sedan to the inescapable moment ahead.

Mourners crowded the cemetery, dressed in dark and muted colors. They seemed to move more slowly and more quietly than normal. Or maybe it was just Kasey's brain working slower, resistant to the changes in her life.

Riley and Von sat on either side of her, near Nick's casket.

The prayers were short and heartbreaking.

Each pallbearer tucked his boutonniere into the full spray of flowers that covered the coffin, then the crowds peeled away from the burial plot.

But Kasey couldn't leave—not yet. She stood and walked to the side of the coffin, slid her hands under the blanket of flowers, and laid her cheek on the smooth wood of the casket. Von and Riley came to her side as the others headed for their cars.

They would receive guests at the farmhouse. Kasey wasn't keen on the idea, but Nick would've wanted it that way.

"Kasey, honey." Riley tried to bring her attention to the present. "Do you recognize that man?" She pointed to their right.

Kasey lifted her gaze from the casket and turned to look.

A very tall man, dressed in black, walked toward them. He had one of his hands shoved deep in the pocket of his trousers, pulling his jacket aside and exposing his slim hip and long stride. Dark glasses rested on his perfect nose.

Even through the tears, Kasey recognized the silhouette. But it didn't make sense. It couldn't be. Her mind must be mixing images from the recent weeks.

She blinked and refocused.

It *was* him. Kasey grabbed Riley's hand and gave it a squeeze. "It's okay." She walked to meet him halfway.

He took both her hands in his—his were warm.

"You're in all of our prayers." Cody Tuggle's deep voice came out slow and calming.

"How did you know?"

"It's been all over the news."

"Why did you come?"

He looked at the ground, pushing the toe of his boot in the grass. "I just knew I needed to. It had to be devastating news to come home to."

"You didn't have to do that."

He placed his hand on her shoulder. "If there's anything I can do to help find Jake . . . or anything, let me know."

Her shoulders folded forward as she tried to drag in air, sobbing into her hands. Cody caught her by the elbow as her knees gave way. Riley ran toward them.

"I got her." Cody swept Kasey into his arms.

Riley pointed to where Von stood just thirty feet away next to a black limo. Cody nodded and carried Kasey to the car. Von opened the door, and Cody released her onto the soft leather of the backseat.

"Thank you." Kasey squinted against the glare of the sun as she peered out of the limo at Cody. "I'm so—"

"Shhhsh. Now who's talking too much?"

She gave him a half smile.

Von shut the door.

Cody extended his hand to Von. "Cody Tuggle.

Kasey just finished a shoot with us the morning of the accident."

"Nice of you to come."

"Anything I can do?" Cody asked.

"I wish there was. She's trying to deal with the grief of losing Nick and the hope that we'll find her son. He was with Nick that morning, but there's still no sign of him." Von swallowed his own grief and shook Cody's hand again. "Thanks. Every friend helps at a time like this."

Chapter Six

Before they'd left for the church that morning, Kasey had picked out three of Nick's ball caps to save from the hundreds he owned. Von had suggested that they put the rest in two small troughs on either side of the front door for folks to take when they came later that day if they wanted them. Kasey had liked that idea. She couldn't bear to throw the hats away.

The limo pulled into the driveway. Kasey flattened her sweating palms on her dress. Friends, family and acquaintances had already gathered at her house and spilled out onto the front lawn.

Kasey's heart fluttered. Most everyone milling about already had one of Nick's hats in hand, and some of the men had them in their back pockets.

Others folded them like a taco to get the curve on the bill just right. Nick had always done that, too. They clung to the caps, a connection to Nick.

Kasey walked from the limo to the front porch and stopped to look at the whiteboard Von had hung on the wall there. On it he had listed the chores required to keep Circle R Farm running for the next three months. The board was nearly filled with the names of neighbors, family and friends who had volunteered to help operate the farm.

"Thank you," Kasey said to no one in particular, overcome by the generosity and outreach of their friends. She was relieved that people with ranching and farm experience would keep Nick's dream alive over the next few months.

Kasey blew out a breath as she, Riley and Von entered the house. "What would I have done without you and Von? There is no way I could have—"

Riley stopped her. "Nick and Von were like brothers. Best friends, just like us. We love you, Kasey. My heart is breaking. I'd do anything to make this better for you. I just don't know what to say. What can I do?"

"Just be here with me."

They held hands. "I'm right here. I'm not going anywhere," Riley said.

Together they braved the endless stream of people, sharing their personal memories of Nick.

Nick as a 4-H leader . . .

Nick as a dad . . .

Nick as a farmer and rancher . . .

Nick as a veterinarian . . .

Nick as a guitar player . . .

Nick as the best darn barbequer around . . .

Nick as one hell of a hunter . . .

Nick, who always lived every moment to the fullest . . .

Nick, the ladies' man before he'd met her . . .

Nick as a steady friend who had never let anyone down . . .

Nick.

"We are going to miss him."

Kasey flinched. Each kind remark seemed to pierce her heart a little deeper. *Nick. I miss you so much.*

The events of the day were catching up to her. Her lips quivered, making it hard to smile. She really wanted to just be left alone.

Nodding continuously, she repeated, "Yes, he was a wonderful man. Thank you."

No one mentioned Jake.

It was too painful for anyone to even say his name. Most of them believed that he'd been swept away in the currents that day. She'd heard the whispers, but she knew better. Jake was out there, and he was wishing for her as hard as she was wishing to find him. She felt it in her heart and soul.

Someone brushed her elbow. Startled, she spun around.

"Jeremy. Sorry, I was off . . . somewhere." She reached up and hugged him. "Thank you for being here."

"It wasn't his time." Jeremy whispered into her hair as he held her. He stepped back and shoved his hands in his pockets with his shoulders slumped. "I'm here for you. Remember that."

She swallowed back the familiar pain. The last time she'd been at a funeral was when Granddaddy had died. That's when she'd met Jeremy. At the time she'd thought that was the worst day of her life, but it didn't even come in a close second to today.

Jeremy had been Granddaddy's trusted mechanic back then. A big deal, because Granddaddy wouldn't let just anyone touch his precious collection of antique cars.

"Where's Grem?" Kasey scanned the room, looking for Grandma Emily.

"She's in the front room holding court, wondering where you are. You know how she has to be the center of attention," Jeremy said with a smirk.

"She was never this bad when Granddaddy was alive." Even when Kasey had lived at the estate, Grem was more than Kasey could juggle without help. Grem ran off good help in record time. Granddaddy had provisioned for Jeremy to maintain his car collection following his death.

Kasey had become desperate after Grem ran off yet another companion. The local service was running out of candidates that specialized in elderly care to send her way. So Kasey sweetened the deal for Jeremy by offering him a live-in situation—complete with full use of the temperature-controlled garage bays on the back of the estate to work on his own antique car projects. In exchange, he'd tote Grandma Emily around and keep things in check on the property. Jeremy had jumped at the chance. He doted on Grandma like Granddaddy used to. Grem adored him.

Jeremy was like one of the family now, and his striking dark hair and blue eyes left many thinking he was related because he looked so much like Granddaddy. *Probably one of the reasons Grem loves having him around.*

"You ready to see the queen?" Jeremy asked, extending his arm.

Kasey managed a grin and took his arm. Grem sat in her wheelchair, next to the fireplace. Kasey crossed the room and hugged her.

Grem held Kasey's arm. "The carriage house is ready, but you should stay up at the house with me for a while, dear. You know, until you feel better."

"Thanks, but I'll be fine here."

Grem scowled.

Kasey stepped back. *What was that for?*

Jeremy must have sensed the mood, too,

because he whisked Grandma Emily off to the side of the small group, turning her back to most of the folks, and whispered something to her.

Grem scowled. She slapped at the wheelchair but Jeremy kept pushing. "What are you doing? For goodness sakes." She twisted around toward Kasey. "Honey, this is no place for a lady to mourn." The old woman's lips pinched. Her too-red lipstick spidered among her wrinkles.

Kasey moved to her grandmother's side and knelt down. "Please don't make this harder than it already is."

Grem looked into Kasey's eyes. "Everything happens for a reason, my dear. Leave this hillbilly farm behind. Live your *own* dreams now."

Was this supposed to be a pep talk? The words hit Kasey like a slap. "Stop it, please." She glanced around and lowered her voice. "I'm sure you mean well, but this isn't helping." Suppressing her emotions, she stood and walked to the window. It wouldn't do any good to get upset with Grem.

Jeremy pushed the wheelchair next to Kasey. "She insisted," he mouthed, then shrugged, set the brake and headed for the door, probably for a cigarette.

Grem grasped Kasey's wrist with her cold bony hand. "Honey, you know I'm right. You're young. Your life is not over." She patted Kasey's arm.

"The dreams, the country, they were *our* dreams.

Nick's *and* mine. I have absolutely no intention of leaving here. This is our home."

The truth was that this place was heartbreak at every turn, but she wouldn't admit that to Grem. Mixed feelings surged through her. One minute she wanted to embrace everything that Jake and Nick had ever touched. Then, a moment later, she wanted to hit the damn road, leave it all behind, and pretend this part of her life had never happened.

Riley stepped between them. "Beautiful service wasn't it, Miss Emily?"

"It was nice." Grem cleared her throat. "Kasey, darling, the photo of Nick and Jake at the service was lovely."

"Thank you," Kasey said, her voice tight. *Sometimes it's so hard to be nice to her.*

She reached for her copy of that photograph on the mantel. Nick and Jake both wore jeans and cowboy hats. The candid shot had captured them so well.

She remembered that day like yesterday. They'd gone to get ice cream at the Pungo Strawberry Festival when something photo-worthy caught her attention. Nick had turned to find her straggling behind—something that happened all the time.

"Where's Mommy? Crazy Mommy is clicking again." Nick had teased.

Jake had reached in her direction and yelled, "Click me, Mommy. Click me!"

And she had. As both her boys had reached toward her, calling her name.

That one moment. So special.

A lucky shot.

Tiny details in the image were the most special to her. The folded ball cap in Nick's back pocket and the scrape on Jake's elbow. Jake had insisted on trying to take one of the goats for a walk; but the goat had other ideas and was faster than Jake. He'd fallen. But that didn't slow him down. Jake jumped up, dusted himself off and finished the walk—bloody elbow and all. He'd never even shed a tear.

Grem's voice carried from a nearby group. "Kasey is my granddaughter. She is quite talented."

Come on, God. Give me a break here. Kasey walked over to her. "Grem, this isn't the time."

She shook her head. "Nonsense, dear. They love to hear about your work."

Grem continued on, telling them that Kasey would be moving home with her.

Kasey clenched her teeth.

The stunning old woman drew a crowd. She looked so sweet, vulnerable, until you got right up close and her fangs started to show.

Riley took control of the wheelchair. "Come on, Grandma. Jeremy is going to take you home." She wheeled her directly to the front door and out onto the porch. "I'm sure this has been a tough day for you."

"Oh." Grem looked taken aback. "Oh, yes. You're so right. You are such a doll, Riley. Yes. I should get back home. The excitement is not good for someone my age."

"There he is now." Riley gave Jeremy the don't-ask-questions-just-get-her-the-hell-out-of-here look. "Can you take her home?"

"Thank you, dear." Grem patted Riley's arm.

Jeremy helped her into the Mercedes and closed the door. "I don't know what gets into the old bird sometimes."

Riley rolled her eyes and shrugged.

Jeremy said, "I didn't get to say much to Kasey. Do they have any leads yet?"

"No. Not a one, but Von is keeping tabs on the investigation for us."

"Yeah. That's good. Will you call me if they hear anything, and if I can help?" Jeremy untwisted the wrapper on a butterscotch candy and popped it in his mouth. He dug in his pocket and handed two to Riley. "Here. Give one to Kasey to remind her I'm just a phone call away. Keep me posted, will you?"

"I will."

Grem tooted the horn, and they both jumped.

"Never a dull moment," Riley said.

Jeremy hugged her, then jogged around to the driver's side of the car.

Riley held the butterscotch candies in her hand with her thumb as she waved goodbye. When they cleared the driveway, she went back inside.

"Is she gone?" Kasey asked as Riley came toward her.

"Mission accomplished." Riley handed Kasey the yellow wrapped butterscotch.

"Jeremy." Kasey took the candy and cracked a slight smile. "He's such a sweetheart."

"Yeah. He's taking her home. The cranky old bat. I can't believe he hasn't quit after all these years."

Kasey shrugged. "He's used to her moods. He earns every penny he makes, that's for sure."

A few hours later, the house finally began to empty.

Riley busied herself in the kitchen with a couple of neighbors. They must have opened and closed the freezer door twenty times as they stored away the food. So much food.

The week after the funeral, the police in Southampton County contacted Kasey about the tape from Penny's Candy and Soda Shoppe. Finally, they had dated proof positive that Jake had been with Nick just moments before the crash.

The news made for a restless night for Kasey, but at least maybe now the police would keep looking for Jake. She'd been worried that they might give up. The combination of renewed hope and fear tugged at her. Even her dreams taunted her, twisting joyful reunions with tragic replays of the funeral. And all of the dreams ended in the woods. She opened her eyes to the sun streaming through a sliver of an opening between the curtains. *Were the dreams a sign? Was there something in the woods that would help her find Jake?* She'd heard of stranger ways of solving cases.

Dutch laid next to the bed. Kasey swung her feet around to the edge and sat up. She rubbed her feet on his soft coat. "Quiet, isn't it, buddy?"

She rolled her shoulders and rubbed her feet on Dutch's back. He groaned.

"Feel good?"

No more back rubs in my future. I'll miss your back rubs, Nick. You gave the best.

Kasey got up, put on jeans, hiking boots, and one of Nick's rodeo t-shirts. In a moment of clarity, she'd decided to go back to the crash site and see if anything came to her that might help her find Jake. Crazier things happened all the time— she had nothing to lose.

She went downstairs and left a note on the counter in case Riley came by.

An hour and a half later, Kasey pulled her car off on the soft shoulder near the accident site. She put her business card on the dash of her car in hopes it would be enough to keep anyone from towing it while she explored.

She stepped over the shiny new guardrail and followed the path of scarred trees that marked the path Nick's truck had taken down the embankment. The incline was steeper than it looked. She sidestepped her way down to the water's edge. Debris marked the high water line left from the storm.

If Jake had somehow climbed ashore, where would he have headed?

She squatted. From this level, Jake's level, she couldn't see the road.

He could've made it to shore if the water had been as low as it was today. She stepped out on the rocks. They were slick, but plenty big to walk on.

She stood in the center of the river on the large rock where Nick's truck had once lain crooked, its interior sucking up water like a sponge.

I probably cried enough tears last week to crest this river.

To her left was a large clearing. She walked back across the rocky waterway, climbed the sloping terrain, and headed to that area.

She snapped off a twig from a tree and poked at the brush in front of her as she walked. No sense stepping on a snoozing snake. "Where are you, Jake? Help me find you."

I'm not crazy.

After three hours of wandering the woods, she knew, crazy or not, that she couldn't stay out much longer. Mosquitoes had begun nibbling on her as if she was a buffet. She swatted at one buzzing around her head.

She hiked toward the highway noise to her car. Her legs ached and so did her heart.

The next morning, Jeremy stopped by. It was Wednesday—the day Grem got her hair done each week. He'd been stopping by every Wednesday since the accident. Kasey wasn't sure if it was Grem's idea or his, but she'd started to appreciate his visits.

Still in her nightshirt, Kasey opened the door. Dots of pink calamine lotion highlighted her itchy mosquito bites.

"What happened to you?" he asked.

"Promise not to laugh?"

Jeremy smiled. "Hell, no. If you're going to make me promise, it has to be funny." He followed her into the living room.

"Fine. I went back to the accident site to see if I could get a connection or idea about where I might find Jake."

He sat down in the chair across from her. "I wouldn't laugh about that. I know how you're hurting. I wish I could fix everything for you right now."

"You're so sweet. It was stupid, I know, but it seemed like it was worth a shot. Better than sitting here wondering."

A glazed look spread over his face.

"I've brought you down, too." She sat next to him. "I'm not very good company these days."

He patted her leg. "Don't be silly. It's just so hard for me to see you so sad."

"I just wish I knew. I've memorized every angle of the terrain near the accident, and I'm no closer to finding Jake. I'm running out of ideas. And to make matters worse, the police don't seem to have the same sense of urgency they had before." Tears slid to her chin. She swept them away with her sleeve. "I know he's alive. I know in here." She tapped her heart. "But I need a glimmer of hope that I'll find him."

"I'm so sorry." He pinched the bridge of his nose and sat silent for a moment. Then he lifted his head and looked her square in the eye. "I have an idea, but I'm not sure you're going to like it."

Kasey's eyes brightened. "Anything."

He started to speak, then paused. "Well." He cleared his throat, then scooched to the edge of his seat. "I know this gal. It's a long shot. She does tea-leaf readings."

She leaned back and rolled her eyes. "Oh, no. You know how I feel about that black magic. It's just tempting bad stuff to come your way. I don't think I could do that."

"No. It's not like that. Tasseography is a divine practice."

She grimaced. "Tassy-whatever-ography doesn't sound divine. It sounds scary."

"Just think about it." He shrugged. "The practice is based on meditation and stuff, so you probably need to believe and trust that it will work. You said you'd do anything."

She wrinkled her nose. "I know, but I don't think I'm *that* desperate. That's just . . ." She ran her hands up and down her arms to chase the nervous tingle that followed the thought of tempting fate with that sort of magic.

"The offer stands. If you change your mind, let me know. I'll set it up."

She was hesitant to even consider it. "You'd go with me?"

"Of course. Anything." His gaze pleaded with her.

"I'll think about it," Kasey said.

"You could ask if Jake's alive. Find out for sure, one way or the other. Maybe get a lead."

"I could ask specific questions like that?" She needed answers, but that magic stuff had always given her the heebie-jeebies. "If I only knew he was safe, it would be easier." She slouched, then shook her head. "No, I'm not ready for that. I have an aerial photographer going up tomorrow to search the area again. He's doing it as a favor. I'm going to photograph his plane for a print ad in exchange. Maybe something will turn up this time."

Jeremy looked at his watch. "I've got to go. Your grandmother will be a real pain in the ass if I pick her up late."

"Like she won't be anyway?"

"Be nice. She's not as bad as you think. She loves you." Jeremy gave her a hug, then left.

Kasey watched him back out of the driveway. The thought of somebody predicting her future or knowing her past sent a tingle down her spine, and not in a good way. Time was slipping away though, and the longer Jake was missing, the more likely it was she'd never find him. Some said it had already been too long.

Even Riley had asked if she wanted to consider a memorial for Jake if something didn't turn up soon.

Kasey couldn't—wouldn't—give up on Jake yet.

Chapter Seven

Kasey stared at the ceiling until the swirled plaster blurred, forming images—silhouettes of better times. She sprawled her leg across Nick's side of the bed. Empty and cool.

She'd promised herself she'd get out of bed today, but that had been yesterday, and today didn't seem as far away as tomorrow had seemed at the time she made that promise.

One month. Exactly one month today since

she'd laid Nick to rest. Everyone said it would get easier with time, but how much time and how much easier?

Although the wounds were still tender, she knew in her heart she couldn't let time keep slipping by. Nick would hate that. He'd lived life to the fullest—never wasted a minute. She hadn't done a good job of either lately.

She sat upright on the edge of the bed and forced her feet to the ground. She held her arms out to the side to steady herself as she stood. Taking slow steps, she made her way to the bathroom and twisted the knobs on the shower.

She stepped out of her pajamas and into the shower, letting the gentle spray wash over her as she prayed for strength. She turned counterclockwise, wishing that would rewind her life to happier times. The water began to run cool so she got out. Wrapped in a towel, she went back in the bedroom and sat at the antique dressing table. She hadn't put on makeup since the funeral, but it was a step, even if she was faking it, toward feeling better. She brushed her hair, then picked out something to wear.

Her favorite pair of khakis hung loose on her now. She cinched the waist tight with a belt. It would have to do.

The melancholy she'd woken up with slid away, now replaced by anger. Nick had given her a wonderful life and then abandoned her.

How could you leave me? You promised you'd always be here.

Kasey went downstairs and walked outside. She looked at the beautiful property, as if through Nick's and Jake's eyes, and remembered each precious day, each moment. She wasn't alone. Dutch wandered around with her every step of the way, like a shadow. The old dog had loved those two Rolly boys as much as she did, and his eyes seemed sadder than normal. Every time she stopped, Dutch pushed his head under her hand. He needed the connection, too.

She went back inside with a plan, with Dutch at her heels. His nails clicked on the hardwood floors like seconds ticking by on a clock.

Kasey picked up the phone and dialed Grem to tell her she was coming by. She made the call short though, because Grem had a way of saying the wrong thing, and all she needed was an excuse to crawl back under the covers.

She wasn't going to give herself a way out today.

It was a beautiful day for a drive. Kasey drove with the top down on the Porsche. She usually loved the wind in her hair and breathing in the air that rushed around the car as she sped along. She'd been known to sing at the top of her lungs without a care about who might hear. No radio and no singing today, though. She was going through the motions for Nick, but her heart wasn't in it.

She punched in the security code at the gates to her grandmother's estate, then idled between the flowering crepe myrtles that dotted the path to the big house. When she reached the end of the driveway, she caught sight of Grem on the porch, waving at her.

Kasey waved and parked in front. The old Porsche had been Daddy's car, his pride and joy. When she'd been little, Daddy would speed down the road with the top down and her by his side. It had cost her dearly to rebuild the old car over the years, but she felt close to Dad when the leather seats wrapped around her like a hug. She'd always been a daddy's girl.

"It's about time. I haven't heard from you in weeks," the old woman complained. "Now get your fanny over here already. The day is half gone."

Had to give it to her for being spunky at her age. "It's only eight o'clock. Most people are just getting their day started."

Grem pursed her lips with a vague hint of disapproval. "Don't be sassing me. Just give me a hug."

Kasey pushed her sunglasses on top of her head and hugged her grandmother.

"Let me get a good look at you."

Kasey stepped back and posed, forcing a smile.

"Goodness dear, you look thin, and you could use a haircut." The old woman took Kasey's hands into hers, then rubbed her thumb over Kasey's nails. "Would you have a look at those nails? My goodness. Are you sure you're my granddaughter?"

"Yes, I am." She rolled her eyes. "I haven't had time."

"Pshaw, you've just been sitting around moping. You've had plenty of time to take care of those little things."

Kasey sat on the top step in front of her grandmother. "Yeah, well that's just it. Those are little things, aren't they? Not so important in the scheme of things."

"Don't dismiss the importance of taking care of yourself. Lucky for you, I had a feeling you would be in a mess. I already called Seth at home. I've made appointments for both of us with him and George this morning, dear."

"Tell me you didn't." Kasey slumped. She like being pampered, and George and Seth were the best stylists around. But they were so full of energy, and she wasn't up to that.

"Yes, I did. If we don't get a move on, we're going to be late."

Defeated, she knew better than to argue. Grem always got her damn way. "Fine. I gather you already have Jeremy lined up to take us."

"Of course, dear. He should be around any

minute. Why don't you put on some lipstick? You look a little pale."

"I look fine." She gave her grandmother a stern look. "Don't push it, okay?" She now remembered why, when she'd lived here, she stayed in the carriage house where she could come and go without bumping into Grem on a daily basis, and why she'd hired Jeremy in the first place. Well, that and the fact that Grem had run off all the other help. Jeremy had staying power.

The older that woman got, the more she thought she had the right to do and say whatever she damn well pleased. That wasn't always pleasant.

Jeremy pulled the Mercedes around. Kasey scooted to the edge of the step and stood, muttering under her breath, "Saved by the Benz."

He made his way to the porch and hugged Kasey. "Glad to see you out and about. We've missed you. You doing okay?"

She nodded, although not too convincingly.

He gave her the don't-lie-to-me look. "Call me. Let me know if you change your mind about the other thing we talked about."

"You know how that freaks me out. I don't see that happening." She put her hand on his shoulder. "But, thanks."

Jeremy helped Grandma Emily into the car. She wouldn't hear of a van or special access vehicle; she'd just stay in the house forever before she'd allow someone to tote her around like that. Kasey got into the backseat and readied herself for what was to come.

The day turned out to be pleasant, even refreshing. Separated by spinning beauty shop chairs and the hum of blow dryers, there was no room for a lot of dialogue with her grandmother. Kasey was thankful for that. However, on the ride home, there was no safe barrier.

"You look like your old self now." Grem looked proud of herself.

"It was a nice day."

"Yes. So . . . are you ready to move back home yet?"

"No."

The old woman raised her hands. A shadow of anger swept her face as she turned and looked out the window.

"What? Why would I move back? I have a home."

Grem spun her sprayed fringe of blued locks around to face Kasey. "Yes, you have a home, and it is with me. Now just come back to where you belong and live like the lady you were raised to be. I want what's best. You've wasted too much time already."

Kasey choked back a gasp. "Wasted? I cannot believe you."

"We all make mistakes, dear." Her grandmother

clucked her tongue, then turned in her seat in a huff.

"Jeremy, pull over." Kasey slapped the back of his seat.

"What are you doing?" Grem's lips pinched into a tight line.

Jeremy caught Kasey's gaze in the rearview mirror.

"Pull over right now or I'm jumping out," Kasey said louder, her voice tight.

Her grandmother's eyes widened. "Don't be ridiculous."

Kasey fumbled with the door handle. Jeremy swerved the car off to the side of the road.

"What is your problem?" the old woman shouted.

"*My* problem?" Kasey shook her head. Her hands trembled. "*My* problem? Is . . . is . . . that you are heartless."

"Dear—"

"Don't *dear* me. I can't believe you. I know you didn't care for Nick. That's fine. You have that right. But he was *my* husband who, whether you like it or not, I loved with all my heart. I'm empty without him. Empty. And my son. My son, damn it. Do you not have a heart at all you old . . . errrrrrrrrr." She pulled on the door handle again—this time it opened, and she jumped out of the car.

"It's not like he was planned," Grem muttered, half under her breath as Kasey slammed the door.

Kasey spun on her heel, fire in her eyes. "I

heard that. I heard you. That was awful. What is making you act this way?" Kasey felt the tingle of red splotches rising on her chest.

Her grandmother rolled down the window. "Get back in this car. Have you gone crazy?"

"No."

"You're going to get yourself killed. You can't just walk along the interstate."

"Who would care?" Kasey balled her hands into fists, pumping them as she marched down the road. "Leave me alone."

"You aren't thinking clearly."

Kasey stepped over to the car and leaned into the window, way in, right into her grandmother's face. "I loved my husband. Having Jake was the best thing I ever did in my life. I don't want to hear your voice. I can't even think about you right now."

Calmness fell over her grandmother's features. "I loved Jake, too, honey. This outburst won't bring him back."

"He *will* be back." Kasey slapped the side of the car. "And you don't know anything about love." She stepped back and screamed to Jeremy, "Drive her home. I swear, get her out of here." She clenched her teeth so tightly that they ached.

"You don't have to live that way anymore."

"Why can't you get it through your thick skull? Nick and I wanted to share those dreams with our son, and I plan to do that." She threw her hands in the air, turned and started walking.

"Kasey!" Grem's voice rose to a screeching level.

Jeremy idled the Benz up to Kasey. "Are you going to be okay?" he shouted across the car.

"Fine. Just go!"

He eased back on to the road.

Kasey kicked the back of the car as Jeremy drove away.

She choked back tears as she walked along the shoulder of the interstate to the nearest exit where she called a cab to take her home. Home, to the farm in Pungo.

Thank goodness, she didn't have to wait long before the cab arrived. Kasey leaned back against the seat and closed her eyes, thankful for the silence on the long ride back. When they arrived, she paid the driver, got out, and went as far as the front porch.

All her good intentions to have a good day had backfired, but somehow she felt stronger for having tried. She loved Nick and she adored Jake. She missed them, ached for them. No one could ever take the good memories from her.

She forced herself to go into the house. There were ten messages on the answering machine. She pushed the button. People checking on her and leaving their condolences. Had it ever occurred to them that if they'd just quit reminding her how fragile she was, maybe she wouldn't be?

When would it stop?

Two messages from Riley, and one from Von, too. One from Jeremy, bless his heart.

His voice was kind and filled with remorse, not that her grandmother's actions were his fault. *"Kasey, its Jer. Sorry about this afternoon. The old lady had it coming, though. She was way out of line. I just had your car loaded on a flatbed tow truck, and it's on its way to your house. I am so sorry about today. She loves you in her own way. Oh. Yeah. I pre-paid the wrecker driver. I used Miss Em's salon account. I figured she owed you, even if she'd never admit it. Call me if you need me. For anything. Bye."*

The guy was a saint.

Quiet settled in the house. Dutch strolled out of the living room where he'd probably been napping in Nick's chair. He'd never done that when Nick was alive, but lately Dutch had taken it over as if he was next in line—man of the house.

Kasey shifted her gaze to the kitchen table where Nick's cell phone lay, attracting her like a magnet. She picked it up and rolled it between her hands. She remembered how she'd cried when she opened the packet from the police, glanced at the phone, and seen there were twenty-three missed calls.

All from her. All made on that tragic afternoon.

The first voice mail had been the hardest for Kasey to listen to. Her voice begged Nick to respond, followed by the muffled sound of the phone being pried from her hand as she realized the officer wasn't mistaken about the news he had given her, and then her crying.

She still called Nick's number sometimes, just to hear his voice.

Chapter Eight

The next morning, Riley sat at her desk staring out the window. Kasey had promised she'd meet Riley for lunch, but she hadn't shown yet. Riley picked up the phone and tried to call her again. Still no answer.

Riley shifted the phone under her chin and dialed Von's cell phone. She tapped her pen on the desk, waiting until he answered.

"Hey, it's me." She closed the folder that lay in front of her on her desk. "Busy?"

"Never too busy for you. What's up?"

"Are you at the house?" She crossed her fingers, hoping that he was.

"Sure am."

"Oh, good. I've been calling Kasey, and she isn't answering. I wasn't too worried this morning, but she was supposed to stop by the office this afternoon. She hasn't shown up."

"Want me to run over and check on her?"

She hated to ask, but . . . "Would you mind?"

"You know I don't mind."

His voice always settled her down, no matter how riled she got.

"Odds are she's in bed. Anything to avoid facing the pain." The past echoed in Von's words. "Don't worry. I'll head over there now."

"Thanks, sweetie. I just have a weird feeling about today."

"No cardinals or ladybugs?" he teased.

"Not one lucky sign all morning. That's when I started to worry."

He often teased her about her strong beliefs in lucky signs. But her superstitions had played in his favor when they'd been dating, so who was he to complain? Her quirky ideas were part of what made him love her so much.

"Don't worry," he said. "I'm on it."

Von closed the phone and headed to his SUV. The keys dangled from the ignition. One of the nice things about living all the way out in Pungo was the low crime rate. No reason to lock up.

He drove along the winding road toward Kasey's place . . . and Nick's. He'd always remember it as their place, together, even though Nick was gone. As he neared the house, he saw Kasey's old Porsche in the driveway. He pulled in and parked behind her car. Out of habit, he skimmed his hand over the hood as he walked past. The metal was cool. She'd probably been here all morning.

Von rapped on the back screen door, and waited for her to answer.

He was no stranger to this house. Over the years, when he and Nick were growing up, Nick's granddaddy had lived here. Nick and Von had spent many weeks on this farm, in this very house. He opened the screen door and rapped on the wooden door.

No sound came from inside.

He twisted the handle, opened the door and stepped inside. "Kasey, it's me, Von. Are you around?"

No answer.

He walked through the house, pausing at the sight of Nick's cowboy hat atop the rack of the sixteen-point trophy buck hanging on the wall. Nick's first buck. That thing had been around for years. He and Nick had hung it on the wall in their first rental back in college. They'd decorated it with a hat and black sunglasses and called him Buck Blue, the third Blues Brother. They'd sung *Soul Man* into beer bottles under that deer head many a night.

Von followed a beeping sound to the answering machine. The LED indicator flashed eighteen new messages. Knowing Riley, the last ten were from her. He slid the switch on the side and silenced the incessant beeping.

He checked every room downstairs, then went upstairs. The wood creaked under his weight.

He gripped the heavy oak banister as he climbed the steep stairs and found the bedroom door halfway open.

"Kasey?" He pushed open the door. Balled up tissues littered the floor and comforter. He noticed a couple of V8 juice cans in the trash. Not even a V8 could straighten you out after the kind of loss she had suffered. He'd been there. He wouldn't wish that feeling on anyone. Apparently this was where she'd spent the bulk of her time, but she wasn't here.

Her car was outside. She had to be somewhere close by.

Maybe she's driving Nick's T-Bird.

Memories of how much Nick had loved that car clouded his thoughts as he left the house and walked across the pasture to the barn. Nick and Kasey used to cruise around, and she'd mouth those famous words, *I love you,* like Suzanne Somers in the movie *American Graffiti.*

Von unlatched the pole gate that led to the big red barn. The antique T-Bird was parked in a garage next to it, untouched.

He walked over to the barn door and slid it wide. Light flooded the vast space. Dust danced in the sunrays and thick cobwebs shimmered in the sunlight.

A rhythmic thump echoed through the large building.

"Hello?" No one answered, but the thumping picked up pace.

Inside he caught a glimpse of Dutch sprawled beneath the ladder that led to the loft. He whimpered as Von got closer, but didn't get up.

"Are you okay, buddy?" He patted his leg. Dutch stood, but wouldn't leave the ladder. "What's the matter, boy?"

He lifted his nose in the air and let out a long low howl like a beagle howl.

"What are you doing out here?" The dog pushed his nose under Von's hand. "Where's Kasey?"

Dutch shook his head, his heavy ears flopping, and yawned.

Von stooped next to the dog and scanned the barn. "Know where Kasey is?" Dutch was over ten years old now, his muzzle gray. He didn't get around as quickly as he once had, but he was smarter than some men Von knew. Dutch seemed to point his nose up the ladder to the loft.

"Kasey." Von climbed the ladder to the loft. It was dark with the exception of a few slivers of light peeking through loose boards. Square bales filled the space. Alfalfa. He recognized the smell.

He swished his hand overhead, grabbed for the string to the bulb that he knew was there and tugged. In the dull yellow glow, he noticed a dark lump on top of a stack of hay bales.

He raced to the end of the barn.

As his eyes adjusted to the darkness, he thought his heart might break.

There was Kasey, lying across the hay bales, dressed in Nick's coveralls, which seemed to swallow her.

Her dirty bare feet hung from the pant legs. She had tissues wadded in one hand and Nick's old farm hat held to her chest with the other. In the crook of her arm, she held Jake's stuffed horse. Nick's first gift to his son, bought on the day the child was born and named after him. Their first day as a family. Jake had dragged that horse around until the time he could walk, then he'd gotten Bubba Bear and that ratty horse was put out to pasture in the toy box.

Von climbed the sturdy stacked squares.

"Kasey."

She didn't stir.

"Hey, kiddo, are you okay?" He wondered how long she'd been up here.

Fear sparked through him. In the extra-large coveralls, he couldn't see if she was breathing. He reached out and rested his hand on her side.

"Kasey, can you hear me?" He nudged her shoulder.

She took in a breath. *Thank goodness.* Relieved, he scooted closer.

"It's me, Von."

Her eyelids fluttered.

He leaned in closer and lowered his voice. "Hey. Talk to me."

She opened her eyes and let out a soft sigh.

He stretched out next to her so they were eye to eye, resting his head on his bent forearm. "You okay?"

"What do you think?" She spoke in a broken whisper.

"I think you're hurting."

She nodded. "You must think I'm cracking up, wearing his clothes." She lifted her coverall-cloaked arm. Her hand didn't even peek out the end of the sleeve.

Von pushed her bangs away from her damp cheeks. He shook his head. "No. I wouldn't judge. I've been right where you are. We all mourn and heal in our own ways."

"I'll never heal."

He stroked her back. "I know it feels that way."

She sniffed and shifted her arm up under her head, wiping her tears on the big sleeve of the coveralls.

"I'm not going to tell you that things will be all right. That was the last thing I wanted to hear when I lost Deidre."

Kasey nodded.

"You just have to take things a day at a time. The truth is, you'll never be the same. But that's okay, too."

Kasey looked away. "There was another shooting on Route 58 last night. Did you know?"

"I heard. I'm checking it out," he said.

"It's like the third or fourth time. Sprays of bullets, no injuries," Kasey said. "What are the odds that, with all those incidents, Nick would be the one to get killed?"

He didn't tell her that Nick's shooting didn't fit the random pattern, or type of gun. A shotgun was used in the other shootings. The casings found by Nick's truck near the accident site were from a small caliber bullet. The police had confirmed that earlier, but that information wasn't something Kasey needed to hear right now.

Von shook his head. "I don't know. Sometimes there aren't any good answers."

"It's not fair."

"I know."

"Nick was a good man. He didn't deserve to die. I can't live without him." Kasey sniffled. She buried her face in her hands, then lifted her eyes to meet Von's. "I need him. He'd help me find Jake. Everybody thinks I'm crazy to believe Jake's still out there. He has to be. I can't live this way."

"You can."

"I don't want to."

"Come here, kiddo." He hugged her close.

She came undone in his arms, sobbing. It broke his heart to see her so sad, to know that Nick wouldn't be back. Nothing he could say could change that. He held her and after a long moment, she quieted a little. "You better?"

She nodded against his shoulder.

"I need to call Riley and let her know you're alive. She was worried about you."

"Sorry."

"We understand. Can you call her?" Kasey look whipped. She was dirty and sweaty. Von tipped her nose with his knuckle. "It would mean more if the call came from you."

Kasey looked down. "I'll call her."

"Thanks."

Von descended the ladder first, then spotted Kasey as she climbed down in the oversized coveralls. They walked out of the barn, the extra long pants swishing with each step she took. Dutch followed behind them.

Kasey wrapped her arms around Von's arm and rested her head against it as they walked.

Chapter Nine

Kasey had other issues to worry about in addition to finding Jake. Gracious volunteers had been running the farm, but they were only scheduled to help for two more weeks. Kasey wasn't prepared to take care of the Rocking R by herself. It was time to find a farm manager, but she had no idea where to start. Pushing that thought aside, she decided to tackle something she knew how to manage.

She walked outside to the RV to get her camera bag. When she pulled her camera out, Cody Tuggle's card fluttered to the ground. She picked it up, her heart clenching when she thought of how kind he had been to come to Nick's funeral and offer his condolences.

She rubbed the raised letters on the card, thinking about the offer to photograph his tour. Maybe joining the tour would be a good escape while the authorities continued their work looking for Jake. She'd heard that the pace on a music tour was so fast that she'd hardly be able to remember what town she was waking up in each day.

That sounds perfect.

The project would keep her name out there while she took some time to sort out her life, too. Downtime was the kiss of death for a freelancer.

Am I really considering this?

She went inside and picked up the phone. Then she put it back down and picked it up four times before dialing Cody Tuggle's number.

The phone rang on the other end. She tensed, almost chickening out, but he answered on the first ring.

"Yeah-lo." His deep voice vibrated.

"Hi," she said, her mouth dry. "Hi, Cody. It's Kasey."

"Kasey? Hey, how are you?" He sounded surprised.

"Makin' it." She drew in a deep breath. "Thanks for coming to . . . well, it meant a lot to me. Thank you."

"Just wanted you to know how sorry I was for your loss. Figured flowers would just get lost in the shuffle and, hell, you probably wouldn't have known who they were from anyway."

"Right. There are so many Tuggles in the world."

"I'm glad you called."

"Did I catch you at a good time?"

"Yeah, sure. I was just getting ready to head over to the studio. We're cutting one last song before we head for the Midwest leg of the tour."

"How's the tour going?"

"We sold out in every city so far."

"No surprise."

"Hey, you never know."

"That's why I was calling." *Don't lose your nerve.* "I was wondering. I mean, well, don't feel like you have to say yes." *Just say it.* "Does the offer to shoot your tour still stand?"

"You kidding?" His voice raised a pitch.

"I don't think so." She looked around the room for an answer. Was she doing the right thing? She didn't have any better options.

"Yeah. Absolutely. We'd love to have you."

"It would be good to be busy. I promise my emotions won't interfere with the quality of my work."

"Don't be ridiculous. If you get here and find you're not up to it, you can leave whenever you need to."

"Thanks, Cody."

"Thank *you*. It will be great to get Arty off my back, too."

"Yeah, he seemed pretty adamant about the project."

"He can be a pain in the ass sometimes, but he's a good guy. He was my biggest supporter when no one was interested. I owe him."

"Then I guess it'll work out for everyone."

"Let me get someone to overnight the full schedule and some materials to get you started. Do you want to fly with me on the jet or tour on the bus?"

"I thought I'd take the RV and follow you all."

"Naw. That won't work. You'd be mobbed. After the first show, I guarantee everyone will know you are on this gig."

"Can I think about it and let you know?"

"Sure. You're welcome either way. In fact, you can switch it up from town to town if you like. I could use some good company on the jet, though. Someone recently said I'm antsy and a chatterbox."

"You don't say." She snickered, shaking her head. The smile felt foreign on her face. *This is the right thing to do.*

"It's true. So I could use an ear," he teased.

"So happens I've got two not being used much these days." That dark hole expanded in her chest again.

"Welcome aboard."

On Monday morning, a Federal Express package arrived from Cody Tuggle's road manager. Kasey glanced at the list of cities, but she wasn't choosy. She needed an escape and location didn't matter. By the end of the following week, she'd be packed and headed for a tour with one of the hottest singers in the country.

When Von and Riley stopped by that afternoon, she told them about her decision.

"Am I a bad mother?" she asked Riley, hoping for reassurance. "I just can't sit here waiting and waiting with no way to help. It's killing me. If I'm working, maybe . . ."

"Hon, I don't know how you've done it this long. You're a wonderful mother. If Jake is out there, we'll find him. Don't you worry about that. The best thing you can do is go on that tour. Work will be good for you. Keep your mind busy and yourself healthy."

"I'll check in," Kasey said. "And you'll contact me with even the tiniest details, right?" She looked from Von to Riley.

Von nodded. "We promise, and I'll take care of hiring a farm manager while you're gone."

One less thing to worry about.

Von gave Riley the look, and Riley picked up her purse. "You know what time it is, don't ya?"

Kasey laughed. "Time for *Cops*?"

Riley nodded. "You know he hates to miss it."

"Hey, it's one show," Von said, looking insulted.

"See ya," Kasey waved and watched them leave, thankful that Von would take care of hiring the farm manager. She braced herself for the arguments that were sure to come when she shared her news with Grem. Calling would be the easy way out, but she owed her grandmother the news in person, no matter how cranky and irrational the old woman was sometimes.

Kasey gave herself a little pep talk, then headed to the estate before she could change her mind.

Jeremy opened the front door just as Kasey took the last step up to the porch. "This is a pleasant surprise. I was going to stop by tomorrow."

"Thanks. I wanted to talk to Grem." She reached up and gave him a hug. "What kind of mood is she in today?"

"Complaining about her arthritis. Didn't like the brand of apple butter I picked out this time. Normal." He nodded toward the sun room. "She's in there."

"Great. Thanks."

"Can I get you some tea? Juice? Crappy apple butter toast?"

"Tea sounds good." Kasey watched Grem from

the doorway of the sun room. She looked tiny and frail sitting in her Queen Anne chair overlooking the gardens. But she never seemed either once she started talking.

Grem turned. "I thought I heard voices. This is unexpected, dear."

Kasey crossed the room and sank into the chair opposite her. "How've you been doing?"

"I'm old. Don't ask. How are you?"

"Same. Not the old part, but the 'don't ask' part."

They laughed.

"I wanted to stop by and let you know I'll be out of town for a while."

Jeremy walked in with a mug of tea and a small plate of toast.

She took both, and they exchanged a look after she noticed the apple butter.

"Thanks. This looks good." She bit into a triangle of toast and moaned. "Delicious."

Grem rolled her eyes.

"Did you just say you were going away?" He set a pot of tea on the table between Kasey and Grem. "I overheard. Where are you headed?"

Kasey sipped her tea. "I have a photo shoot."

"Where?" Grem asked.

"I'm shooting Cody Tuggle's tour. He's a country singer. I'll be heading to Nashville, then up and down the coast."

"Now that's my girl. That sounds like a big deal." Grem looked pleased.

"It is." Kasey nodded. "Von and Riley will be my eyes and ears here while I'm away, in case anything comes up about Jake."

Grem placed her hand on Kasey's arm. "I think it's the right thing to do. Your career is important. Keep me posted, won't you?"

"I will." Kasey sighed in relief. She'd expected a lot of drama, but her grandmother had taken the news quite well.

A non-event. Thank goodness for that.

All she had left to do now was to pack.

"When will you leave?" Grem asked.

"Friday," Kasey said.

Jeremy straightened. "So soon? How long will you be gone?"

Kasey shrugged. "I'm just going to see how it plays out. I wanted to let y'all know, but like you said, it's soon." She got up and stepped over to Grem's chair. "I need to run some errands and start packing."

"I'm sure you'll do an amazing job," Grem said. She hugged Kasey. "I'm so proud of you."

"Thanks. Love you," Kasey said over her shoulder as she walked toward the door.

Jeremy stepped between her and the front door.

"Wednesdays won't be the same," he said.

"From what I hear about these music tours, I may not even know which day *is* Wednesday." She laughed.

He didn't.

She cocked her head. "What's the matter?"

"I just hate the thought of you being gone. I mean, Jake—and now you."

"And Nick," Kasey said. "Nick's gone. We don't have any leads on Jake. I can't take it anymore. The waiting. The sitting here doing nothing. It's killing me. We've talked about this. You know how it's tearing me apart." She bowed her head, her jaw tightening. "You're the last one I expected to get any heat from."

He hugged her. "Sorry. I'm overreacting. Jake will show up. I feel it, too. I'd just hate for you to be gone when he does."

Kasey hitched her purse onto her shoulder. "Me, too, but it's not like I'll be in the jungle. I can be on the first plane back. I'm praying for answers."

"Me, too," Jeremy said. "Let me know what you need from me. You know you can count on me, right?"

"Of course."

On Wednesday morning, just after nine, there was a loud knock at the front door. Kasey ran down the stairs, swung around the newel post and answered it. A courier handed her a package. "Need your signature, ma'am."

More tour stuff.

She took the pen from the young man's hand and scribbled her signature next to the X, then took the package. She kicked the door closed and opened the stiff envelope. Over the last two days she'd felt an excitement that she thought she'd never feel again. She'd had fun reading all the details of the promo for each city on the tour, knowing she'd be a part of the action.

Kasey pulled the contents from the envelope, excited to see what they'd sent her now. Her hands recoiled as if she'd touched a hot stove. Paper fluttered like angel wings to the floor.

Her hands trembled.

She fell to her knees and swept the sheets into a pile. Two flimsy slips of cardboard, three blank sheets of paper and two pictures—printed on an inkjet by the looks of their quality.

Her breathing became rapid and shallow.

She grabbed the two pictures from among the cardboard and paper, then ran to the phone and speed-dialed Riley.

"Good morning." Riley answered on the first ring.

"You're home. I need you." Kasey's words ran together.

"Slow down. What's the matter?"

"Get over here, now. Bring Von," Kasey said, still staring at the pictures.

"Are you okay?"

"I don't know. I'm not sure what to think. Please hurry." Kasey hung up the phone, and stared at the pictures in front of her.

Chapter Ten

Kasey was sitting in the middle of the kitchen floor, a picture in each hand, when Von and Riley let themselves in through the back door.

Riley raced to Kasey's side. "What's wrong?" Riley slid to the floor next to her and took one of the pictures from Kasey's shaking hands. "Is this why you called?"

Kasey nodded.

Riley studied the picture, passed it to Von, then looked over Kasey's shoulder at the other.

"Why would someone send me these?" Kasey whispered.

"Are these pictures that you took?" Von asked.

She shook her head.

"Careful handling them then." Von leaned in for a closer look.

One picture had been taken from a distance. Nick's silver truck lay cocked to one side in the middle of the river. Steam rose from the hot engine. The other picture was more of a close-up, but the quality was so poor that, had Kasey not seen the first photo, she wouldn't have known that the picture was of Nick's truck.

"Why?" Kasey repeated. "I don't understand why someone would send these."

"I have no idea," Riley said. "A cruel joke?"

Riley studied the picture more closely, then handed it to Von.

He took the pictures to the kitchen counter where the light was better.

Riley helped Kasey to a chair at the table.

"Where did you get these? Email?" Von held the flimsy paper to the light.

"A courier. I assumed the envelope was from Cody Tuggle's tour manager. I had to sign for them."

Von raised a brow, then tore a piece of paper off the grocery list hanging on the side of the refrigerator. "What time?"

"Just a few minutes ago."

"Did you notice the color of the vehicle?"

"White? No. I don't know. Maybe a light color. A car." Kasey rubbed her temples. "I didn't pay attention. I'm sorry."

"Was there a note, or just the pictures?"

"There were a few pieces of blank paper and some cardboard."

"Where are they?"

"In the living room. On the floor."

Von gathered the evidence, then dialed the lead detective on the case to bring him up to date. Kasey and Riley sat silent at the table.

A quick rap at the front door shifted their attention.

"Hello," a man called.

"Who is that?" Riley asked.

"I'm in the kitchen," Kasey called out, then turned back to Riley. "It's Jeremy. He comes by after he drops off Grem at the salon."

Jeremy stepped into the kitchen. "I saw Von's car out front. Anything new?"

Von hung up the phone and joined them at the table. "Someone sent these to Kasey." He slid the pictures in front of Jeremy.

Jeremy reached for them.

"Don't touch them," Von said too late. Jeremy already had them in his hands.

"Wow." Jeremy leaned in closer. "Is that—? That's Jake in the truck, isn't it?"

"What?" Kasey's eyes went wide. She jumped to her feet and looked over his arm at the picture. "I didn't see any . . . give me that." Kasey grabbed the picture from his hands. Riley rushed to her side.

"I don't see anything." Riley glared at Jeremy.

He shrugged.

Kasey ran her finger across a shadow. "No. He might be right. Look. Is that the outline of my baby in the backseat?" She handed the picture to Riley. "Excuse me." She ran to the bathroom, crying.

Riley slapped Jeremy's arm. "Why the hell did you do that?"

"What?" He rubbed his arm. "You don't see it? This could prove he's alive. Someone had to be there to take these pictures."

"It doesn't prove anything. It's just plain mean," Riley said.

Von stepped over, his voice low. "Don't give her hope, man. She's just started acting like herself again."

"Do what you want. She's like family to me and if I see hope, I'm giving it to her." Jeremy plopped down in one of the kitchen chairs.

"And we're not?" Riley's jaw tensed. "She's my best friend. Don't make this worse for her."

Kasey came back into the kitchen with a handful of tissues, her eyes red and puffy. "What the hell do I do now?"

Riley wrapped her arms around Kasey.

"How can I leave now? This just makes it worse."

"Kasey, don't do this to yourself. Von will follow every lead. You know that. We'll update you every day. I promise. But, honey, you really need to work. You need to get your feet moving again. It's not going to get any easier."

"I don't know."

"You can't do anything to help the investigation. You'll just be waiting again."

Kasey looked to Jeremy. "You haven't said anything. What do you think?"

He stood. "You need to do what you think is right. You know I'll support you no matter what. Doesn't look like you need my help anyway." He glanced at his watch. "I've got to pick up your grandmother."

"I understand. Thank you for coming by." Kasey gave Jeremy a hug, then walked him to the door. She glanced over her shoulder then grabbed Jeremy's arm.

"Wait," she whispered. She tugged him out the front door and out of view.

He followed her lead, with a look of bewilderment on his face.

"You *can* help." Kasey closed her eyes, gathering strength.

He took her hands into his own. "Anything. What?"

"If I knew he was safe or not—just one way or another—I could at least live my life. It's the uncertainty of it all that I can't stand." She steepled her fingers under her chin. "If you'll come with me. I mean, oh gosh, I can't believe I'm doing this. Call that tea-leaf lady. You'll come with me, right?"

"Of course. Yes. I'll take you, be there every step of the way." He held her hands in his. "Thanks for letting me help."

"I hope I don't regret this."

"You won't," he said. "I'll call you later tonight, as soon as I have the details."

Kasey watched him drive off in Grandma Emily's Mercedes.

Riley stepped up behind her. "What was that all about?"

"Nothing." Kasey reached for Riley's hand and

squeezed it. "I think I should call Cody and let him know I'm considering not coming on Friday."

In just a few hours, the Rolly farmhouse buzzed with renewed energy as the detective and Von pieced together the information and the source of the pictures. Von had already tracked down the courier. But the point of origination on their docket was a different courier located outside of Richmond.

As the debriefing wound down, the detective gathered the courier packet and contents. He promised to have the lab expedite the test for trace evidence.

"This could prove Jake's alive? It's proof, right?" Kasey prayed he'd tell her what she wanted to hear. She raised her eyes to meet his level stare. "I mean, there's a chance—"

"Mrs. Rolly, there's a chance until we find proof otherwise. We're going to do everything we can. An investigation like this takes time."

That wasn't what she'd wanted to hear. He'd given her hope, but not any more or less than she had the day before. She picked up her cell phone from the end table and dialed Cody Tuggle's direct line.

"Yeah-lo."

"Hi, Cody. It's Kasey Phillips."

"Hey. Getting excited? We can't wait for you to join us. Nashville is always a kickin' town."

"Yes, but that's why I'm calling. I might not be coming this Friday. I'm not sure yet, but there's a lead on Jake."

"A lead? That's great. You do whatever you have to do. What can I do to help?"

"Nothing. I mean, we're not even sure it's a lead. Someone sent me some pictures of the accident. I'm probably fooling myself, but I didn't want to leave you hanging at the last minute, so I thought I'd let you know."

"Thanks, but I'm flexible. This project might be the end of the world for Arty, but not for me. Your son comes first."

Cody Tuggle was nothing like the man in the gossip rags. He was kind-hearted and gentle, and she couldn't have happened onto a better friend.

Von and Riley left to give her some time alone.

Kasey couldn't eat. She couldn't rest. She sat. She stood. But mostly she paced the living room with Dutch at her heels. The detective had left just hours ago, yet she still prayed each minute for the phone to ring.

When it did, the caller wasn't someone with news about Jake, it was Jeremy.

"I just got off the phone with Lala," he said. "She's in town."

Sheer black fright coursed through Kasey's veins. Although she'd never heard the tea-leaf lady's name until now, she knew whom Jeremy was referring to and every alarm in her head was ringing. She hoped the name Lala wasn't just more proof that this was crazy la-la-land kind of stuff. *I hope I don't regret this.* "When?"

"She can do a reading for you tonight, or next Tuesday."

An icy chill seemed to paralyze her. "If I wait, I won't do it. Let's do it tonight."

"Want me to come get you?"

"No, it's too far. I'll meet you. Hang on." Kasey rummaged through a drawer for a pen, then grabbed a cereal box to write on. "Where?"

"We could use the carriage house. Your grandmother is already in bed. She'll never know."

Kasey dropped the pen and blew out a breath. "I'm on my way, then."

Please let this bring me some answers.

When Kasey got to the estate, she drove past the main house to the carriage house. She'd lived there for years, so at least the surroundings were a comfort. She walked inside. Jeremy sat across from a tall woman with a long braid. She wore jeans and a t-shirt.

The woman looked normal enough, but the whole thing didn't feel normal. "How do we do this?"

"Relax," the woman said. "You can call me Lala."

Nodding, Kasey held back a nervous giggle.

Lala sat with the elegance of a ballerina.

"Where will you be most comfortable?" Her voice was velvet-edged and strong.

Kasey took a seat on the adjacent loveseat. "Is this okay?"

Jeremy got up and disappeared into the kitchen. When he walked back into the room, he carried a wide black tray. It shone in stark contrast to the white porcelain teapot and wide-mouthed cup and saucer arranged in the middle.

Kasey placed her hand over her heart, wishing it would stop beating so hard.

Lala reached over and touched her. "Don't be afraid."

After a brief discussion about the process, Lala poured steaming water over loose tea leaves in the cup and handed it to her. "Hold this in the palms of your hands as it steeps."

Kasey accepted the cup and gave Jeremy a worried glance. He hung by the kitchen. Watching.

"Focus on your question."

Kasey closed her eyes and focused all her energy on Jake. Her hands trembled. If this helped, it was worth every bit of the fear that consumed her.

Lala's low voice broke the silence. "When the tea is cool enough, sip it. But don't drink it all. Leave the last sips and tea leaves in the bottom."

Kasey steadied herself and took a sip.

Is this tea making me lightheaded? Relax! You're doing this for Jake.

She drank most of the tea. Lala took the cup,

then swirled the contents with purpose. She picked up a square paper napkin from the tray, placed it in the center of the saucer, then flipped the cup upside down on top of the napkin.

Kasey wondered how long this would take, and if her courage would sustain. *All my hopes are trapped under a china cup.*

Lala righted the cup. She inspected it. Slowly. Methodically. Then she scribbled on a paper at her side. She never uttered a word.

Kasey leaned in, trying to decipher what Lala had written. The scribbles made no sense.

"So much here," Lala said, her voice louder, confident—almost vibrating. "A lot of emotion in your life."

No kidding.

"There *is* an answer to your problem. The answer is in your circle, but yes, new friends are coming your way to help." Lala twisted the cup and drew another symbol on the tablet. "Does the letter L mean anything to you?"

Kasey looked up. *L?* "No. I don't think so."

"It's a strong L. Lee perhaps? Any connections to a Lee? Place, person?"

"No."

"It's in front of you, so perhaps you haven't intersected just yet. But soon." She nodded and twisted the cup again. "Good news is coming your way."

I can't believe I fell for this.

Lala pointed a long finger into the cup and tipped it toward Kasey. "This egg and the smaller one near it represent success or perhaps a business opportunity." She pointed to the side of the cup near the handle. "See here, this is the anchor—the answer to your problem. It's close. And here, the angel. She's good news."

Everything from that point forward was a blur. Kasey's mind clung to those words.

The answer.

Good news.

As Kasey drove home, she realized nothing the mysterious Lala had said was specific.

Smoke and mirrors.

Why had she let herself fall for such a scheme? She knew better. Clutching the steering wheel, she looked into the starry night and hoped she hadn't just done something that would backfire on her with some kind of bad karma.

God, please forgive me. I'm desperate.

Exhausted by the time she got home, she went straight to bed.

She closed her eyes to the images Lala had scribbled across that page. Hieroglyphics inspired by clumps of messy wet tea leaves that looked like nothing to her told Lala a story. Or was it just what Kasey had wanted to hear?

Kasey prayed that dreams of Nick would soothe her worries during the night.

• • •

The next day was a long one, but Kasey promised herself she'd put last night behind her. When the phone rang, she tripped over Dutch as she lunged for it.

"Hello?" she said as she steadied herself.

"It's me."

Riley's voice was a welcome one, but not the one she'd hoped to hear. "Hi."

"Sorry. No more news. Von's still working on every angle and so are the police."

"Why does everything take so long? I mean, you can get almost anything on the internet in mere seconds. But when the information is important, it takes so long. It doesn't seem right."

"I know. I thought I'd come do a sleepover tonight, if you want. Might make the waiting easier. Or heck, maybe we'll have news by then and we'll be celebrating."

Kasey smiled. "Von won't mind?"

"Not at all. Are you kidding? He'll be happy to have all the pillows without a fight."

"That would be great. Thanks, Riley." Kasey's jaw dropped. *Riley—Lee. Maybe that was the "L," the Lee, Lala had referred to?*

"I'll be over as soon as I finish cooking dinner for him. I'll bring you something."

"Don't bother. I can't eat," Kasey said.

"Well, you need to. You need your strength. I'll see you shortly."

110

Kasey hung up the phone and curled up on the couch. Dutch sat in front of her, resting his chin on her leg. She stared out the picture window at nothing until the daylight started to dim.

No lights out here in the country.

No neighbors.

No family.

No life.

Headlights streamed into the now dark living room where Kasey still sat huddled on the couch next to the house phone and with her cell phone in her lap. She turned on the lamp when Riley stepped onto the porch.

"It's me," Riley said, as she let herself in.

Kasey responded with half a smile. Her stomach growled in response to the familiar smell of home cooking. "You made chicken and dumplings." Riley knew it was her favorite.

"Comfort food. Lord knows we deserve it." Riley dropped her purse in the corner and put a paper sack on the coffee table. She retrieved two covered bowls and spoons from the bag, handed one to Kasey, and snuggled next to her on the couch with the other. "At least try."

Kasey swirled her spoon in the bowl. "Any news?" She lowered her head and blew across the top of the piping hot broth.

"A little, but don't get excited. Whoever sent the pictures went to some trouble. They've traced the package back through two couriers to the origination point, but they didn't ask for any identification at origination."

"Great."

"It gets better. You won't believe who the paperwork says the pictures were sent by."

Kasey raised her eyes and held Riley's gaze. "I'm almost afraid to ask."

"You. It says they were sent by Kasey Phillips."

"Why would I send those pictures to myself?"

"You wouldn't. This is a case of bad record keeping or a good cover up. They put your name in both the *To* and the *From* blanks on the shipping form." Riley took a bite of chicken and dumplings, then set her bowl on the table. "There's one other thing."

"What's that?"

"The package originated in Nashville."

Kasey blinked as she realized the connection. "That's where I was headed to pick up Cody's tour."

"I know."

"If my baby is in Nashville . . ." Kasey set her bowl next to Riley's. "Do you think Jake is alive and in Nashville?" She shook her head. "This doesn't make sense. Why would he end up so far away?"

"Don't get your hopes up. I mean . . . wait . . . I know that sounds awful. I want you to have hope. We all want to find him, but this doesn't mean . . ."

"I know. I know. I could drive myself crazy. Or maybe I am, and I printed bad unfocused pictures and sent them to myself."

Riley put her arm around Kasey and they shared a laugh. The first one in a long time and Kasey wasn't sure if the tears were from how good it felt to laugh, or how anxious she felt about Jake at the moment.

Kasey's cell phone rang.

Riley reached for it. "Want me to get it?"

"Would you?"

Riley snagged the phone and answered. "Kasey Phillips's phone. May I help you?" Riley's eyes went wide. She mouthed "Cody Tuggle" to Kasey, and Kasey nodded in response. "Yes, she's right here. No, I think she'd want to speak to you. One moment."

Kasey took the phone and filled him in on the latest details.

"Nashville? Then I *can* help. We can get the word out. I have promo spots on radio and television in every stop on this tour. We can post a picture. What Amber alert can't do, maybe the Tuggle country music fan club network can."

"I wish."

"No. I'm serious. I can slip that in on every stop. What are they going to do, tell me to shut up?"

"Maybe."

"It's a risk I'll take. Come on out to Nashville as scheduled. If your son is anywhere near there, you'll be that much closer when they find him. I'll jet you wherever you need to go."

"Really?"

"Yeah. And if it's not a good lead, the tour will be a good distraction for you."

He was right. "I can't thank you enough." Kasey hung up the phone, feeling hopeful and more confident in her plan.

Riley raised a brow and smiled. "Is the trip back on?"

"It is."

Chapter Eleven

When Kasey landed in Nashville, she headed for baggage claim. The rush of being on a schedule again was a welcome diversion. As soon as she stepped off the escalator, she spotted her driver. The black-suited man was as short and stout as the capital letters that spelled out her name on the sign he held in front of him. She introduced herself.

He nodded. "Schaffer, ma'am. I'll be your driver while you're in town. How many bags do you have?"

"Four," Kasey said, then felt the need to explain. "Four in all. One for clothes, and three full of equipment and supplies."

He grabbed a cart and headed to the baggage carousel just as the belt started chugging and an array of bags eased past. Cody's road manager had sent special stickers for her luggage which made the four cases easy to spot.

The driver grunted while lifting her equipment onto the cart. Kasey cringed.

"Ready, ma'am?" he asked, as he lifted the final one into place.

"Thank you," Kasey said, then followed him to the limousine, trying to figure out how to ask for a favor.

He opened and held the door of the stretch limo. She slid onto the fine leather of the backseat. The car shifted from the weight of her bags when he loaded them into the trunk. He rounded the limo and got in.

"I know you're supposed to take me to the hotel, but would you mind stopping at this address?" Kasey handed the driver a piece of paper noting the address. "I don't know if it's on the way." She watched for a response.

"Not a problem, miss." He punched the address into the GPS, then eased into traffic.

A few minutes later, he parallel-parked the car in front of *Victory Courier Service*.

"Thanks. I'll be just a few minutes." Kasey opened the car door, but the driver was around to her side before she stepped out. She felt herself flush.

He held the door. "Take your time."

She got out and stood there for a moment. *What*

do I think I'm going to find out that the cops didn't? The thought froze in her brain. While on this tour, she'd do everything she could possibly do to find Jake. If she rattled a few cages along the way, so be it.

Neon signs indicated that the shop was open for business. Filled with determination, Kasey walked to the door. Three giant bells on a single piece of twine jingled as she entered the small shop, then stepped to the counter.

A balding white-haired man looked up from his newspaper and peered at her over the top of his glasses. His plaid western shirt had seen better days, but its rosy orange color matched his cheeks.

"How can I help you today?" he asked with a warm smile.

"Are you the owner?"

His long wiry brows seemed to dance above his eyes. "Yes, ma'am. Is there a problem?"

"Oh, no, nothing like that. You spoke to the police earlier this week about a package."

His smile faded. "Yes. The one the lady sent to the courier in Virginia?"

"That's the one." *Thank God, he remembers.* "Do you remember what she looked like?"

He studied her. "Yes. Yes, I do."

Her heart raced, and she prayed she wouldn't screw up anything the police had already done. Was he going to answer?

His face softened. "I remember her because, you see, she was wearin' one of them fringy coats. Kind of looked like a hippy from back in the sixties. She'd have been a looker back then, but you're too young to know what I mean by that. She was tallish. Long, straight brown hair. Said she was just passing through."

"You're sure?"

"Positive. Why do you ask?"

"I'm Kasey Phillips. The package was sent to me."

He wagged a crooked finger toward her. "No, young lady. You are *not* the lady that sent that package."

She nodded. "Oh, I know. Do you think if I sent an artist over, you could describe her well enough for them to sketch a picture?"

He tapped his finger to his temple. "Mind like a steel trap. I can do that."

"Excellent," she said, her voice jumping as high as her hopes.

"You seem pretty excited about that. Mind me askin' what this is all about? Police wouldn't share much."

"No, sir. I hope you can help me." She told him the story of the accident and Jake's disappearance.

He reached across the counter and patted her arm. "I'm so sorry."

"Me, too. I pray for any lead that might help

me. Mr. . . . Where are my manners? I'm sorry. I didn't get your name."

"Lightner."

She grabbed a business card off the counter. "I'll have someone call and set up a time to come by as soon as possible, Mr. Lightner."

"That'll be fine. I hope I can help." His brows wiggled again. "I bet you're a wonderful mother."

She pressed her hands to her heart. Her eyes welled. "That's a nice thing for you to say. Thank you." She shook the card his way as she backed out of the store. "I have someone waiting on me, but we'll be in touch."

He waved goodbye, shook the paper open, and turned his attention to the morning news.

Back in the limo, Kasey couldn't contain her excitement. She thanked the driver so many times for stopping that he rolled up the window between them.

She dialed Von and passed along the news. Once he finished fussing at her for going to the courier service, he agreed to arrange for a sketch artist to visit Mr. Lightner and follow through with the lead.

A newfound sense of strength came over her. She relaxed against the fine leather, basking in the knowledge she was doing everything she could think of to find Jake.

The driver looked at ease as he maneuvered

through the traffic, then parked in front of the hotel. Kasey was greeted by a concierge who escorted her to Cody Tuggle. As they passed through the lobby, the concierge introduced himself as David Allen. He was so proper she didn't dare ask if those were his first and middle names, or first and last, though she wondered. He told her the bellman would retrieve her bags and deliver them to her suite. She hadn't expected this level of opulence in décor or service.

David Allen led her to a private elevator and punched in the code for the penthouse. When they reached the top floor, they stepped into a marble sitting area with a skylight overhead and faced a set of huge double doors. David Allen pulled a gold key from his suit pocket and twisted it in the lock.

Kasey entered the grand room. White marble floors glistened as bright as fresh Aspen snow. Carpeted areas sectioned off the space with pile so deep her high heels sank, making it hard to keep balance. She followed through the huge space toward the hum of conversation. An impromptu interview area had been arranged at the far end of the room—two large black leather chairs and stage lights that burned so bright she sensed the sizzle from yards away. Near the interview area, Cody sat with a paper cape tucked into the collar of his white shirt. A pretty blonde dabbed his forehead with a sponge.

"You made it," Cody said, leaning to dodge the woman who was now coming at him with a huge makeup brush. "I was getting worried."

Kasey hadn't considered that her little detour would be noticed by anyone but the driver.

Cody spoke to a dark-haired woman who then crossed the room to greet Kasey.

"He'll wrap up in just a little bit. I'm Annette. I run the publicity campaign for his tour." She extended her hand.

Kasey accepted the handshake and introduced herself.

Annette's dark hair swung across her shoulders as she spoke. "Cody filled me in on your son. I'm so sorry. I can't even imagine . . ."

"Thank you." Kasey took in a deep breath.

"He's getting ready to do an interview with the local TV affiliate. You're just in time. He said you'd have a picture. We'll get them to show it at the end of the interview, and Cody will explain the situation. I hope it helps."

"You don't know how much this means to me." Kasey took a manila envelope out of her shoulder bag and handed it to her.

"It won't hurt Cody's reputation any either. I have a hard time getting him to do interviews. He's always hell bent on staying off camera, but then paparazzi just make up stuff about him. That's never good. You're in the biz. You know."

"All too well," Kasey said.

Annette tugged the photographs out of the sleeve.

"They're all the same. I made fifty copies." Kasey had taken the picture after a long day at a picnic. Jake had been sweaty and dirty—all boy—and clutching his Bubba Bear to his chest.

Annette took in a quick breath and her eyes went glassy. She rubbed her fingers under her nose. "He's adorable," she said in a compassionate tone.

Tears teased the rims of Kasey's eyes. She couldn't let that start. Not here. Not now.

"Thank you for all your help." She excused herself before she lost control.

Kasey poured herself a glass of water and filled a small plate with food from the huge spread that had been laid out for the crew. She took a seat and watched Cody and the television host. Cody looked nervous. Stiff. He'd been the same with her on the photo shoot at first.

Once the interview got going, he loosened up and the real Cody came out—charming and full of humor. Toward the end of the interview, Cody asked the host if she would do him a favor.

"Of course," she gushed. "Anything for you, Cody."

Cody shifted gears—from playful musician to sentimental man.

He cleared his throat and leaned forward,

resting his forearms on his knees and forming a steeple with his fingers. Kasey guessed that the camera-man was zooming in on him.

"Bad things happen all the time. Usually to really good people. I have a friend, a real nice lady; she's had a rough time. Long story short, her son is missing. We're going to flash a picture for you. If you've seen this child, please call the toll-free number below, or contact the station here."

Kasey held her breath. She might as well because her throat was suddenly so tight that no air could pass through it.

Cody looked her way, then repeated the phone number and the description of Jake.

She tilted her head and mouthed the words, "Thank you." A dormant strength awakened inside her, a welcome feeling that she really wasn't alone in all of this.

"If your tip brings this little man home to his momma, I'll pay a generous reward for the lead."

Why hadn't I thought of that?

The producer called from the side, "Aaaaand, that's a wrap."

Cody thanked the interviewer, then the entire crew, appearing much more relaxed since the camera had stopped rolling. He made his way over to Kasey.

"The segment will air across the Nashville area on the six o'clock news," Cody said. "Don't worry about the reward. I'll pay it."

"You're doing enough just getting Jake's picture out there," Kasey said, still amazed by his generosity.

He grabbed an Orange Crush from an ice bucket and twisted off the top. He took two long swigs. "Those lights are hot."

"You're changing the subject."

"Yeah. I'm the star. I get to do that." He winked. "Did you want to change before we go over to do the sound check?"

"You always get your way?"

"Pretty much." Cody picked up a white phone from the bar and, in what seemed like less than a minute, the concierge was back to escort her to her quarters.

Quarters. Excuse me. Talk about first class treatment.

Kasey stayed close to Cody on the tour, jetting from city to city and staying in constant contact with Riley for updates. She became a part of the group in no time flat. They even had her wearing a tour do-rag of her own by the time they arrived in the third city.

She found it easy to get caught up in the excitement that filled the arena when Tuggle hit the stage. Every show sold out, and she'd gotten creative with the concert shots, even perching high among the lights in Austin, Texas.

Cody had been right. She couldn't have

followed along in her RV, even if the tour stops had been on the east coast. The pace was too fast, the crowds intense. Women cried when they saw Cody Tuggle on stage and swooned when he grabbed the mic and sang. Traveling with Cody turned out to be easiest for Kasey because they were gone before the crowds finished cheering, miles away while the fans still held lighters in the air, begging for an encore.

Within a week, they'd played Nashville and three cities in Texas. They'd drawn a full house in Beaumont, Austin and Corpus Christi, but tomorrow night's show in San Antonio had sold out in record time. They added a second show the following night to accommodate the demand. The added date meant a tricky travel timeline as they moved east, but the road manager assured them they could squeeze in another show.

In each city, Cody used his stardom to get the word out about Jake. The radio and television stations were open to helping out. Kasey had never felt safer with so many people on her side working to find her son. In San Antonio, the local radio show even put Kasey on the air. They activated their Country Super Star Alert system. The 800-line had received some calls, and Von and a team of specialists ran down all the leads. So far, nothing had panned out, but at least they were trying. Riley kept Kasey up to date with daily reports.

• • •

After the final song at the second San Antonio show, Kasey and Cody were whisked away to catch the jet. There was no time for any of them to wind down after this show. Even the band had to move out in a hurry.

On the private jet, Cody sat in his usual spot—a large reclining seat that had been supersized to fit his huge frame. She strapped herself into one of the seats in the front of the plane where Annette and the road manager liked to go over their plans.

After a smooth takeoff, Kasey stared out the window as the lights of the city dimmed beneath them. Cody strummed his guitar. She could just barely hear him humming over the white noise of the plane.

The flight from San Antonio to New York was long compared to the little hops they'd made over the past week between the Texas cities. Kasey downloaded images to her laptop and worked on them for a while until Annette stretched out on the couch. Afraid the clicking and typing on the computer would bother her, Kasey shut it down for the night. She took a novel out of her bag, moved to the other side of the plane, turned on a single overhead light, and pulled a plush velour blanket over her legs. She snuggled into its warmth and read while Cody strummed a soft melody behind her.

Lost in the novel, she never heard Cody put

down his guitar or move through the cabin until he sat in the seat next to her.

"Can't sleep?" he asked.

"Winding down. You?"

He reclined the seat and rested his hands on his stomach. "I'm always geared up for a while after a show. Music is what I always wanted to do. Even as a kid. It's like living a dream every time I set foot in front of those folks and share my songs. Sometimes I think my heart will just burst from the happiness I feel."

"They sure love you."

His blue eyes narrowed. "No news yet? About Jake, I mean."

She shook her head, holding her raw emotions in check. "No. They've had some calls, but nothing that's turned into a lead. Yet."

He patted her arm. "It's still early, and we have a lot more towns."

"Needle in a haystack. That's what it feels like sometimes, but I can't give up," she said.

"You've got your head on straight. If you still feel he's out there, he is. Go with your heart. God'll let you know when it's time to do otherwise."

It was the first time she'd heard him reference God, but she could tell by his tone it wasn't the first time he had.

"I'm sure you miss your husband, too."

A tumble of emotion assailed her. "You can't

begin to imagine." She'd never forget a single detail of Nick's face, the love in his eyes. "We were soul mates. We hadn't even known each other long when he asked me to marry him." Kasey paused. "Why am I telling you all of this?"

Cody shrugged and leaned back. "I have that effect on all the girls."

"I bet." Kasey laughed and continued, "He married me even though I was pregnant with another man's child. He loved that baby as if he were his own, with never so much as a word that he wasn't." A thoughtful smile curved her mouth. "We were the kind of couple that never had to say a word to know what the other was thinking. Nick gave my life meaning."

"You were lucky." Cody's voice was gentle. "Smart to recognize such a rare blessing and hang on."

She turned to him. A look of sadness passed over his features. "That sounds like experience talking."

His brow wrinkled. "I've made some mistakes in the past. Left some pretty special people behind in my pursuit of a music career."

"Sounds like you didn't leave the memory behind."

"Memories." The beginning of a smile tipped the corners of his mouth. "They won't keep you warm at night."

"You got that right." Her reborn zest for life

comforted her. "They say people come in and out of your life for a reason. Thank you for being here for me now."

"It works both ways," he said. Their eyes locked, but neither of them moved. Cody reached up and clicked off the overhead light. "We better get some rest. Tomorrow's another big day." He closed his eyes, took a deep breath, and let it out slowly.

She couldn't take her eyes off him.

This man, who shouldn't have a burden in the world, was helping carry hers.

An angel. A guardian angel. I pray Jake has one, too.

New York City whooped it up big with the country band. Who would have thought a bunch of city folks could get down country-style? But they did. Since the band wasn't leaving town that night for the next show, they treated the sold-out crowd to a good old-fashioned jam session as the encore. Kasey wasn't sure who was having more fun, the band or the fans.

The band was in good spirits from the impromptu jam, and Annette was thrilled that Cody had come to her about doing a couple extra guest spots while they were in town—something he rarely did. He wasn't big on self-promotion, preferring his music to stand on its own. Yet he seemed to think that helping Kasey was a worthwhile way to use his celebrity. He did all three morning shows for the networks, and even two late night shows.

The next morning, Kasey sat across from Cody watching for his reaction to the latest set of proofs.

"You gonna get that?" he asked.

"Oh. It's me?" She dug in her purse for the phone. "I never get calls in the morning." Kasey's heart pumped as she flipped open the phone.

"Hello?" *Please be a lead,* she prayed.

"Your grandmother is in a hell of a tizzy." Jeremy spit out the words like pellets. "You better call and explain to her soon, else I'm liable to just leave. She's driving me crazy."

"What's going on?"

"Nothing, until your grandmother picked up those gossip papers at the grocery store. There you were, right on the cover."

"Me?"

"Well, you all tucked down in the arms of that rock star."

"You've got to be kidding me." *Oh. My. God.* She mouthed to Cody.

"The picture was bad enough, but the article all but has you cheating on Nick while you were married, and offing Jake to be with Cody Tuggle."

Blood pounded in her temples. Was this Grem just trying to get attention again? "You better be kidding, and if you are your joke is not funny."

"You haven't seen it?" His tone made it clear that he wasn't kidding.

"Which one?" Her jaw tensed.

Cody's eyebrows rose.

Kasey pressed the speaker button on her cell and held the phone so Cody could hear.

The sound of papers shuffling came from the other end, then Jeremy said, "The one I have here is *The Insider*. She has another one in the other room. Does it matter?"

"If *The Insider* is running the story, everyone else will have it by the end of the week." Kasey's temper rose, and Cody's nostrils flared with fury to match. "Tell Grem to quit reading that trash. You know none of it is true."

"Yeah, like that will happen," Jeremy said. "You know how she loves that celebrity gossip."

He was right. "Tell her the story's not true. I'll call her when I cool down. I appreciate the heads-up." She threw the phone in her purse and dropped her head into her hands.

She glanced up at Cody. His lips were thin with anger. They exchanged a knowing look, a been-there-done-that-and-this-t-shirt-sucks kind of look.

Kasey said, "Houston, we have a problem."

Chapter Twelve

"What should we do?" Kasey hoped Cody would have an answer.

Cody reached for his phone. "I'll call Annette. She'll know who to contact." Before he could dial her number, she called him to tell him the same news. They spoke while Kasey lugged out her laptop and brought up the internet to search for the article.

It was easy to find. It splashed the front page of their website.

Unfortunately, the angle of the photo used on the cover of *The Insider* made Cody and Kasey appear a bit snuggly. It was just the other night. Cody had been shielding her from a heavy crowd of screaming women as they ran to the limo after the show in New York.

She twisted the laptop screen toward Cody who was still talking to Annette.

He winced.

The article was pure smear—anything to hike sales. Cody's reputation made profitable news, only this time she was caught right in the middle. She called Von to warn him and see if he could help insure it wouldn't hinder the investigation.

Annette ran damage control, and Von tried to keep the investigation from getting sucked into the mayhem. At noon, the Southampton County Sheriff was scheduled to make a statement to the press on Kasey's behalf. She was thankful for their willingness to publicly support her and dispel the nasty rumors. The focus could then return to their quest to find Jake.

The morning was supposed to have been leisurely, but they'd spent just about the whole time doing damage control until the driver came and whisked them away to the airport to head to the next city.

On the plane, Kasey second-guessed joining the tour and every move she'd made.

Once they were in flight Cody stepped behind her seat and rubbed her shoulders. "Don't worry. The crisis will blow over before we land in Connecticut. If it doesn't, I'll clear the air in the next interviews. Annette is a miracle worker when it comes to stuff like this."

"I'm so sorry. If I'd just taken the bus with the guys, this wouldn't have happened." Kasey put her laptop aside.

"Don't be silly. Besides, I like having you with me." He squeezed her shoulders, then came around and sat next to her. "You're a special lady."

"I think you're pretty special, too," she said. "I don't know what I did to deserve such a great friend, but I sure am thankful for you."

"No, I mean really special." He held her gaze.

"I'm so relaxed around you. I can be myself. You don't even seem impressed by me. I like that."

Kasey laughed. She was impressed all right. Impressed he could be this down-to-earth with women falling at his feet every day.

"Seriously," he said. "Not just anyone can adapt to this kind of lifestyle, or fit in with this group of assorted nuts I consider family."

"It's not hard. I feel like a princess," she admitted, but reminded herself that this wasn't her lifestyle.

"I know it's crazy timing, but I had to tell you how I feel." He held a finger to her lips before she could respond. "Don't say anything. I just wanted you to know."

It was true that being with Cody was easy, but her heart wasn't open to those kinds of thoughts. He was a welcome distraction and he'd saved her when she didn't think she could bear to go on, and a wonderful man, no argument there, but . . .

"Don't get me wrong. I can see us being great friends—lifelong friends, but my life is a mess. I married my one true love and my heart is in a million pieces. I've been so worried about my little boy I've barely grieved for Nick. I won't say I'll never be in a relationship—because never is a risky test—but I can tell you right now I can't even imagine it."

Did I just turn down Cody Tuggle? They'll certify me crazy for sure.

"You don't have to explain," he said.

"My only priority is my son. Being a mother to Jake was the best thing I've ever done. I have to find him. I appreciate your help. If he's out there, it's your help that is going to bring him back."

"I'm glad I can help you."

She cocked her head. "My turn to change the subject." She wiggled her brow trying to lighten the mood. "Have you ever been close to getting married?"

"Close? Sort of."

"So there was someone special. What happened?" Kasey settled in for the story.

"It was a long time ago. She was ready. I wasn't. She found someone who was. End of story."

"Ouch."

"You can say that again." Cody recoiled like he'd been slapped. "Guy swept in while I was doing a string of bar gigs. He owned an Italian restaurant. Stuck the ring right in the middle of a plate of spaghetti. Didn't sound so romantic to me, but she went for it."

"You should hear how Nick proposed to me."

"No spaghetti, I hope."

"No. He slipped a rubber fishing worm around my finger. I wore it for a week until we had time to get a real ring."

"I'd love to have seen that."

"It was sweet."

"Guess you had to be there."

"Yeah. Like I said, when it's right you know it, and even something hokey like that comes off like Prince Charming." She smiled. It was nice to remember the good times with Nick. "Any of those early hit records about her?"

"Just about every one of them. Damn near broke my heart, but I wanted to perform. Music is in my blood. She just couldn't wait."

"Sorry."

"Yeah. Were y'all married a long time?"

"Nope. I must have gotten a dozen proposals over the years. Riley teases me that I could have a charm bracelet from all the rings guys insisted I keep. Things just never felt right until I met Nick. I knew the day I met him that he was the one."

"That's how I felt about Lou," Cody said with a nod. "I know exactly what you mean."

"Lou? That ought to have stirred up a few rumors."

"Hey, don't laugh. Her name was Bettie Lou. We just called her Lou for short. Bettie was too prissy for her."

Kasey twisted in her seat and belted out a verse of *Bettie Lou's Got a New Pair of Shoes*.

"Funny. Do you think that's the first time I've heard that?" Cody laughed and shrugged it off. "Be nice."

"Sorry. Have y'all kept in touch?"

"No." A big grin spread across his face. "We

135

didn't part on the best terms. She probably has two kids and a dog. I blew it. Why bother?"

"You never know. Marriages don't last. People change. She could've been your one true love."

"You believe in that crap?"

"Sure." Kasey folded her hands in her lap. "I do. Mine was perfect." She shrugged. "You ought to look her up sometime. It might be fun to catch up, live in the past for a little bit."

"Maybe I will—if you don't think I'm your one true love." He said it playfully, but there was a glimmer of hope in his words.

"You've been a wonderful distraction, but I could never live in this world, and you could never live in mine."

With that, he tipped her nose. "Never say never. That's risky."

"Touché."

"I'll let you get back to your work," he said.

She shifted her laptop back into her lap and tried to concentrate on the behind-the-scenes pictures she'd shot. This tour had stolen America's heart, and by being on tour with them, Kasey had the chance to show the real man behind the music and provide fans a peek behind the scene. This group, the band and crew, really seemed like an extended family—Cody at the center. That came out in the pictures. Fans would love them. There was no trail of half-dressed groupies in his life. He poured every ounce of his energy into his performances.

A positive vibe came through in all of the pictures. She was excited to be the one behind the camera to share this aspect of Cody with the world

Kasey smiled at the shots of the band and crew cooking burgers and eating off paper plates—far from the glamour people would expect to see from such a successful band. And even though Cody was the reason they all were on tour, he acted like one of the gang. The guys and gals enjoyed the simple things and the meaningful things. The few band members who were married had wives and children in tow. Unlike a mechanic who never turns a wrench when he gets home, or the landscaper whose yard is full of weeds, the band members jammed almost every night into the wee morning hours. It wasn't work but rather what they truly loved.

But the group's creativity didn't stop at music. They'd rigged a basketball net on the back of the bus. It probably wasn't regulation height, but no one seemed to care. They played hard, cutthroat to the point of needing a designated referee for their games.

There were touching moments too, like when Cody visited the children's hospital to say hello to some of the young patients and brighten their stressed parents' days. Kasey let children take pictures with her big camera and promised to email their shots to them. The children were elated. The smiles and tears in the parents' eyes, as they watched their sick children glow with the excitement, was a reward she wouldn't soon forget. Cody's schedule had been tight, yet no one would have known. He moved at a leisurely pace and gave one-hundred percent to those folks. The children and their parents had been his priority at the time. Everything else had to wait.

At the end of each week, she completed proof sheets so Arty and Cody could choose favorites along the way. That helped her make sure the shots encompassed the diversity they needed for the book. It was already being hyped.

Kasey posted the top three blooper shots on the bus bulletin board after each concert. It was quickly becoming a tradition. She easily picked up on some of Cody's quirks, like his love for barbecue. Barbecued chicken, ribs, pork, beef, goat, even potatoes and corn. If someone barbecued it, he'd eat it. Not only did he love to eat barbecued anything, he also loved to grill. They had a fancy one loaded right there on the bus, and Cody spent a lot of time grilling for the gang.

Kasey had captured dozens of pictures of Cody in different barbecue eateries, big and small, across the country. It was in a small barbecue shop in Texas that they'd teased about Cody becoming the next Bobby Flay and having his own barbecue cookbook. Arty Max grabbed that idea like a pit bull on a steak. He'd already pitched it to a New York publishing house, and they were thrilled with the idea. Kasey and Cody agreed to go to the famous Annual Texas Goat Cook-off over Labor Day weekend to kick off that project.

The tour was successful—from the west coast across the Midwestern plains, and now working its way up and down the east coast. Sometimes they hit four cities in as many days with little downtime in between. The tour had been well organized, yet there were a few times that Kasey wasn't sure which city they were in. Itineraries posted on the plane and buses helped everyone stay on course.

Kasey was exhausted, but it felt good to have control over something again. She had plenty of sad nights, but more often than not, she was so tired she didn't have time to think. She thanked God that Cody had turned up when he did and offered her this escape. The photography work was mindless. She got lost in the creativity, and no one needed or wanted anything from her. What a relief.

The busy schedule relieved her from making any major decisions and of the emptiness at home. She just followed along. Even in the hurried pace of it all, she knew that Christmas was around the corner. She hated to think of facing it alone.

The whole Tuggle clan and all of their family members would gather at Cody's ranch for a three-day Christmas celebration. They'd invited her, but she didn't want to bring anyone down so she'd declined.

"You can't skip Christmas," Cody insisted.

"I can try. I know I can't wish it away, but the holidays are going to be hard and I don't want to drag anyone else's down with me."

"You won't. You have to come."

She shook her head. "I—"

"I happen to *know* you don't have anything better to do. You may as well join us. You can get more pictures. Who knows. You might just have some fun while you're at it."

"Okay, okay. I'll come. But if I get weepy, you have to promise you'll send me to my room."

"It's a deal, but I plan on making sure you're fine."

On Christmas Eve, they'd sung Christmas carols into the wee hours of the morning, then everyone exchanged gifts. Kasey had created collages for each of the band members and road crew to commemorate their role in the big tour. Everyone loved them. It was what she did best, and the project had kept her mind in a good place.

She got gag gifts from the road crew, and her obsession with red licorice garnered her more of the stuff than she could eat in a lifetime. The drummer had even taken the time to weave hundreds of red licorice ropes into the shape of a cowboy hat.

The break for Christmas proved to be fun and relaxing. As much fun as the break was, the band and crew, including Kasey, were all ready to get back on the road.

The first show after Christmas was in Raleigh, North Carolina. A buzz filled the air as over eighteen thousand fans piled into the arena. Once the opening band cleared the stage, Kasey took her place down in front. Tonight she'd take the final pictures. Tomorrow morning she'd head home.

Cody opened with his first number-one song. The crowd went nuts, singing along. Fourteen songs in, the crowd was just as engaged. They didn't even notice that she'd moved out of the orchestra area to the catwalk above them. She zoomed in on the audience for reactions and captured a wide-angle panoramic.

By now she knew how many songs they'd play before Cody's first wardrobe change and the order in which the last three songs were performed. She had all the pictures she needed, so she let the camera swing on her neck strap and sat cross-legged on the catwalk, high above the stage. The last song, one of the few ballads Cody had recorded, was her favorite. She wiggled into a comfortable position and waited for the final song.

But Cody didn't follow the six-chord fade into

the song he usually closed with. Instead, he took the mic from the stand and swung his guitar to his back. He repositioned his hat, a nervous tic. She'd noticed that a while back.

"Can I get personal with ya for a minute?" he said.

The audience cheered.

"You've been terrific, Raleigh. I want to play something special."

They went wild.

"It's a song I've been workin' on for the past couple of months."

A hush came over the crowd; only a couple of whistles broke it.

"You may have heard that I've been trying to help a friend get the word out about her missing son."

Kasey gulped. *What is he doing?*

"You might not have heard that we've been photographing this tour for a book. You're part of that. The book will come out next fall. I hope you'll buy a copy. Not for me, but because twenty percent of every book sold is going directly to the National Center for Missing and Exploited Children."

Kasey reached out to steady herself. His overwhelming generosity was dizzying.

The crowd hooted and howled.

"I knew I could count on your help." Cody shaded his eyes and looked to the projection booth. "Johnny, will you put that picture up for me?"

Jake's picture filled the floor-to-ceiling backdrop.

Kasey snapped her mouth shut in utter disbelief, her gaze clouded by tears.

"Thanks." Cody looked back at the picture, shook his head, then turned back to the crowd. "This is Jake. He's been missing since Hurricane Ernesto came through these parts a while back. If you see him, would you please contact the police? His mother, a very dear friend of mine, she's looking for him." He swung his guitar back around. "This song is called *A Mother's Love*."

No one in the band joined in. It was just Cody and his guitar.

Kasey clutched the metal railing with both hands as she listened, recognizing the melody immediately. She'd heard it a hundred times in the plane.

She was drawn into his words, and then the bridge

A child is born and placed in the arms of
   his mother.
A powerful love, and a bond like no other.
There to protect, to guide and to grow,
A love as strong you'll never know.

By the second verse, the band members joined in.

When Cody sang the bridge, the crowd sang along. Every mother in the crowd must have felt this song to her core. The audience swayed below Kasey as she cried.

When the song ended, Cody turned his back to the crowd, knelt on one knee and dipped his hat to Jake. Then he rose, faced his fans, and waved as he headed off the stage.

Kasey would usually have been backstage well before now, but her knees were like jelly. The house lights would come up in about three minutes. She couldn't stand, much less descend the ladder from the catwalk. She watched as the fans cheered for Cody, hoping he would come back on stage. He rarely did.

The house lights came up. Kasey watched from her spot in the sky as people shuffled toward the exits. Roadies moved in to unhook cables and disassemble what they'd just assembled a few hours ago.

She pulled her feet underneath her and stood, holding the rail to steady herself. Then she headed for the ladder and made her way to the stage level. As she stepped on the last rung, Cody startled her.

"I couldn't find you." He steadied her by the hips as she climbed down. "You had me worried."

She reached up and hugged him. "That was a beautiful song. Thank you."

He held her tight, rocking her in his arms. "You're welcome. You're a beautiful mom."

She let go and stepped back. "I can't believe I'm leaving tomorrow."

"You don't have to," he said, and raised a brow.

Kasey paused, but only for a second. "It's time. I have to handle things at home. I'm not sure I'm really ready, but I know I can get through it now."

"I understand. It's been good having you around. Real good." There was an awkward silence. "A driver will take you home tomorrow."

"You don't have to do that. I can rent a car."

"Don't be silly." They walked down the tunnel to the SUV that would shuttle them back to the hotel. "It's taken care of."

The driver leaped from the car when he saw Cody, but Cody waved him off, opened the door himself, and helped Kasey in.

They rode in silence on the twenty-minute drive to the hotel. The driver let them out at a back entrance.

"Hey, guys," Cody said to the two security guards who stood nearby. He gave them a nod, and he and Kasey disappeared around the corner.

Cody took her hands in his. "I'm not very good at goodbyes."

"It's not goodbye. We'll be in touch."

He nodded. "Count on it."

She hugged him.

He held her for a long moment. "You take care of yourself, and please let me know if you need anything. Anything. I mean it."

She nodded.

"Keep me posted on Jake, too."

"I will."

He hooked his arm. She threaded hers through his. They got on the elevator. When it stopped on the twenty-third floor, Kasey backed out.

"Thanks again," she said.

"See you soon." He tipped his hat.

She wondered if he was trying to be cute, or hiding how he felt. The elevator doors closed. The chime sounded on the floor above, the penthouse, where he was staying. She turned and walked to her room, humming *A Mother's Love*.

Chapter Thirteen

The day after the Raleigh concert, Kasey said her goodbyes to the band members. It was a lot harder than she'd expected, kind of like when she'd left her friends for the summer after school let out.

As the limo moved into traffic, she noticed the glossy white box on the seat. A perfect Tiffany-blue bow crossed over a card—from Cody. He'd done so much for her. Opening the box seemed so final.

Cody isn't the only one that's not good at goodbyes.

She pushed it aside and decided to wait until she got home to open it.

Home.

It was time.

Kasey wondered if Dutch would act as if she'd only been gone a day.

The smooth ride lulled her to sleep. By the time she woke up, she was close enough to home to recognize her surroundings. Her stomach swirled a little when the limousine pulled into the drive-way.

Her RV and Porsche were parked side-by-side in front of the house, next to the crumpled metal heap of Nick's truck. Her heart spiked as she relived the moment when she'd seen it in the river. There was no fixing it. She should've sent it to the crusher, but it was hard to let go of anything that had belonged to Nick.

The driver came around and opened her door. She stepped from the limo and stretched while he got her bags from the trunk.

"You can leave them on the porch."

The driver had sweated through his starched white shirt by the time he heaved the last bag onto the porch. Relief washed over his face when he closed the trunk.

Kasey handed him a stack of bills.

"It's been taken care of."

Of course it has. Thanks, Cody.

The limo kicked up a cloud of dust as it drove down the lane.

Leaving her alone.

Standing on the porch, she wrapped her arms across her body and took it all in. Not ready to go inside, she walked down to the yard and followed the edge of the wooden fence that outlined the pastures. The air seemed fresh, the sounds from the animals familiar. Birds chirped and there was that gentle buzz she'd grown to love.

Goats called out as if they recognized her and hoped for a handout. One of the older does came to the fence. Kasey recognized the animal as one of Nick's favorites. She twisted off a small sprig of pine needles from the tree next to the fence and dangled it over. The goat nibbled the needles, then stepped up on the fence with its hooves to get closer, begging for more. Kasey petted her nose.

She brushed her hands on her jeans and sat on the white bench under the trio of river birch trees. She and Jake had spent so many afternoons in this spot while Nick worked the horses and goats. Thunder rumbled and the north sky grew dark. Nick would know if it would rain or not. He'd said he could smell it.

She crossed the yard to the front porch. The swing swayed as the wind picked up. She, Nick and Jake had spent countless hours in that swing. Nick had combed his fingers through her hair and dropped kisses into the crook of her neck. Even now, the memory caused the same shiver of seduction.

Kasey's tears still fell, but not as often. Now her loss seemed more of a dull ache, not so fresh and pink.

Huge raindrops splattered against the metal roof and dotted the sidewalk. She opened the front door, and Dutch ran outside to greet her. He panted and pranced from paw to paw, his tail whacking the front door.

"Calm down, old boy." Thunder clapped in the distance. Dutch ran back into the living room. He hated storms. She rolled her luggage into the foyer just as the wind sucked the front door closed with a slam.

"It's okay, Dutch," Kasey consoled the dog. He looked bigger than she remembered, and grayer. "Did you miss me?"

She walked into the kitchen and flipped on the light. A huge stack of mail cluttered the edge of the counter.

Mostly junk, I bet.

She tucked the phone under her chin and dialed Riley. "I'm back," she said as she sorted through the mail.

Riley squealed. "I've missed you like crazy. How's it feel to be back home?"

"Good," she admitted.

"Did you meet the new farm manager?"

Kasey looked out the window toward the barn. "No, and I didn't see a truck out back. He must be gone for the day."

"Maybe. He's working out great."

"Thank you so much for hiring him for me. I wouldn't have known what to ask or where to start."

Riley said, "Don't thank me. That was all Von. I bet Dutch was happy to see you."

"You better believe it. He about knocked me over when I came in."

"I'll probably do the same thing when I see you. Be ready."

"Thanks for the warning." Kasey laughed.

"Why don't you come over for dinner tomorrow and fill us in?"

"Sounds good." It was weird to have no schedule. No calendar to check. Kasey hung up and carried the mail into the living room.

The rugged maleness of Nick filled the space. Being away must have been healing, because it was easier now to be around his and Jake's things. More comforting than painful to touch them, to be close to them.

Nick's cell phone lay on the end table where she'd left it. Kasey had kept the account open just so she could hear him on his voice mail. She dialed it, and listened: *"Hey now. This is Nick. You just missed me, but leave a message and I'll get right back to ya. You can count on it. Later. Bye."*

Short and to the point. Good thing, too, because every time she listened to it, she held her breath.

If the message went on any longer, she might pass out.

There were several new voice mails. She held the cell phone to her chest. It was true. You couldn't hide from grief. All she'd done was postpone it.

Kasey took a deep breath, then went back to flipping through the mail. She tossed the trash into one pile and made a "keeper" pile that was much smaller. She caught herself in mid-toss, looking at an envelope that stood out from the rest. It wasn't a slick window envelope and wasn't metered bulk mail.

The return address was Emporia, Virginia. Handwritten addresses, not in a scrolling script but in a man's rushed scribble.

She ran a manicured nail under the edge of the flap and pulled out the letter.

Chapter Fourteen

Kasey read the letter twice. She recognized the name of the sender. Riley had taken down messages while she was away, and his name was among the callers. He hadn't specified what he wanted, so Kasey hadn't returned his calls. The letter was as cryptic as the phone messages. Chaz Huckaby wanted Nick to call him.

She picked up the phone and punched in the long distance number. The call was long overdue.

"Huckaby, can I help ya?" the man answered with a southern twang.

"Um, hello. Is this Chaz Huckaby?"

"It is indeed," he replied with enough energy to charge a battery.

"I'm returning your call, and responding to a letter you sent my husband. I'm married to Nick Rolly. You've left a couple of messages for him." She stalled, not wanting to get to the part where she had to say the words—that Nick was gone.

"Oh, uh . . . yeah. Just need him to give me a ring, princess." His voice held a rasp of excitement.

"Yes." She cleared her throat. "About that. Mr. Huckaby, he won't be returning that call. He . . ." The words caught in her throat.

"It's Kasey, right?"

How does he know my name?

"Yes. How did you know?"

"Nick talks about you all the time. Is he okay?"

"No. He was in a car accident." She heard the squeak of a chair on the other end of the line. "He didn't . . ."

"Oh."

She heard the gasp of realization—thankful she didn't have to finish the sentence.

Chaz said, "I am *so* sorry."

"Me, too."

"I wondered why he hadn't returned my calls. I just figured he was busy. I didn't know."

She couldn't respond.

"Nick is a good man, and that little Jake is the apple of ol' Nick's eye—no question about that. Yours too, I'm sure. How's he taking it?"

"You know my son?"

"Yes, ma'am. I got to know Nick and Jake pretty well."

Who is this man?

"May I ask how? I'm sorry, but your name isn't the least bit familiar. And the letter you sent doesn't make sense."

"I guess it can't hurt to tell you now. Under the circumstances, I guess it's time the secret was shared."

"Secret?" The word stabbed her heart. "Nick and I didn't have secrets."

A hearty chuckle came over the line. "Yes, yes. Maybe secret was the wrong word. Surprise. Yes, a surprise is a better way to say it."

"You're confusing me."

"Your anniversary is week after next, right?"

Kasey blinked in surprise. She hadn't even thought about that, but he was right. "Yes, sir. It is . . . would have been." Tears balanced on her lashes.

Who was this stranger who knew Nick, Jake, and even her anniversary date?

"While you were doing those photo shoots, your husband and son were trekking out here to work on a surprise for you."

"I dialed a long distance number. Where are you?"

"Near Emporia. The town's called Adams Grove. Nick bought a house out here last year. Beautiful land, but it needed a lot of work and fencing. Anyway, Nick and Jake loved it. They decided that it was the right thing to do."

"What was the right thing to do?"

"Surprise mommy, of course." His laugh carried a unique force, like a riptide tugging you in.

"Nick wouldn't make a major purchase like that without telling me."

"I don't know about all that. What I do know is that Nick did a lot of talking about living in the moment. He said y'all had dreamed about property further out from the hustle of Virginia Beach. Said he thought this one was perfect. He loved you a lot, said you worked too dang hard. He was excited about surprising you—said this house would be your dream home."

His warm laugh and deep southern accent were comforting, but what he was saying just didn't make sense.

Kasey asked, "Do we owe you money? Is that why you're calling?" She wondered how many more things she'd have to figure out on her own.

His hearty chuckle boomed across the line. "No. No, ma'am. This property is paid for lock, stock and barrel. He's got the deed somewhere. In fact, the renovations were all paid up front, too. I've been trying to get to Nick because we had a deal that I would get all the renovations done for him before your anniversary. It was going to be a surprise."

"I'm surprised all right."

"I'm sorry for your loss, Kasey. It's okay if I call you Kasey?"

"Yes. Of course."

"Nick was an easy partner, and I considered him a friend. And that little boy of yours . . ." he choked on the words, ". . . he was a little bundle of energy, cute as a button in those boots and hat. I'm sure it's been hard on him—losing his daddy."

She swallowed hard, thankful that Chaz rambled on so she didn't have to address the comment about Jake.

"They both loved you very much. They talked about you all the time."

"Thank you, Mr. Huckaby."

"I'm sure Nick would love for you to see what he'd been working on. When would you like to come?"

"I don't know. Can I call you back? I'm afraid I'm a bit overwhelmed."

"Of course. Tell you what. I'll keep an eye on the place for you. That's no problem. You take your time. Call me when you're ready."

"That would be great. Thank you. Where did you say it is again?"

"It's out past Emporia—not far off of Route 58."

"Now it makes sense." It came out as almost a

whisper. This explained why Nick had been on Route 58 that day.

"Are you okay?"

She held the phone with both hands. It suddenly weighed a ton. She knelt to the floor to keep herself from falling. "Mr. Huckaby, when did you last see Nick and Jake?"

"Let's see. I left that afternoon for my daughter's wedding. Would've been the last Saturday in August. Right before the hurricane."

Her jaw went slack. "I bet you were the last person to see Nick."

"Oh, my." His voice was low and quiet.

"Nick died on Route 58. They were supposed to have been on the Eastern Shore. At least that's what he'd told me. But now it's all starting to make sense. He was up there at that house."

"Probably," Huckaby said. "No. Not probably. He was here. I remember."

"Mr. Huckaby, let me get my thoughts together and call you back. I do want to meet with you. I want to talk to you about that day and see what Nick was up to, but my head . . . well, I don't know . . . this is just too much for me to absorb right now."

"Take whatever time you need. I'm here whenever you're ready. You just let me know what I can do. All right?"

"Thanks. Goodbye." Kasey hung up the phone. The news made her shiver. She reached for the throw on the back of the couch and spread it across her legs to chase the chill—it smelled of Nick's cologne. She breathed in the familiar scent. "Nick, what were you up to, you sneak?"

At first, she felt angry, even a little betrayed. She and Nick didn't have secrets. At least she didn't. But then she thought about the times they had sat outside, she leaning back between his legs, taking in the starry view and dreaming of a quieter place. The beautiful farm was Nick's heritage, but the green line of Virginia Beach encroached a little more each year. Now the once peaceful and serene countryside was often disturbed by the blazing sound of jets from nearby Oceana Naval Air Station practicing maneuvers.

The pleasant memory of those dreams made her smile. They'd talked about what their home would look like. What it would be like. They'd looked at a farmhouse the summer before last, but a change in Kasey's schedule kept them from making an offer on it and someone else had snatched it up. Nick wouldn't have wanted to lose another perfect place. But how had he kept it a secret? It must have been torture for him. How sweet that he'd planned to surprise her for their anniversary.

Had Nick not been thinking of her, trying to surprise her, maybe he would still be here today.

She wished she could turn back time and change the events that had landed her in this terrible place.

Chapter Fifteen

Kasey pressed redial on Nick's cell phone. His voice was a comfort. *"Hey now. This is Nick. You just missed me, but leave a message and I'll get right back to ya. You can count on it. Later. Bye."*

Like a junkie when it came to his voice, she needed to hear it, yearned for the soothing sound of it. At least now the tears didn't flow every time she heard him; instead she felt warm inside. She missed him like crazy. She tugged Jake's little denim jacket off the coat rack and breathed in the smell of Fruit Loops that still filled the pockets. Jake loved the green loops best. They matched Daddy's tractor.

Dutch walked over and pushed his nose under her hand, licked the salty tears from her cheek, then snagged a couple of the stale Fruit Loops from her hand.

She glanced at the clock. It was close to seven, but she had a feeling that Chaz Huckaby would answer no matter what time she called. She punched in his number.

"Mr. Huckaby?" Kasey asked.

"Yes, ma'am. Who's calling?"

"This is Kasey."

"Well, hello there, Ms. Kasey. I was hoping you'd call back. Your husband put a lot of love into that property for you. I know he'd want you to see it."

"I'd like to. Can you give me directions?"

"I can. But why don't you meet me in Emporia at the shop here, and I'll drive you over?"

"If it's no trouble . . ."

"None at all. It'd be my pleasure. When would you like to come?"

"I'd like to come right now, but I guess morning will have to do. Can I call you when I'm on my way?"

"You bet." He gave her the address of his store. "I look forward to talking to you in the morning."

Kasey felt close to Nick and Jake as she hung up the phone. She called Dutch, who came running to her. They went outside. She sat on the back porch, and Dutch bounded out into the yard.

Frogs and crickets chirped in the night. She pulled a tissue out of her pocket and blew her nose. She must have scared Dutch because he came bounding back up the stairs.

"Come on, boy, let's hit the sack."

She went back inside and locked the house. Dutch followed her upstairs and sprawled out on the floor as she got undressed and slipped under the covers. She hung her arm over the side of the bed to pet Dutch—needing the connection as she tried to relax. But she was too anxious to sleep.

Conversations between her and Nick replayed in her mind. Talks about their dream home in the country. How they would decorate it. A simpler life. He would've loved it if she'd have stayed home and been his wife, Jake's mom, and scrapbooked all day. She had planned to do that . . . someday. But she'd put it off too long.

When the alarm sounded, it was just a reason to get up because she'd been peeking at the clock almost every fifteen minutes all night.

She was dressed and out the door in record time, only to find a hard frost on her windshield. She slid behind the wheel and turned the key to start the car and get the defroster going. Not a click. Not a groan.

"Damn this old car and its crappy electrical system!"

She slapped the steering wheel and went back inside. Von would help her, but she wasn't ready to tell him about her conversation with Chaz. He'd tell Riley and they would all have to go, and she didn't want to share this yet. She wasn't sure what to expect, but she was sure she wanted to go alone.

The keys hanging on the rack next to the door caught her eye. She could take Nick's T-Bird. She'd ridden in the antique car a million times, but had never driven it. Nick had tried to talk her into driving, but she liked being his passenger.

"What the hell." She snagged the Ford key-chain off the rack, grabbed her purse, and headed out back where the car was parked.

"Come on, Dutch. Let's check this out."

He ran ahead of her toward the barn and sniffed around the car while he waited for her to catch up.

She lifted one edge of the cover on the car and whipped it in the air to push it back. Dust sparkled in the sunlight as she swept the cover back and let it fold onto the ground behind the car. She opened the car door, then just stood there for a moment. Her fingers trembled as she grabbed the steering wheel and slid behind it. She twisted the key in the ignition. The engine turned right over. The gas tank was full, ready to go.

"Meant to be, I guess."

She pulled the directions from her purse and tucked them in the console, then idled the light blue car out from under the shed roof and drove up to the house. She put Dutch inside, jumped back in the car, and headed west.

Nick's favorite AM sports station blasted through the crackling static on the radio. No surprise there. She turned down the volume and smiled at the memory of the playful banter she and Nick used to have about sports radio.

This early in the morning, the drive was easy, the traffic light. As she made her way toward Emporia, she stopped at the site of Nick's accident. She hadn't been there in months. The trees still bore bruises from the impact. She walked a short distance down the road, squatted next to the first bruised tree, and prayed for her boys, remembering the day that had changed her life forever. She wished someone had recognized the woman from Mr. Lightner's sketch, but that lead had led absolutely nowhere. It seemed no matter how hard she tried, she couldn't catch a break.

Nick, do you even know how much I miss you?

She reached for the tree and steadied herself. Nick's absence burned deep to her core, but she still felt that Jake was alive—somewhere.

A noise came from the woods.

Jake?

No, just a white-tailed deer scurrying for cover.

Kasey forced herself to get back in the car and continue her journey.

The road sign showed just eleven miles to Emporia. Two turns off of Route 58, and she was in front of Huckaby's shop. Parking places were scarce along the curb of the Main Street address, so she parked a block down the street and sat in the car for a minute.

Am I really ready to do this?

She gathered herself, then headed up the sidewalk toward Huckaby's store. The hand-lettered sign on the old Main Street building read *Huckaby House* and, in smaller letters, *Real Estate & Renovation Supplies & Rifle Range.*

"Talk about a jack of all trades," she said with a giggle.

She made her way to the door thinking there

162

must be a diner nearby—the smell of bacon permeated the air. She twisted the old brass knob on the tall wooden door. Bells tinkled as she stepped inside and closed the door behind her. The air was stale, as it often was in these old buildings, but the shop looked clean and ship-shape. Any other day she would have loved to rummage through all of this old stuff. Reclaimed mantels, corbels, and rows of stained glass panels lined one side of the space. On the other side, wooden shelving lined the wall, and bins overflowed with original doorknobs and hardware. Heaven for any picker or renovator.

A grayish-blond man with a bushy moustache and Captain Kangaroo bangs wheeled around the corner of a display counter.

"Good morning," he boomed. His joyful smile was as genuine as the white of his name tag.

"Hi. You must be Mr. Huckaby."

Kasey extended her hand. Even without the name tag, she would have recognized his energetic voice.

"Call me Chaz. You made it here quick." He stepped back and took a good look at her. "How did I not guess? Jake has your eyes and chin."

She smiled. People always said that. "Is now a good time?"

"Absolutely." He called over his shoulder. "Ben, I'm heading out."

In the back of the shop, a man raised his arm over a counter, signaling he'd heard.

Chaz nodded. "All right." He jingled his keys in his pocket and held the door open for her. "Let's go. I'll drive."

"Okay. Let me grab my camera."

Kasey didn't say a word on the ride, but he didn't seem the least bit bothered by her silence. He hummed the whole way there. She noticed the hearing aid in his ear and wondered if he realized he was humming out loud.

They turned off the main road onto another that was heavily treed and winding, paved but narrow, with no painted lines. She could see why Nick would like this area. The land wasn't hilly, yet rolled just enough to add interest. Huge old trees lined the edge of the road, marking their territory. The terrain was a nice change from the flat land in Tidewater.

After two miles of passing only trees and a cotton field, Chaz slowed the truck. Ahead, a white clapboard single-story house with a red tin roof sat at the end of a long blacktop driveway.

"This is it," she said. Kasey knew. She and Nick had talked about it enough that the picture was clear in her mind. The house was a perfect match.

"Yes, it is." Chaz looked pleased as he parked the truck in the driveway. "It's nice, isn't it?"

The porch ran the length of the house. At the far end of the porch, a swing hung from chains—just like at the Rocking R.

White vinyl fencing outlined the fields for as far as she could see. When she and Nick had repainted all the fencing at the farmhouse last year, she'd told him she wanted vinyl. He'd argued that she was a city girl and there wasn't anything like good old wood. She smiled at the vinyl. She hadn't even known she'd won that battle. He had done this for her.

An old barn stood at the top of the hill in the back.

"How many acres?" she asked.

"A little over two hundred, a lot of it trees. Good huntin' back here." He opened the glove box and retrieved a keychain.

She slid out of the truck and walked toward the house, her camera bag on her shoulder. Chaz hung back for a moment, giving her the space to see the dream as Nick had seen it.

A red tricycle sat abandoned on the front porch. She could picture Jake, pedaling until he was sweaty, racing across the front yard and up and down the smooth asphalt driveway.

After a bit, Chaz joined her. "Ready to see inside?"

"Yes." She smoothed her hands on her pants and stepped toward the door.

Not only was the house renovated, it was, for the most part, decorated and furnished. It matched every detail they had discussed and a few she knew were all Nick's—like the oversized leather recliner with the remote control balanced on the arm that was not too far from the big television.

Just like at home.

Nick was everywhere in this space.

"It's exactly how we planned." She turned to face the large stone fireplace. She knew just what picture belonged over it: the one of Nick and Jake.

Chaz stood near the door, allowing her to take the time she needed.

In the master suite, a wall of windows overlooked pastures that backed against the thick tree line. Goats? She walked back out to Chaz.

"Who has been taking care of the goats?" she asked.

He laughed. "Oh, they're no problem. The 4-H club comes out twice a week to check on 'em. Nick has an automatic feed and water system out there. Not much to do most of the time."

"Of course he does." She smiled. "How many are there?" She put her hand up, "No, let me guess. One buck and twenty does?"

"Yeah. I think so. You psychic or something?" His fluffy moustache wiggled as he spoke.

"Hardly. I just know my husband. Twenty does and a buck—the perfect starter herd. I've heard him say it a million times." Her eyes welled with tears, but she felt happy to be standing here in the middle of this dream.

Several male cardinals flitted in a tangle of bright yellow forsythia. They whistled back and forth. Kasey thought of Riley. If Riley had been here, she'd remind her that the birds were a sign. A lucky sign.

"Cardinals, good luck," she said quietly, and she believed it, because this was the first day she'd felt like herself in months.

"What do you think?" Chaz asked.

She hugged her arms around herself. "I think I married the most wonderful man in the world."

He nodded.

"Are you in a hurry?"

"No, honey, I'm not in a hurry. You take all the time you need."

"Do you mind if I take some pictures?"

"Not at all. I'm just gonna sit out here on the swing. You go on."

She wandered through the rest of the big house—big enough to fill with the additional two children that she and Nick had hoped for. But there wouldn't be any more babies in her future. Shaking off the gloomy thought, she continued touring the rooms.

Nick had designed the most amazing darkroom and lab for her, and right off that room he'd built what she knew he intended for her framing and scrapbooking projects. In a large L that lined two entire walls were slanted, counter-height work surfaces that lifted to offer storage. Her heart tugged at the sight of the bins with cubbyholes, perfect for designer scrapbook paper, and peg-board with hooks for scissors and other supplies. He'd thought of everything. In the closet there were slots to store glass and mat board without damage.

"Amazing."

She carried her camera from room to room, photographed the house inside and out, from every angle. Then she walked outside and took pictures of the landscape. Breathtaking.

She walked over to the porch. "Thank you for everything, and for your part in this surprise. It's wonderful." Kasey nodded in appreciation. "I could live here."

"It's yours. No reason you can't."

Realization struck. She felt lighter as everything became clear. "You're right. I guess I could."

He nodded.

"Yes. Yes, I can, and that's exactly what I'm going to do."

"You'll love it. I grew up around here. The people are nice. It's a great place to raise that little boy of yours."

She wasn't ready to talk about Jake. Did Chaz really need to hear about that right now? Her heart couldn't take the switch in emotions and right now she felt happier than she had in a long time. No sense screwing that up.

"How soon could I move in?" Her mind hummed on all cylinders, thinking about how to make this happen.

"It's Nick's gift to you. You can stay tonight if you want to."

She put her hand over her mouth and nose and breathed in. Her eyes tingled, but this time the tears weren't filled with sadness. She felt joy, or peace—something good inside. "No. But I *will* be back soon."

Chaz smiled and put his arm around her shoulder, dropping the key into her hand. "Welcome to the neighborhood, Kasey. It's all yours."

She clung to the keys, holding them close to her heart.

Chapter Sixteen

Kasey tapped the steering wheel as she drove. She felt alive again. For the first time in months, she had a clear direction.

Until she and Nick had fallen in love, she never would have considered living outside of the city limits. In fact, many times she'd considered moving to New York City, Chicago, or even Atlanta to get closer to the action. No one had been more surprised than she when she felt so at home in Pungo with Nick. Of course, that was because Nick had been there. Even so, she could picture herself living in that adorable home on Nickel Creek Road.

She laughed when she realized Nick could be short for Nickel.

Funny coincidence. I bet you noticed it right off, didn't you, Nick? A selling point, right?

He'd thought of everything. She wouldn't have to pack much except for her clothes and a few personal items. Her dreams with Nick could still survive, and she intended to live them. Nick and Jake would always be in her heart. No one could cheat her out of that.

Nick would have wanted her to live in their new home in the country and hire someone to run the Rocking R. She could leave the farm in the hands of the caretaker for 4-H. There were funds already set aside to make that happen. It was just a matter of taking the time to do it.

Kasey relaxed back in the seat. She could almost smell Nick's cologne. Her mind told her that it was just the car, but her heart felt close to him, as if he was watching over her. That made her happy.

She enjoyed driving the Thunderbird. No wonder Nick had loved this car. It didn't handle like her Porsche, but it sure got a lot of looks. She'd take the T-Bird with her. The car had meant too much to Nick to leave it behind. Maybe Von and Riley could drive up one weekend and bring it to her.

Everything fell into place so easily. Not one difficult decision to make. Moving to the house on Nickel Creek had to be the right thing to do.

Kasey couldn't wait to share her plans with Riley and Von. She knew they'd be supportive.

Grem, on the other hand, was another story—the one snag in an otherwise perfect plan.

Get the difficult conversation out of the way first.

Drawing in a deep breath, she dialed her grandmother from her cell phone, but hung up before it rang.

Popping in unannounced might be a better plan.

Excited to share the news, she almost bumped the slow opening gates as she drove onto her grandmother's estate. She parked by the front door and took the steps two at a time, almost bouncing her way across the porch.

She knocked twice and pushed the front door open. "Grem? It's me, Kasey."

Grem was a creature of habit. At this time of day, she'd be in the sun room off the kitchen, watching the birds flutter from feeder to feeder in the lush gardens.

Kasey's heels clicked against the wooden floor. Grem practically had her nose to the window glass watching the birds.

"Haven't you been back for a few days?" Grem asked in a condescending tone.

She must have seen Kasey in the reflection of the window, because she hadn't turned around.

It's going to be one of those visits.

"Yes, a couple. But I was out of town this morning." Kasey walked over, gave her grandmother's shoulders a squeeze, and kissed her on the cheek. She'd promised herself she wouldn't let the old woman's foul mood get to her today. "I'm good. How are you?"

Grem folded her hands in her lap and lifted her chin. "I've been better. An old body has aches and pains, you know."

Kasey nodded. "I'm sure, but you're a tough cookie."

Tough old bird is more like it.

"Yes. Well, what would you know?" she muttered. "Off running the roads like a groupie for months."

"I called every week and you had my numbers. You could have called any time, although you chose not to." Kasey tried not to lose her patience. "Maybe I'm the one whose feelings should be hurt."

"My feelings are not hurt, young lady. It's just common courtesy to stay in touch with family."

"Right. Okay. I'll do better."

Grem touched Kasey's arm. "Thank you, dear."

Jeremy walked in and leaned against the doorway. "I thought I heard your voice. I didn't recognize the car at first."

"Oh, yeah. Nick's. It's been under a cover for months, so I took it for a drive."

Grem gave her the stink eye. "You're not driving your father's car?"

She rolled her eyes. "It's not Dad's car anymore. It's mine. And no, I'm not driving it. The darn thing wouldn't start. Probably the battery or alternator again. So I drove Nick's."

Grem pursed her lips as though she didn't approve.

"What did you decide to do with the truck?" Jeremy asked.

"I guess I'll have it towed. I don't know why I thought I needed it at home with me. It seemed like the right thing to do at the time."

Jeremy popped a butterscotch into his mouth. He extended one her way with a nod.

"No, thanks."

He shrugged and shoved the candy back into his pocket. "Want me to have someone stop by and check out the Porsche?"

"That'd be great. Granddaddy was right. He always said you were the best all-'round problem-solver ever born."

"Rest his soul," Grem said, her voice floating like a prayer.

Jeremy nodded. "Consider it done."

"So, dear. Don't you think it's about time to move on, then?"

"I'm trying." Kasey cleared her throat.

"Good. I suppose you could park Nick's car in the back garage. That thing's been empty for years."

"What are you talking about?" Kasey asked.

"When you move back. I suppose you will want to bring his car with you. You can store it in the back garage."

"Who said anything about moving back here?"

Grem gripped the arms of the wheelchair with both hands. "You agreed it was time to move on, didn't you?"

Kasey looked out the window. It was now or never. "Actually, I did come over to let you know . . . I'm moving."

"There you go then. I knew you'd come to your senses."

Kasey braced herself. Where to begin? "Did you know that Nick bought a house out near Emporia?"

Grem shook her head. "How would I know that, dear? It's not like Nick and I were close." She rubbed her elbow. "Emporia? Why, for goodness sake, would he buy something way out there? No one lives out there."

"That's not true, Grem."

Jeremy shrugged and walked out of the room toward the kitchen.

"It's a long story, but when I got back in town there was a letter and a couple of phone messages. That's how I found out that Nick had been working with this guy on our dream home in the country as a surprise for our anniversary this year."

"A secret?" Grem looked pleased, as if anything that marred Nick's character was a point in her favor.

"Not a secret. A surprise. A romantic surprise."

"Whatever." The old lady clucked as if she wasn't buying it.

"I went there this morning," Kasey said.

Jeremy came back into the sun room, ice clinking in his glass. "Alone?"

"Yes. Alone. I drive all over the country alone. Why would that surprise you?"

"Yeah. Well, I know that. I mean, well, I'd have gone with you," he half-mumbled.

Grem's right eyebrow shot up like a question mark. "Why didn't you tell us before?"

"I didn't even really know what I was going to see." Kasey refused to let either of them dampen her renewed spirit. "It's absolutely perfect," she gushed. "Our dream house."

"That's very nice." Grem patted Kasey's hand. "You should make good money when you sell it. You can never have too much put aside for a rainy day." She leaned forward in her wheelchair and spoke to Jeremy. "Will you help Kasey get her things to move back into the carriage house? This is good timing; the cleaning lady was here just yesterday."

Jeremy faced the old woman. "Sure."

"I am not moving back here," Kasey said.

"Into the carriage house. Of course. I know."

"No. I am not moving here at all. I'm moving to the house that Nick built for me."

Grem frowned. "You can't. It's too far away. I'll never see you."

"You're moving there?" Jeremy asked.

Kasey shot him a you're-not-helping look. "It's less than eighty miles away. Jeremy can drive you out, and I'll come visit. We don't get together that often now, and I'm less than twenty miles away. What's the difference?"

"The difference is, you never should've left to begin with."

Kasey's mood dipped. "Please don't."

"That man ruined your happiness."

"Stop it. That man *was* my happiness." Kasey put her hands up in front of her, trying to resist the urge to say anything hurtful, even if her grandmother deserved it. "I'm leaving. I wanted you to be the first to know. I hope once you think about it, you'll be happy for me."

"Jeremy." Grem's voice rose. "Tell her she can't do this."

"I'm leaving. I'm not having this argument." Kasey stormed out the front door and got into the Thunderbird. She threw the car into gear and floored it, spinning the wheels as she headed for the gate.

In the rearview mirror, she saw Jeremy standing with his hands on his hips in the open doorway of the house.

Chapter Seventeen

Kasey wasn't about to let anyone else ruin her excitement today. She'd pick up boxes on her way home so she could start packing.

Of course, that turned out to be easier said than done. What happened to the days when you could stop in at the grocery or liquor store and pick up as many boxes as you wanted?

With folks so environmentally conscious, you can't even get a good box for free anymore.

Determined to have her way, she stopped at Target and bought six large plastic containers with lids—probably a better plan anyway since she could use them for storage later.

She went home with her blue bins and considered what she needed to pack. She'd never been a lister or a planner, but she sure could use those skills today. Maybe she should call Riley. She was the queen of listing and planning.

Kasey lugged the bins into the house and left them in the middle of the living room. She decided that her first priority was to develop the pictures of her newfound paradise. That would remind her just how wonderful it was since, during their brief visit, Grem had managed to suck all the happy out of her day.

There was nothing like being up to her elbows

in solution to lift her mood. Digital photography was fast, but she truly loved developing film. She could hardly contain her excitement as she lifted the pictures out of the developer solution and they came to life in front of her. They captured the serene beauty of the countryside.

Nick had matched her vision of their dreams so well, he might as well have been in her head.

She sat at the kitchen table, one foot tucked under her, the other swinging to the rhythm of the happy beat of her heart. Five enlarged photographs covered the table in front of her. Scrapbooking materials littered the rest of the table. She snipped, glued, and mounted several pictures onto large colorful pages of the scrapbook that held her dearest memories from over the years. Today she added the pictures that chronicled the trip with Mr. Huckaby to the Nickel Creek house. Today had been a good day.

The sound of a tap on the back screen door startled her. She was relieved when Riley pushed the door open with a *yoo-hoo*.

"I didn't hear you drive up," Kasey said.

"I walked over." Riley went to the refrigerator, grabbed a bottle of water, and took a swig. She sat next to Kasey. "Your grandmother called me all in a huff. She said something about you being ungrateful, losing a grasp on reality, and that you were going to live in the woods. What is that all about?"

"She's a maniac, isn't she?"

"Hey, these pictures are beautiful." Riley moved one of the two enlarged landscapes in front of her. "The colors are amazing." She tapped her fingernail on the table as she looked over Kasey's shoulder at the scrapbook pages she was assembling. "Is this where you were this morning?"

"Yep." Kasey layered colored paper under the pictures, then added a couple squigglies around them with a colored marker.

"Nice house," Riley said.

"Isn't it?"

"Whose house is it?"

"Mine."

"Yours?" Riley looked confused. "You bought a house?"

"No. Nick did."

Riley eyed Kasey. "What . . . *exactly* . . . do you mean?"

"Don't look at me like I'm crazy. I know Nick is gone."

Riley sighed.

"When I got back into town, there was a letter in the stack of mail. That's how I found out about the house. Nick had been working on this place before . . . before the accident. It was going to be a surprise. Isn't it wonderful?"

Riley picked up the picture of the house. "You didn't know about it?"

"Not a thing. I guess you didn't know either."

"Nope." Riley shook her head and looked more closely at the pictures.

"So sneaky, but it makes me love him more than ever. Do you think Von knew?"

"You would think so, but he never mentioned anything. It's cute. Where is it?"

"Only about an hour and a half away. I think Nick was coming back from there the day of the accident. Chaz Huckaby is the guy who was coordinating all the renovations. He remembers seeing Nick and Jake that day. The house is off of Route 58."

"You're kidding."

Kasey shook her head. "I met with him this morning. He knew both Nick and Jake. He confirmed the last time they were up there. It fits."

"Oh, my gosh. That's wonderful. I mean, it's more proof that Jake was with Nick."

"I feel stronger than ever that we'll find Jake."

"Kasey, while you were away there were a couple more shootings."

"They have to catch the gunman."

"Well, that's just it. They did."

"You're kidding. Why didn't anyone call me? Do they have Jake?"

"No. Nothing new on Jake. The gun used in those shootings was a shotgun. The casings at Nick's crash site . . . they don't match."

"No?"

"Nope. That information was never released.

Von thinks someone may have been copycatting, or actually targeting Nick."

"Why?" Kasey felt the blood rush from her face. "No one would target Nick. Everyone loved him." She stood and walked to the window. "Von thinks Nick's accident wasn't random?"

"He's been working a few angles. He'll find out who was responsible."

"I'm not sure I want to know a person that would want to hurt Nick."

"I hear ya. So what are you going to do with that house? There must be a huge mortgage on it. Are you in debt? I mean, you didn't know about it, right?"

"No debt. I have the deed and the key."

"Cool. That's a nice-looking place. I bet it will bring a pretty penny."

"Oh, I can't sell it."

"That's understandable. I guess it wouldn't be hard to rent out."

"I'm moving there."

"You're what?"

"Please don't try to talk me out of it. Grem was so ugly about it this afternoon. Trust me on this. Moving there is the right thing to do. At least for now. I haven't felt this alive in months."

"No wonder your grandmother is going off the deep end. She'll never be able to control you from an hour and a half away. You sure this is the right thing to do?"

"Yes. It is the most peaceful place. No neighbors. It's like the wilderness."

"The wilderness? You won't be afraid?"

"No way. I've traveled all over the world, and to some of the most dangerous cities in the US, for work. I can manage a little rural life."

Riley laughed. "I don't know. Even this much country living is a stretch for two city girls like us, and we're like within mall distance."

"I'll have Nick and Jake watching over me."

Riley looked around. "How will you move all this stuff?"

"I'm not going to. The new place is furnished. I'm just going to pack a few things and take them out there with me tomorrow. Do you want to come along?"

"You aren't wasting any time. Are you sure you want to do this? I'm going to miss you. I don't think I'm ready for you to move."

Kasey put her hand on Riley's. "I'll miss you, too. I can't stay here, though. When you see the Nickel Creek place, you're going to know why I have to be there. It's . . . a feeling. It's safe."

"I'm being selfish. You know I'll support any decision you make. So do you need Von to help you pack?"

"I think I can get what little I'm planning to take into the RV. If y'all could bring the Thunderbird up for me, that would be great. My car is acting up. Jeremy is going to come by and take a look. Probably the electrical system again."

"Again?"

"I know. Hopefully, Jeremy can fix it tomorrow. I'll come back with y'all and drive it up on my next trip."

"Whatever you need," Riley said. "Von loves a road trip."

Chapter Eighteen

Kasey woke to a gray and drizzly day—not a perfect day for a drive. But she'd already put the few boxes and the plastic bins she intended to take with her into the RV, and her heart was ready to be in Adams Grove. Rain or shine. She flipped on the television and watched the forecast. The meteorologist called for morning drizzle with clearing skies in the afternoon. According to the fancy radar, the sky would clear from the west, so she'd get better weather sooner by driving to the new house.

She called Riley, who must've known there was no talking her out of the plan, because she didn't even try.

They agreed to hit the road at ten o'clock sharp.

They pulled out onto the highway right on time and it was a regular convoy. Riley drove Von's SUV, following Von in Nick's T-Bird, behind

Kasey's lead in the RV. All they lacked were CB radios and cool nicknames. They had driven for about forty-five minutes when they took the exit to Route 58 where the scenery became far more rural. The Cotton Gin was Kasey's mental halfway mark. As soon as they passed the long row of warehouses, she punched speed dial to Riley's phone.

"Breaker, breaker, Lucky Charm," Kasey said in an exaggerated southern accent. "This here is Shutterbug."

Riley laughed and responded in kind. "Ten-four, good buddy."

"Halfway home," Kasey said.

"That's a big ten-freakin'-four, because my butt's already numb. I hate driving Von's truck."

"I know, but thanks for doing it," Kasey said. "I'm glad you're sharing this moment with me."

"My pleasure, treasure. Now hang up. It's nasty out here. We don't want to cause an accident because we're not paying attention."

"Breaker, breaker. Ten-four. I'm signing off. Over and out." Kasey pressed end. It would be hard to live so far away from Riley, but she chased those doubts away.

Forty-five minutes later, the convoy paraded into the driveway of the house on Nickel Creek Road. Just as the forecast had promised, the late morning sky was bright and clear.

They stepped out of the vehicles and stretched.

"It's even prettier than the pictures," Riley said as she caught up to Kasey.

The rain had made everything look fresh and green.

Kasey reached for Riley's hand and gave it a squeeze. "I know. Wait until you see inside." Every tiny doubt that had crept in had drifted away as soon as she pulled into the driveway today.

This is home.

Von nodded and said, "I can't believe he didn't tell anyone. This might be the only secret Nick Rolly ever kept in his whole life."

"I know. I can't believe it either." Kasey thought about how Nick couldn't even keep a Christmas present a secret. "He was terrible at keeping things to himself."

"Yep. That was Nick." Von wrapped one of his arms around his wife, the other around Kasey. "It must have meant more to him to surprise you. He loved you so much."

"I know." Kasey's voice softened. "I was lucky."

"I grew up out this way, you know," Von said, dropping his arms from around them. "There's great hunting and fishing around here."

"That ought to come in handy for me." Kasey laughed.

She and Riley walked toward the house.

"I'm going to check out the manly stuff." Von turned and headed to the huge garage. "I'll get the T-Bird stored away and under the cover the way Nick would've wanted."

Riley and Kasey went inside.

"Wow. I love the open floor plan," Riley said. "This is amazing. Nick even did all this decorating? Picking out paint colors and furniture? Everything?"

Kasey nodded. "Everything."

Riley walked through to the kitchen and looked out back where Von opened the garage doors. They were the carriage house kind.

"Look, a perfect rainbow!" Riley pointed to the east. A long rainbow with bands of yellow, orange, pink and purple spread high and wide.

"Rainbow, good luck," they said at the same time and high-fived.

Kasey smiled. "I knew it, and you should see all the cardinals."

Riley nodded. "It does feel like a lucky place. I'm going to miss having you so close, but I can see why you'd want to be here. I'll visit a bunch, I promise."

"I know, and there are always phone calls and instant messaging." Kasey opened one of the boxes and put things away.

A few minutes later, Von came in the house carrying two boxes stacked on top of each other.

"Thanks, honey," Riley said, reaching for one.

"You should see that garage. It's sweet."

Kasey smiled. "Nick sure did love his man cave, didn't he?"

"Can't blame him," Von said as he went outside to get the last of the boxes.

When Von came back, Chaz Huckaby was with him.

Chaz made himself at home, heading right for the kitchen. "Hi, folks. I stopped by to surprise ya with a basket of local goodies. My wife makes the best applesauce cake in town. Just wanted to officially welcome you."

Kasey dug into the basket and took out the cake. She unwrapped it while Chaz told one of what must have been his favorite stories to Von —the same ones she'd heard the day she met him. No surprise, the two men hit it off. But then it seemed that Chaz never met a stranger. He was just that kind of guy.

"What size piece do you want, Chaz?" Kasey asked, offering him some cake.

"I'm not staying. Besides, I've got to watch my weight." Chaz rubbed his belly. "Thanks, but y'all enjoy it."

Kasey served up the cake on small plates and took them out to the deck. The four of them sat at the wrought iron bistro table. Nearby, the out-door kitchen had a gas grill and a fire pit for smoking brisket. Nick's specialty.

Von moaned when he took a bite of the

scrumptious dessert. He waved his fork toward Kasey. "I hope this town teaches you to bake like this. This cake is delicious."

"Don't hold your breath. I'm not sure I have that gene," she said. "I'm a lost cause in the kitchen."

"Told ya my wife makes the best applesauce cake. It's good." Chaz nodded and looked for confirmation.

"Oh, yeah." Von took another bite and twirled his fork. "Kasey, you'd better suck up to Chaz's wife before each of my visits."

"Now that I can do," Kasey said.

Chaz didn't stay long, and they quickly finished the chores they'd plan to complete today. Von agreed to take care of the transition of the Rocking R to the 4-H camp Nick had provisioned in his will. They all agreed that the old farmhouse and its contents should remain untouched for a year to give Kasey the chance to decide what she wanted to do with the things she'd left behind. Even without Kasey around, the Rocking R was never empty. Local 4-H-ers came and went to take care of their project animals and pitch in as needed.

The sun began to sink, turning the sky bright orange and pink above the horizon.

"I guess it's about time for us to head back," Von said. "We'll want to get home before it's too late. I need to feed the dogs, too."

"Are you sure you want to come back with us tonight?" Riley asked Kasey.

"Yep. Jeremy said he'd have my car ready, and I have that meeting in Richmond tomorrow with Prescott Banks to go over the final contracts for the annual International Auto Show."

"You can't do that online or by fax?"

Kasey rolled her eyes. "Nope. Those folks are so old school. They still require me to meet with them, even after doing that show for ten years. If it didn't pay so darn well I wouldn't bother."

"I hear ya. It's a sweet contract," Riley said.

"It is. Anyway, I'll come back here after that."

"It doesn't look like you want to leave." Riley raised a brow.

"It's hard. But I need to go back. I'm good."

"Let's load up then," Von said. He picked up his plate, stacked their plates on top, and took them to the kitchen.

Riley washed the dishes, Kasey dried them, and then they all headed out to Von's SUV. They talked about the property almost the whole way back.

Beneath a starry sky, Von pulled into Kasey's driveway. "Home safe and sound," he said.

"Thanks for everything, y'all." Kasey hopped out of the truck. "I appreciate ya."

"We're happy for you. This is the right thing to do," Von said. "We're here for you, no matter what decisions you make. You know that."

"Thanks. I know." Kasey waved as they backed out of the driveway.

She was lucky to have such true friends to support her.

Jeremy had left a note under the windshield wiper of her car. The Porsche was ready to roll. Perfect.

Kasey went inside, reviewed the list Riley had made for her, and started piling items near the door. Since her meeting in Richmond was mid-day she wanted to get as much pulled together tonight as possible. She hoped the meeting would wrap up early so she could drive to Adams Grove while it was still daylight.

Home. It felt good to have a place that felt like a home again. Now if she could just get a lead on Jake and bring him there, life would be perfect.

Chapter Nineteen

The next morning, the Porsche started right up and Kasey left for Richmond to meet with Prescott. She twisted the knob on the radio to pick up a better signal and landed on an oldies station. She sang along with the Bee Gees and wondered if she'd make it to the appointment on time. Glancing between her speedometer and watch, she calculated she should have about ten minutes to spare.

She watched her speed since this stretch of road had a reputation for speed traps. Even so, as she cleared the next corner and saw the cop parked in the median with the radar gun pointing out the window, she couldn't help but tap the brake out of habit. But instead of her car slowing down, it sputtered and choked. She gave it some gas and it smoothed back out. Relieved, she steadied her speed, but as she turned the next corner the engine went silent.

The steering became a chore without the power of the engine. She veered to the side of the road as the car slowed to a coast. In her rearview mirror, she saw a big rig barreling her way.

"No!" She slapped the steering wheel and cranked frantically on the ignition, but nothing worked. The car slowed to a crawl. She bounced in the seat, willing the car off to the side. Just as she made it to the shoulder, the semi swerved to the oncoming lane to avoid hitting her. The force of the wind pushed her tiny sports car the rest of the way off the road.

Her heart raced.

"Jesus!"

She released the steering wheel and leaned forward against it. Her heart pounded so hard she thought it might honk the horn.

"That was too close."

Her heart took its sweet time slowing down.

"Daggone it." She pounded the steering wheel, got out of the car and walked to the rear where she opened the hood over the engine compartment.

She stood staring at the engine with no idea what she was looking at. She reached in and wiggled some wires, then pulled out the dipstick and checked the oil. Having been spoiled by the mechanics and Jeremy, she'd never seen any reason to learn much beyond the basics.

She hadn't seen an exit for miles and didn't see one on the straightaway ahead. Heck, she hadn't passed anything except woods for at least three miles. How far would she have to walk to the next town or gas station?

Maybe that radar cop would come this way.

She went back to the driver's seat and tried the key. Nothing.

She flipped open her phone, then rolled her eyes. No bars. No Service. "The one time I have an emergency, the doggone thing won't work."

Hiking up the road wasn't a good option. Kasey didn't have the time to walk for miles or the strength to carry all of her camera equipment. She couldn't risk leaving it behind for someone to steal, either.

She walked about thirty feet forward to see if she could get a signal on her phone. No luck. She even held the phone in the air hoping it might miraculously catch a wave or something. Of course, that didn't work either.

Why did I take this route instead of Interstate 64? Just to torture myself by going by the accident site again? When will I learn?

If she didn't get a move on soon, she'd be late for her appointment. The International Auto Show was too good a gig to screw up, and really the first real job she had scheduled since the tour. Prescott Banks wasn't the type to take being late lightly. Old fuddy-duddy.

Cars passed, but no one even slowed down. She hoped that radar cop would break for lunch and ride this way. He'd have to stop and help. Wasn't it his duty to serve?

She looked at her watch. Not even five minutes had passed. It sure seemed longer standing there alone on the side of the road. Maybe the jokers who passed weren't familiar with a rear engine car or were afraid they'd have to help her change a tire. All she needed was a phone and a ride. She slammed the cover over the engine and opened the trunk at the front of the car, praying that would change her luck.

The late January afternoon was sunny and warm. In the southeastern part of Virginia in January, it could be twenty-eight degrees and sleeting one day and in the high sixties the next. It really wasn't unusual to have a few spring-like days sandwiched between snowfalls.

She scrounged around in her purse for a clip, fastened her hair up off her neck, and popped a piece of gum into her mouth. When she turned around, she almost swallowed her gum.

An antique baby-blue T-Bird was parked right

behind her. The dark-haired man behind the wheel looked just like . . . *Nick?*

Coughing to get the gum out of her throat, she reached into the car for her bottle of water. When she stood back up, the man was out of his car.

She exhaled. His car had a vanity plate. It wasn't Nick's. Wishful thinking or her mind playing tricks on her. But the T-Bird looked like Nick's car, and the man had looked like Nick in silhouette.

He walked toward her. "You okay?"

She cleared her throat, trying to shake the chills that had scampered up her spine a moment ago. "I've been better."

"Broke down?"

"Not exactly a picnic spot." Kasey regretted the snarky response as soon as it left her lips.

He raised a brow and smirked as traffic whizzed by. "What's the matter?"

"I don't know. She just sputtered and quit." Kasey propped her hand on her hip. "A big rig almost ran over me."

"Probably electrical," he said.

"Wouldn't be the first time."

Is he going to help me, or just make friends? "I'm late. Can you get me to a town so I can rent a car, or get a cab into Richmond? I have an appointment I can't be late for."

He's too good-looking to be a murderer. Isn't he?

"You live in Richmond?"

"No."

"Oh." He shoved his hands in his pockets.

"I just moved up this way."

Why did I tell him that? Because his mouth moves like Nick's—soft.

"Really? Where?"

"Over in Adams Grove."

He met her gaze. "You must be the girl Huckaby has been talking about. The old Miller farm?"

"You know Chaz Huckaby?"

"Who doesn't know Chaz Huckaby? Are you over on Nickel Creek Road?"

"Yeah. That's it."

"My mom lives over that way."

"Really? Small world. It's beautiful out there."

"When's your meeting?"

"One-thirty."

He looked at his watch. "You're going to be late."

She waved the useless phone at him. "I know, and I can't even call them and let them know." She held the useless cell phone up in dismay. "My phone won't work out here."

He pulled his phone off a clip on his belt and dialed a number. "Hey, Bobby. I need your wrecker out on Route 58." He looked around to get his bearings. "Just west of Capron near the old store . . . Okay . . . Sure . . . Black Porsche . . . Seriously . . . An hour? Great. Thanks, man."

"An hour?" She tipped her head back, frustrated. "I knew I should've left earlier."

"You can make it if you leave now."

She motioned toward the car. "Yeah, well that isn't happening."

"Why don't you take my car? I'll wait for the wrecker. Bobby's place is right there by Huckaby's shop. We can meet up later today. After your meeting. Sound good?"

Is he serious?

"What makes you so sure I won't steal your car?"

"I'm not worried," he said.

"Shouldn't take but a couple hours."

"You can buy me dinner at Jacob's Diner around five. Can you get back by then?"

"Yes. Definitely."

"Have you been there? Jacob's Diner, I mean. Best darn chicken anywhere."

Kasey shook her head. "No. I haven't been anywhere but Huckaby's, but I know the way there."

"It's on the same block."

"Are you for real?"

"Sure." He thumped the trunk of the Porsche. "You did know the engine isn't up here, right?"

"Yeah. I thought maybe people weren't stopping because they thought I had a flat."

"Good thinking. I'm sure this classic is as important to you as mine is to me," he said. "I'd say if you run off with mine and I end up with yours, we're about even. But you look honest, and you're a neighbor. You better get going."

"You're not kidding."

"No, now scoot. Geez, you city girls sure are full of suspicion."

"I'll need my equipment." She leaned across the driver's seat and grabbed her briefcase and camera bag.

"Need any help?"

"Thanks." She handed him the heavy case, then headed toward the T-Bird with the bags hiked up on her shoulder. She put the equipment in the passenger's seat, then stood with one foot in the car, watching him as he walked back to her Porsche. "I really appreciate this."

He turned, smiled, and saluted her.

She scrambled in her purse for a second, looking for a business card, then ran to his side. "Here's my card. I'll see you at five. Promise."

He smiled and tucked the card in his shirt pocket without even glancing at it. "I'm not worried."

She slid behind the wheel of the T-Bird and started the engine. What a stroke of luck. She opened the door and half stood. "I didn't even get your name."

He turned, walking backwards. "Scott."

"Thanks, Scott. I owe you. Big time."

"Get moving. You're late. But don't speed or you'll be later."

"Yeah, I've heard about the ticket-crazy cops out here. Thanks." The country had its advantages. She pulled the car out into the traffic, waving to her new friend as she passed by.

Chapter Twenty

Kasey felt an odd sense of déjà vu as she drove Scott's T-Bird. The car was so much like Nick's. She wasn't sure if it was the same year or not. Even though she'd photographed many older cars in her career, she'd never paid close attention to their model years.

She turned on the radio. No AM sports station here. The sound of a country song with a catchy beat filled the car.

She pushed the gas a little harder to keep the T-Bird at the posted speed limit of sixty. This car didn't have the power of her Porsche, but she was on her way, thank goodness.

The bars on her cell phone lit up. She picked up the phone to dial Prescott and let him know she might be running late.

Just as she punched in the numbers, a siren wailed behind her.

She pulled over so the policeman could pass, but he followed her off to the shoulder of the road. *I know I wasn't speeding.* She put her phone on the seat and cranked down the window. A young officer walked up to the car, one hand on his hip, the other on his gun. The gun looked proportion-ately large for such a small guy

"Good afternoon." She smiled her best give-me-a-warning smile. It had never let her down.

"License and registration, ma'am."

She handed him her license, then looked in the glove box for the registration. "I'm sorry, officer. The registration doesn't seem to be here."

He smirked. "Why doesn't that surprise me?"

She pushed her sunglasses to the top of her head. "I don't know. Happens all the time, huh?" Isn't this where he was supposed to notice her pretty brown eyes and winning smile and let her go with just a warning?

"Ma'am, please step out of the car."

She blinked in surprise. "Excuse me? For what?"

"Ma'am." He shifted the hand on his holster. "I asked you to please get of the car."

"Yes. Okay." She fumbled with the lap belt and then with the door handle of the unfamiliar car. She stepped out on to the pavement feeling humiliated. There was a lot of traffic. She would swear that cars were slowing down and people were staring at her. Funny how no one had been interested when she was broken down on the side of the road, but they all wanted to see this.

"I'm in a hurry, but I wasn't speeding," she explained.

"Please step around to the back of the car here, ma'am."

"Is something wrong?"

"Anything you want to tell me?"

"I'm late?"

"Put your hands on the trunk of the car, please."

Kasey took a step back from the officer. "Now wait a second."

He dipped his head in a very serious way. His voice was calm but firm. "Ma'am. Do as I say, please."

She rolled her eyes, shaking her head.

Unbelievable. What else could go wrong?

She spun around and placed her hands on the trunk of the car. Just like on *Cops*.

"Do you have any weapons or anything I need to know about on your person or in the vehicle?"

"No-oo." Kasey suddenly felt guilty though she knew she had no reason to. "Absolutely not."

The officer peered into the car. "What's in the bag?"

"Camera equipment."

"Out taking pictures?"

"I'm late for a shoot in Richmond. I'm a photographer."

"This your car?"

She shook her head. "No."

"I didn't think so." He pulled one arm behind her back.

Her eyes shot wide. She looked over her shoulder

at the officer as he pulled her other arm behind her back.

"What the heck are you doing?" Kasey said. "I didn't do anything. I wasn't even speeding."

She heard a zipping sound. Her hands were bound behind her. "That's what happens, ma'am, when you steal a car. You get caught eventually."

"Steal? No. You don't understand."

He pushed her toward the cruiser. Passers-by stared.

"Yes, ma'am. I'm sure you have a story to tell me. They all do. We'll do that in town."

"I told you the truth. My Porsche broke down. I borrowed this car to get to my meeting."

"Your Porsche?" His look told her that he didn't buy her story.

"I swear. Run the tag. You can check."

"You'll have to just get in the back of my Caprice Classic because my Ferrari is in the shop," he said with a smirk.

"Go back and look. My car is on the side of Route 58."

"Whose car is this?"

Her mind went blank.

What was his name?

"He stopped to help me. It was . . ."

Come on, what was his name?

"It wasn't Nick . . . It was Scott."

"Yeah, okay. Good guess from the license plate." The officer nodded at the vanity tag on the back of the car that read GR8SCOTT.

"I promise I'm not lying." She pulled away from him, but he grabbed her and guided her to the back of his car. He pushed down on the back of her head and forced her onto the backseat of the cruiser.

"This can't be happening to me."

The officer walked back to the T-Bird. He removed the keys from the ignition, pushed the lock on the door, and slammed it shut. He sauntered back to the cruiser as if he thought he'd just saved the world. Kasey was so angry she couldn't even look at him.

He got into the car and snatched the transceiver from the dash to call in the details of her arrest. She didn't bother to listen. It didn't sound like anyone *else* was listening to him either, because no one responded.

There was no way she'd get to her meeting on time now. Just when things had been going so well, too. Her last hope drifted out of sight as they pulled onto the road heading to who-the-heck-knew-where.

Kasey leaned forward and spoke through the partition that protected him from her. "Sir. Excuse me?"

"Yes, ma'am."

Yechh. If he called her ma'am once more, she'd clobber the little guy. Good thing he'd tied up her hands. "What's your name?"

"Taylor," he said with a northerner-come-south drawl that made it sound like there was an extra L in there somewhere. "Dan Taylor."

"Sheriff Dan Taylor?"

The young man smiled. "Deputy Dan Taylor."

She flopped against the back of the seat. *Deputy Dan. Well this just gets better and better. Sounds like a cartoon character.* There was nothing she could do about this now. She might as well relax and resign herself to rescheduling her appointment with Prescott. Hopefully it wouldn't compromise her arrangement with his company. It was one of her favorite jobs. The new prototypes were fun to photograph. But she sure couldn't tell Prescott she'd been arrested on suspicion of grand theft auto.

The cruiser stopped. Kasey looked out the window. *Spratt's Market* in huge letters spanned the side of a concrete building. Market? Geez, was he going to parade her all over town?

He had better not leave me out here while he goes grocery shopping.

Deputy Dan got out of the car and opened her door.

"You're taking me to the market?" She couldn't refrain from the smartass tone that came with the statement.

He glared at her, less than amused. "Let's go."

Frustrated, she puffed not-so-nice names for him under her breath and scooched to the edge of the seat. With her hands bound behind her, getting out proved to be harder than she'd imagined.

The deputy helped her to her feet, then spun her around to face a brick building with the words *POLICE DEPARTMENT* emblazoned across the front.

"I stand corrected," she mumbled.

"Walk." He gave her a little push.

She glared at him. "I'm walking."

I'll have his badge, damn it.

They made the short walk across the parking area and through the heavy wooden doors of the building. Once inside, Kasey stifled a laugh as she looked around. The place resembled the set of the old *Andy Griffith Show*. The desks and gun cabinets lined the right side of the space, and four barred jail cells—all of them empty—were situated on the left side. Did they have a town drunk who slept off a night or two here as if it were a modern-day Mayberry timeshare?

He parked her in a scarred wooden chair next to a metal desk that had seen better days. She wiggled and shifted in the chair, trying to get comfortable with her hands secured behind her. He opened a couple drawers, searching for something, and came up with a checklist.

I'm probably his first arrest.

Deputy Dan used his finger to keep his place as he read the list.

"Name?"

"Kassandra Phillips."

"Address?"

"You've got my license. It's all on there."

He shot her a look.

"Fine." She gave him the information and wished like heck she'd taken I-64 instead of Route 58 this morning.

Deputy Dan leaned in toward the screen to review what he had entered, backspacing more than he typed. He struck the keys with a slow monotony that had her wanting to offer to type for him.

"Look. Don't I get a call or something?"

"Not yet."

She tried to remain calm. "Can you take this thing off my wrists at least?"

"No. It's policy. Until I put you in the cell, you must remain restrained. It's for my safety."

Pretty good damn policy, too, because she'd had about enough of this ridiculous situation and felt pretty sure she could kick his scrawny ass.

He asked her again about the vehicle.

"I already told you. His name is Scott."

"What's his last name?"

"I don't remember."

He picked up the keys from the desk and dangled them. "Scott is on the keychain and on the license plate. You may as well tell me the truth, lady. You aren't doing yourself any favors here."

"So you're arresting me because I borrowed a car without asking someone's last name. Or is it because I didn't have the registration? Why did you stop me anyway?" Kasey became more agitated.

"I stopped you because I know the owner of this car."

"Great. Call him, then."

"I tried. He didn't answer. But I know he wouldn't let anyone borrow it. He loves that car."

"Well, he did. I told you he offered to wait with my broken-down Porsche. He was going to take it to the garage for me. He let me use his car to go to my meeting."

"Until I can reach him to clear you, I'm not letting you go."

He walked her to the cell furthest from the front door and cut the zip-tie from her wrists before releasing her into the small space. The heavy metal-barred door clanked as it closed behind her.

"How long can you hold me here?"

He ignored her and walked through a doorway at the back that led down what appeared to be a long hallway.

"What about my call?" she yelled after him.

She sat in a chair in the corner of the cell and

watched the clock tick off the minutes. After fourteen minutes and twenty seconds, the deputy returned. Kasey jumped from the chair, ran to the bars and clutched them, her hands on either side of her face. She hated to imagine how she looked. "Can I please make that call?"

The deputy picked up a cordless phone off the desk and handed it to her through the bars. "Here you go."

"Thank you." She nodded, then turned her back and dialed Prescott's number. Thank goodness, she knew the number by heart. "Hi. This is Kasey Phillips. I was supposed to meet with Prescott this afternoon. Can you let him know that I have been . . ." she turned and eyed the deputy with disdain ". . . unexpectedly detained and am not going to be able to make our meeting?" She nodded, listening. "Yes. I understand. I'll get back with him to reschedule . . . Sorry . . . Yes . . . Goodbye."

She ended the call and began to dial Riley.

"Ah-ah." He shook his finger at her. "One call, Ms. Phillips."

"But I need someone to get me out of here."

"One call is the policy."

She thrust the phone through the bars. "Don't you ever bend policy?"

"No, ma'am."

"Of course you don't." Figures she'd get the one no-testosterone, law-abiding rookie in the state. "How long do you plan to keep me here?"

"Until I can talk to the sheriff."

"Have you called him? I'd love to talk to him."

"Been trying all afternoon. No answer. It's his day off."

She plopped down in the chair and put her head in her hands.

The clock ticked to five o'clock. Now, technically, she could be accused of stealing that car. She was supposed to be meeting Scott right now. Deputy Dan cleared his desk.

Holy crap, is he going to leave me here all night?

"Sir. Deputy Dan."

He looked up from the pile of paperwork he'd been shuffling around. "Yes?"

"Could you take me down to the diner next to Huckaby's in Emporia?"

"You think we're going to take you out to dinner? We'll feed you, but you'll be eating in your cell."

"No, I mean I can clear myself if you'll take me there. I was supposed to meet the owner of the car there at five." She pointed to the clock. "He should be there waiting for me."

His keys jingled on his hip as he walked to the door.

Her hopes sprang. "Are you going to check?"

"I'll be back."

She sat, keeping one eye on the door. A few cars passed the building at long intervals. What the hell was she going to do? Why had she wasted her call on Prescott instead of calling Riley?

I am such an idiot.

Kasey's stomach growled. The deputy had been gone for over an hour and she was hungry. She hadn't eaten all day.

The front door swung open. She hoped the deputy had some food in tow. But it wasn't the deputy who walked inside. It was a different man, and he didn't give the wall of jail cells a second look. He headed over to the second desk in the room, a bigger one in the corner behind glass partitions, as if he were looking for some-one.

She walked to the cell door, watching the visitor. "Scott?"

He jerked his head up.

It *was* him. "If you're here to report your car stolen, you won't need to do that. The deputy arrested me not long after I left you. He wouldn't believe that you loaned me your car."

"You're kidding. That's why you didn't show. Why didn't someone call me?" He unclipped his phone from his waistband and glanced at the screen. "Damn. I must have accidentally turned it off after I called the tow truck for you."

"Thank goodness you're here. I didn't know your last name, and Deputy Dan wasn't buying my story. Maybe he'll believe you and let me out of here."

"I can do better than that." He headed toward the cell keys that hung on the wall.

"No. You can't break me out. He has all my information."

A wide grin spread across Scott's face. "That's funny. I had you pictured as an adventurous type of girl."

"Yeah, but a law-abiding one."

He opened the cell door.

Kasey didn't budge. "You're gonna get me in more trouble than I already am. With my luck, I'll be the one they make an example of, and I'll end up in one of those women's prisons with Big Bertha callin' the shots. No, thanks."

"I wondered what happened to you when you didn't show up for dinner. I've never been stood up before." He shook his head. "Kinda hurt my feelings."

"I'm so sorry. I've been here all day. I'm starved."

"Come on, let's get something to eat."

"No. You just sit tight until that crazy deputy gets back so you can clear my name."

The front door of the building opened, and Deputy Dan stepped in.

Kasey knew she was in trouble now with the door to her cell wide open.

"Hey, Sheriff," the deputy said.

Kasey looked at Scott in surprise. "Sheriff?"

Scott shrugged. "Would appear so, huh?"

She dropped to the chair.

He turned his attention back to his deputy. "Dan, let's review the case back here." Scott pushed open the door to the back of the building and Deputy Dan scrambled in behind him, apparently eager to please.

Kasey sat there, dumbfounded.

After a couple of minutes, Scott returned by himself. He headed straight for the cell and motioned for her to come out. She complied. Scott handed Kasey her purse and camera bag.

"Thanks."

"I tore up the paperwork. I'm sorry. I was trying to help you. I sure didn't mean for your day to turn out like this. Can I buy you dinner?"

She smiled. How many times was this guy going to rescue her today? "I *am* starved."

He put his hand on her shoulder. "If it's any consolation, your car's fixed."

She brightened. "Thanks. What do I owe you?"

Her response seemed to amuse him. "Oh, I think I'll still owe you before we're even. Let's grab some dinner."

"I'm only driving if we take my car," she said emphatically.

"How about we walk? There's a great little place up the block."

"Even better."

Chapter Twenty-One

Kasey dabbed her lips with the paper napkin. "I'm going to bust. That was the best fried chicken I've ever had."

Scott nodded. "Hope you saved room for dessert. Kay makes the best cobblers and seven-layer chocolate cake ever."

"U-u-u-ugh! No way. I'll have to take a rain check. I am beyond full."

He leaned forward. "A rain check? That sounds promising."

Scott was easy to be with. Small talk had turned into heart-to-heart sharing and laughter during the last hour. Of course, the biggest laugh was over her almost-arrest by his overzealous deputy, and he'd assured her that all the evidence had been destroyed.

She was glad to learn that the little four-cell jail was not the official holding area. That portion of the building was part of the National Register of Historical places. Deputy Dan had done her a favor by not putting her in the general population, which was down that hall. It was harder to forgive Deputy Dan, though.

Kasey and Scott made easy conversation. When she mentioned Nick's accident, she was surprised to hear that he was familiar with the case.

"A lot of us helped out on that search. Even my Aunt Ida Claire. She came out of retirement to see if she could uncover anything."

Kasey almost spit out her sweet tea. "I'm sorry. Did you say 'Aunt I declare'?"

He laughed. "Okay, well if you say it like that, it's kind of funny. It's Ida. Her middle name is Claire."

The name tickled her. She started laughing and couldn't stop.

"Well, that was easy." He leaned forward. "I like seeing you smile. You have a nice smile." A serious look crossed his face. "I really am sorry about what's happened to you. I mean, about your husband and all. It was awful."

She lowered her eyes.

Scott reached across the table and patted her arm. "So what made you move up this way by yourself? I mean, a city girl and all."

"Chaz Huckaby called and told me about the property. My husband worked with him for a while—renovating the house as a surprise."

"Wow. Some surprise."

She nodded. "Yeah. They made a deal to get it done by our anniversary. Chaz didn't know about the accident. Well, not that it was Nick anyway. He'd left some messages, but they were cryptic, and I just hadn't had the energy to call him back until recently. At first I thought I was coming to see what I needed to do to unload the place. But when I saw it, I felt so close to Nick and Jake. I knew I wanted to live there . . . *needed* to live there."

"Tell me about Jake."

Kasey grinned. "He was three at the time of the accident, but if you asked him, it always looked like four. He had trouble getting his fingers moving in all the right directions to show his age. He's four now."

She pushed the dishes to the side and leaned her forearms on the table. "I know some people think I'm crazy for believing he might still be alive, but I know he is. I feel it." She brought her hands to her heart. "In here. I just know it." She put her hands in her lap and met his gaze. "You think I'm nuts, too."

"No. I don't. Mothers have a sense like that about their children." He leaned on his forearms, mirroring her posture. "Let me tell you a story. When I was ten, I was riding a mountain bike on the hills by the old pit with some other kids. I fell and broke my leg. We weren't supposed to be on the man-made piles, but you know—boys."

She nodded.

"Anyway, one of the other kids ran home and called an ambulance. When the paramedics wheeled me into the emergency room, my mom was already there waiting. Turned out no one had called. She just knew. She told me that years later."

He did understand.

"You're kidding?"

"Happened again a few years ago. I was shot during what was supposed to be a routine traffic stop. She already knew I was injured, but not dead, when the guys at the station called her."

"I like your mom."

"Everyone does. So . . . tell me more about Jake."

"Gosh, he's a bundle of energy that never stops. Such a little man tromping around in cowboy boots and a hat like his daddy. He slept in those boots more than once." She paused. "He's just— I don't know—fearless. He's strong and deter- mined—wise for such a little boy."

"Got any pictures?" Scott asked.

"Of course I do." She dug around in her purse for her wallet. She flipped it open and handed him the pictures.

"He looks like you."

"Thanks."

He handed the wallet back to her. "Think you'll like living in the country? It's a lot different."

"Sure. It's quiet. That'll be nice."

Scott snickered. He'd known plenty of folks who thought the country would be nice until they got here. Then all they wanted to do was turn their quiet paradise into the city. They'd complain about the very things that drew them to the wide- open spaces to begin with. Scott had first-hand knowledge of how a city girl could have trouble feeling at home in the country.

"Don't be so quick to think you'll fit right in. We don't have good shopping around here, you know."

"I'm internet savvy. The UPS man comes this way, doesn't he?"

He nodded. "Sure. Well, maybe you'll surprise me."

He raised his tea glass, and she raised hers to meet his.

"Welcome to our little neck of the woods. I hope you settle in and don't regret joining us." He tipped his glass to hers, then took the last swig of his sweet tea. "I'm having a few people over Sunday afternoon. I'll throw something on the grill. Nothing fancy. Will you come?"

She hesitated.

"I thought you'd like to meet a few of the locals, and I do make the best steak in town."

"True, and making new friends is part of starting a new life." She nodded. "Yeah. Thanks. Deputy Dan won't be there, will he?"

"No. I'm thinking you might need some time to cool off before you see him again."

"You got that right."

He drew a map on a paper napkin, then turned it to face her and talked her through the directions. She pointed out the window of the diner—left and then right. "Okay. So that way, right?"

"Tell you what. I know exactly where you live. Why don't I just pick you up at one?"

"No. That's too much trouble. Plus you'll be getting ready for your guests."

He shook his head. "Nope. I insist. Not a problem. They won't get there until around two. You can help me get ready. I could use an extra hand."

She felt relieved because she didn't know her way around yet, and all the roads looked the same. All trees or all crops.

"Deal."

They shared a smile and a handshake.

"I better warn you," she said. "I'm not too good in the kitchen."

"Thanks for the warning." Scott dug in his front pocket, peeled off the money to pay the bill, and put it on the table for the waitress. "Ready?"

"Yep."

They walked back up the street to the station and around back to where both their cars were parked. Scott had made the deputy retrieve his car from the side of the road while he and Kasey went to dinner.

She told Scott goodbye and started her Porsche, relieved to hear the hum of the engine. Driving these country roads at night was a daunting new experience. There wasn't a streetlight beyond the small town, and she'd never driven these roads in the dark before. It seemed much darker here than the surroundings of the farm in Pungo, but then when she first moved to Pungo she remembered feeling that way, too. She tightened her grip on the steering wheel.

Okay, little animals, no darting out in front of my car.

The mailbox with *PHILLIPS* in reflective lettering came into view. She let out a long sigh. She'd thought to put Rolly on the box, but since she never took Nick's name, it seemed a little creepy to do it now. At least, that's what Riley had said when she'd shared the idea with her.

Kasey pulled into the driveway and got out of the car. After a few steps, she realized that it was so pitch black she couldn't see her way to her front door. This place brought a whole new meaning to the word *dark*. She made a mental note to check the timer on the garden lights and to leave the porch lights on.

Inching her way back to her car, she fumbled with the key to get it into the ignition. The headlights brightened a path to the door. She unclipped the house key from the key ring and ran to the house and unlocked the front door. She turned on the porch light, then headed back to turn off the headlights.

Something scampered in the bushes.

In an all-out sprint, she ran to retrieve her car keys and then raced back as fast as she could. She slammed the door behind her, heaving deep breaths. When had she become such a sissy? Or gotten so out of shape? She squeezed her left side to alleviate the cramp, probably from the heavy dinner she'd just consumed.

Adrenaline surged through her veins as her anxiety rose with each creak and noise from the darkness outside. She tried to shake her skittishness by flipping on the lights in every room and turning on the television.

"There. That's more like it."

Chapter Twenty-Two

Kasey had fallen asleep watching television. She woke to bright sunshine and birds chirping outside and every light in the house still on. That felt ridiculous now.

She turned off the TV, and got up to make some coffee.

Being arrested hadn't been the least bit funny at the time, but after the nice dinner with Scott, she'd begun to see the humor in the chain of events. She'd always been a fly-by-the-seat-of-her-pants kind of a girl, but not once had she ever been in real trouble. Riley and Von would get a big laugh out of this. Grem would've had an all out hissy fit if she'd known Kasey had flirted with a criminal record. Thank goodness she hadn't had to call Grem for bail.

Welcome to Adams Grove.

She started the coffee, got her laptop from her office, and sat at the kitchen bar. After all the action of being on tour, it felt weird to sit still with nothing going on around her. She checked her email, then went to Cody Tuggle's website. One click on the events page and she saw that they were in Florida tonight.

Good place to be the last week of January.

She got up and poured a cup of coffee, then sat back down. After a show, Cody didn't wind down until after nine in the morning. He'd be up. She picked up her phone and dialed his cell number.

"Hey, Kasey. I'm so glad you called."

His enthusiasm reflected her own. Their friendship had grown so much over the last few months. "Not a bad time?"

"No. Everything okay?"

"Yes. Everything's fine. I was just thinking about y'all and thought I'd check in. I do have some news."

"About Jake?" Cody sounded hopeful.

"No. Nothing there yet, but I moved."

"Moved? You just got home."

"I know. It sounds crazy, doesn't it?" She explained the whole story—from Chaz Huckaby to the house. Cody seemed to understand her immediate connection to the place.

"I think you did the right thing. You sound good. Real good."

"It's just a little hard to embrace all the quiet after the pace of the tour."

"You can always come back," he said as if the answer was obvious. "I *do* have a seat on my plane that's empty."

"I'll keep that in mind. I'll email you the mailing address and phone number in case there's anything we need to handle on the book. If you ever get back out this way, stop on by."

"By the way, I need to thank you."

"Yeah? For what?"

"I have some news, too," he said.

"What's that?"

"Annette tracked down Lou for me. She's divorced. I'm thinking about giving her a call."

Kasey smiled. "True love. You know it when you feel it. Good luck."

"Thanks." His voice softened. "I'm glad you called. We've missed you around here. Keep in touch, will you?"

"Count on it." She hung up feeling connected in a good way.

The weather was chilly, but not as frigid as the first week of February could be. Kasey spent all day Saturday taking pictures and getting to know the new property by snapping off rolls and rolls of film. She'd test out her new darkroom developing the film. She looked forward to that.

The landscape, trees, the goats, and anything

that came in view of her lens was fair game. She made a mental note to drive into town and get a book on birds. She'd caught several on film. Beautiful ones. But she had no idea what kind they were, and some things were just more convenient to have in book form rather than having to Google around on the internet.

She liked exploring the place, although it would have been more fun with Dutch by her side. He was good company, but Von convinced her that the old dog would be better off with the familiar surroundings and the constant attention of the 4-H-ers who frequented the Rocking R. It killed her to leave him behind, but the fifteen-year-old dog probably wouldn't do so well being uprooted. It was the right thing to do for him even if it was hard for her.

It was after five when she came back into the house. She turned up the heat and took a warm bath. Wrapped in her favorite robe, she popped popcorn for dinner.

Accepting Scott's invitation to his cookout tomorrow had seemed like a good idea at the time, but now she wished she hadn't accepted. She couldn't go empty-handed. Nick had stocked several bottles of wine in the rack, but wine didn't seem like the right thing to take. She hadn't stocked the pantry yet, but then her cooking skills weren't that good anyway. She didn't want to embarrass herself in front of her new neighbors. Maybe she could backtrack her way to the market in the morning and pick up something.

She climbed into bed, exhausted from the fresh air. A dog howled in the distance and she wondered if it might be a coyote. Not that she'd ever heard a coyote howl, except in those spooky Halloween soundtracks. Taking in a couple of long, cleansing breaths, she reminded herself she was safe here, and tugged the covers over herself.

Kasey's body clock woke her at seven. She stretched herself out full-length pointing her toes under the sheets. The extra-high mattress required a leap to the floor, as had the one she and Nick had shared before. The height had been no problem for him. He'd been tall. The bed was so high she literally had to climb in and out. She jumped to the ground and raised her hands over her head in an exaggerated gymnast's flourish, as if she'd nailed the landing.

Nick used to tease her about her bed dismounts, shouting out scores as if he was a judge on *Dancing With the Stars*. He'd built a little stool to keep next to the bed, but she liked the bouncy dismount better. He pretended to spot her sometimes, just so he could cop a feel. As if he needed an excuse for something they both liked anyway.

I miss you, Nick.

If Nick and Jake were here, this house would be full of comforting boy howls and playful banter. Instead, it was quiet.

Will I ever get used to the quiet?

Kasey made a cup of coffee, sat at the table in the corner of the kitchen, and looked out over the pastures, fully aware that Nick had this view in mind when he designed this space. She closed her eyes and squeezed her coffee cup. Tears tickled her bottom lashes. She felt the familiar warmth of Nick in the room. She blinked and shook off the thought. It was still too hard to go there—the wounds still too fresh when she missed him as she did now.

If she was going to find something suitable to take to Scott's cookout, she needed to get busy. She got dressed and drove to town without one wrong turn. There weren't large quantities of anything in the little market, but to her surprise there was most anything you could want, including some things you wouldn't expect—like fishing poles and waders.

Deviled eggs would be easy enough. She could probably pull that off. She'd made them a couple of times. But if she didn't peel the eggshells off just right, all the eggs would be gouged. That would be embarrassing with people she didn't know—even with people she did.

She was a photographer, not a cook. She was good at creative stuff. Grem sure as heck never cooked, and it wasn't something Kasey had ever learned to do. She spotted the waders again and had an idea. Tossing them in the cart, she picked up a few other things and headed to the register, pleased with her purchases. On the drive home, the feeling of accomplishment lifted her mood. She still had plenty of time before Scott picked her up at one.

As she approached the house, she was surprised to see a man leaning against a car in her driveway, his legs and arms crossed, waiting.

Chapter Twenty-Three

Kasey pulled her car to a stop next to him.

"Jeremy? What are you doing here?" she asked as she got out of the car. "Is everything okay?"

"Housewarming. I brought presents." He lifted a big basket with a gingham kitchen towel draped across the top.

Kasey started to hug him, but a sweet aroma captured her attention. She released him and lifted the cloth draped over the basket. "What smells so—Lemon poppy seed?"

"Of course."

"My favorite. I can't believe you drove all the way out here to bring me muffins. How did you find it? My GPS couldn't even find the address."

"It's not that big of a town," Jeremy said with a

slight hesitation. "Internet. You can find anything online. You don't mind, do you?"

"Heck no, especially when you come with fresh baked goods."

Jeremy's face lit up. "How've you been?"

"Fine. Great, actually." She walked back to her car to get the groceries. Jeremy followed her, carrying the basket.

"Need some help?"

"Yeah. Thanks." She loaded his free arm with one bag, lifted the other, and headed to the house. Her expression grew serious. "Did Grem send you to do her dirty work?"

"No. She doesn't know I'm here. I came on my own."

"Oh." She blinked in surprise.

He followed close behind her. "She *has* been down since you left, though."

"I don't know why. I've only been gone a few days. It's not like we used to see each other every day."

He shrugged. "I guess it's just knowing that you're farther away. She's not getting any younger, just crankier."

"You got that right." She laughed. "She'll be fine. She has her friends."

"This time I think it's different. She had me take her to the doctor yesterday."

That got Kasey's attention. "Grem hates the doctor."

His brows flickered a little, and his dark eyes softened. "I thought you'd want to know."

Kasey knew she should check on Grem, but all their conversations ended up being about her moving into the carriage house, and that wasn't going to happen. It made her feel guilty as hell.

"Is she okay?"

"Seems to be. They ran some blood work. I guess she'll hear those results next week. I'll keep you posted."

"Thanks."

Jeremy put the basket on the kitchen table. "Nice place. How do you like living out here?"

"I love it."

He raised a brow. "I can't picture you this far out in the country."

She unloaded the shopping bags. "It's not like I'm beating my laundry on a rock or dipping water out of a well."

"It's a lot farther away than you were before."

"True." She leaned against the counter. "I'm surprised Nick never mentioned this place to you and Grem. He never was good at keeping a secret," she said. "Seems like he would've told someone." She shrugged, not really expecting an answer.

"Didn't look like there were any fast food or delivery places nearby. You could starve out here."

"I'll just have to cook."

"Is that burnt popcorn I smell?" He sniffed. "Hope he installed a smoke alarm."

"Ha ha, so I'll know when dinner is done. Funny. And yes. That's what I had for dinner last night."

Kasey was happy to see Jeremy, but she didn't have much time before Scott came to pick her up. She hadn't expected the unannounced company. Even though Scott wasn't a date, she'd feel awkward if Jeremy was there when he arrived. She needed to get a move on. How was she going to get rid of Jeremy without being rude? She put the rest of the groceries away. She put the waders, a potted mum, and some ribbon on the table.

"What are you doing?" Jeremy asked, pulling up a chair.

"A project." She took a pair of scissors out of the kitchen drawer and cut one of the waders down to a manageable size that would hold the potted plant. She folded the top of the boot over, cut slits in a row around it, ran a ribbon through the slits and tied a perfect bow. She wiggled the pot down into the boot until the bright flowers nestled into place.

"Cute," Jeremy said.

"I'm not done. Wait here. Be right back." She rushed down the hall into the darkroom. She dug through bins full of pictures that weren't keepers but were too good to toss, and found what she was looking for. As she turned to stand,

228

she slammed right into Jeremy. Her heart leaped into her throat.

"You scared me to death." She swatted him on the arm and took a deep breath, hoping to slow her racing heart. "I didn't hear you come up behind me." She was inexplicably irked.

"Sorry. I followed you."

Kasey pushed past him. "Don't scare me like that again."

"See. You are antsy about living out here, aren't you?"

Irritated by his mocking tone, Kasey said, "No. Not at all." Why was he challenging her?

She took the handful of photos back to the kitchen table.

"Well, I won't hold you up. I just wanted to let you know about your grandmother and see how you were settling in. Give you the housewarming gift."

She wiped her hands on her pants. Thank goodness. He was finally going to leave. She still needed to get ready. "I'll walk you out. Oh, and thanks for the muffins. The dish towel matches the kitchen. That was sweet."

He just stood there for a moment, which was a little awkward. She made her way toward the door, hoping he would follow. He did, and she walked him to the car. He got into the car and rolled down the window, tossing something her way. She caught it in mid-air, then opened her hand. A butterscotch candy.

Of course.

She waved, feeling a little bad for being annoyed by his surprise visit.

Back in the kitchen, she cut the pictures and positioned them onto the boot, gluing and layering them into place. She hadn't decoupaged anything in a long time. Hopefully the lacquer would dry before Scott arrived. She opened the first drawer in the kitchen to toss the butterscotch candy into it. There were already a few in there.

Old habits. Jake had probably emptied his little pockets in here on his visits. Before meals, it was their routine for Jake to empty his pockets of all his collections into the kitchen junk drawer. She missed that. Sometimes he'd have little army men or rocks, and oftentimes candy or Lucky Charms marshmallows that he'd tucked away.

She took a deep breath and turned her attention to the project before she got all misty-eyed. The planter turned out so cute, she thought about keeping it for herself. She gently placed it into a large paper sack and set it next to the door before she changed her mind.

She showered, blew her hair dry, and put on jeans and her favorite denim shirt. Her wide leather belt popped as she tugged it through the loops. She twisted to get a good look in the mirror, and pouffed the bottom of her shirt.

The idea of the cookout—of meeting a bunch of strangers—made her stomach queasy. *It's just a casual get-together, and the chance to meet new neighbors.* She shoved her hands into her back pockets and rocked side to side, trying to burn her excess energy.

A few minutes later, Scott pulled the Thunderbird into the driveway. Even though she expected to see it this time, the sight of the car still made her heart skip a beat.

Scott tooted the horn twice.

Kasey picked up her camera bag, grabbed the paper sack, slammed the door behind her, and went outside to meet him.

"Hey, girl," Scott said as he climbed out of the car.

"Hey, yourself." She walked to the passenger side.

He followed behind her and closed the door after she'd settled into the seat. With a click of the lap belt, she was ready to go. "All set."

Scott got into the car and nodded toward the paper sack, her purse and the camera bag all shoved onto the floor board. "Do you ever travel light?"

"I have to have my camera with me. Occupational hazard."

"I suppose." He pointed to the side of the house. "Who does the RV belong to?"

"Me."

He gave her a sidelong glance. "*You* drive that thing?"

"Yep. For work. I used to do a lot of work on the road before I married Nick. That *thing* is fully equipped—darkroom and all my backdrops, lighting and stuff. A self-contained photo studio. I haven't used it much over the last couple of years, but I'm afraid no one would be interested in buying it."

"Sounds cool." He nodded, looking impressed, then put the car in reverse and backed out of the long driveway.

Big puffy cotton-candy clouds filled the sky. The kind of clouds that somehow never get in the way of the sunshine, even though they're everywhere.

The silence was a bit awkward. Kasey asked, "How far away do you live?"

"About eight miles."

"You said your mom lives out this way?"

His mouth curved as if he was on the verge of laughter. "She lives at the other end of Nickel Creek, near the river."

"I haven't been to that end of the road yet."

He turned to her, his thick hair skimming his shirt collar in the back. "It's nice. There's a boat ramp down that way, too. Most people take Bradford Junction Road to get to it, though, so your road is pretty quiet." Scott looked relaxed, one of his arms propped on the console as he drove.

"Yeah. It is quiet. I think I've seen two cars in the last two days." She looked out the window as he turned off the main road. "Hey, this is a regular neighborhood."

He chuckled. "What did you expect? Cows?"

"Quit laughing. But yeah, maybe."

He drove past the row of houses, a mishmash of new and turn-of-the-century buildings. Scott's house was at the very end of the road, nestled amidst huge old trees. "The river runs behind the house," he said as he parked the car.

He offered to help her with her bags, but she insisted on carrying them herself. Kasey followed closely behind him to the side door. She could see the water from there.

"You *are* right on the water."

"Yep. I grew up on these rivers, boating and fishing with my dad." He pointed down the slope to a boathouse and dock. "I have a pontoon boat and a fishing boat. We'll have to go out some-time."

"That sounds like fun."

Inside, the house was tidy but lacked a feminine touch. It had an open floor plan. From where she stood, she could see the living room, dining room and kitchen. In the living room, a stone fireplace stretched across one entire wall. Its heavy wooden mantel appeared to be hand-carved. Oversized leather and suede furniture looked comfortable enough to nap in. She found herself mentally redecorating the place in something other than shades of brown.

The kitchen was huge and very upscale. It looked like something off the Food Network, with tons of cabinets and a fancy multi-burner gas range. It even had two ovens. An array of food cluttered the counter, an assortment of pots nearby. She felt totally inadequate already.

"I take it you're a pretty good cook?" Kasey couldn't hide her surprise or keep from feeling a little jealous. He even had things prepped and ready to go without a mess.

He blushed, grinning. A dimple became visible on his left cheek. "Yeah. I've been a bachelor a long time. I had to learn to cook or starve, and I figured out pretty fast that I couldn't live on take-out with the limited options we have in this town."

"I'm impressed."

He pulled fresh ingredients out of the refrigerator. "Are you going to show me what you have in that huge paper sack?"

"I'd love to." She placed the paper bag on the center island, its black granite countertop cool to her touch. "It's a little present to thank you for springing me out of jail and inviting me over."

He cocked his head. "Really? That wasn't necessary." He set aside what he had in his hands and rubbed them together like an excited eight-year-old. "But I love surprises."

He reached into the bag and pulled out the planter. Kasey waited for his reaction.

"Neat." He smiled, but then lowered his eyebrows. "How did you get so many pictures of my car?"

"It's not your car, but only you and I have to know that."

"It looks just like mine."

"They're pictures of my husband's Thunderbird."

Scott looked surprised. "Your husband's? He had a car just like mine?"

She nodded. "I know. Isn't that crazy? It's in the garage behind the house.

"I have to admit something about the day my car broke down. When I turned around and saw you getting out of that Thunderbird to rescue me, I thought that big rig had hit me—I'd died and Nick had come to take me to heaven."

"No wonder you were all out of sorts that day."

That memory was still so sharp. "Oh, yeah. You got that right."

"It does look just like my car." He put his arm around her shoulder and gave her a friendly squeeze. "Thanks. That was thoughtful. I love it."

"I'm glad." She casually leaned against the island. "I hope you love it so much that I'm off the hook for any cooking assignments. I warned you—my talents lie elsewhere." She scrunched her face.

"You're off duty." He pulled a bar stool next to the counter and patted the seat. "Here you go. The best guest seat in the house."

She hopped up on the chair, happy to follow the order.

He poured two glasses of wine, then chopped and sliced. Kasey sipped wine and watched him move around the kitchen like a *Top Chef*. She picked up a magazine featuring do-it-yourself projects from the counter and flipped through it as they talked.

Kasey held the magazine up in front of her. "You must be kind of handy if you're going to take on any of these projects."

He tossed a wooden spoon in the air and caught it behind his back. "I'm full of untapped talent."

"Impressive." She put down the magazine and applauded.

"My mom got me that subscription for my birthday. I *have* built a few things I saw in there. A deck box, the picnic table, and a rocking horse for some friends who had a baby boy last year." He tossed salad as he spoke.

"You are talented." She picked up the magazine and flipped through it again, paying closer attention this time. "This is really cute." She turned the magazine to face him. He leaned over as he smoothed olive oil over baked potatoes and rolled them in kosher salt.

"The swing?"

"Yeah, isn't it cute? I love the stars and stripes. My Jake would love it."

"That's a five-minute job," he said.

"Yeah, right. It's adorable." Kasey smiled as she pictured Jake swinging, pumping his legs to go as high as possible. In the photo, the swing's plank seat hung from thick ropes that knotted beneath it. She left the magazine opened to that page and laid it on the counter.

Scott opened the pre-heated oven and slid the cookie sheet of potatoes inside. Ears of corn, still in the husk, lined the counter. Beside them was a plastic container of steaks in a marinade of herbs that tickled her nose.

Scott washed his hands and dried them on a dish towel.

"Come on, we have some time. Let me introduce you to Maggie and show you the boathouse before everyone gets here. Better grab your jacket."

"Maggie?"

"You'll love her."

She put on her jacket, and he led her out of the kitchen through the back door. They walked down a path to the water's edge.

A black lab ran up to Scott with her tail wagging. "This is Maggie."

Kasey stooped down and let the dog sniff her hand. Once Maggie gave her an approving lick, Kasey patted her head.

"How's my girl today?" Scott asked. "You ready for some supper?"

Maggie spun in excitement.

"Maggie, show Miss Kasey what you've been up to while I get your food."

Maggie headed to the boathouse that bordered the dock at the bottom of Scott's property. She barked and led Kasey to the back of the building to a smaller room.

Kasey raised a brow and looked in Scott's direction.

"Lassie doesn't have anything on my Maggie."

"All-righty then." Kasey followed in Maggie's footsteps.

In the corner of the room was an empty kiddie pool. Well, not really empty. It was filled with a dog's bed and puppies. *Lots* of puppies!

Maggie stepped gingerly into the middle of the pool, then sat proudly next to her litter, thumping her tail.

"Miss Maggie, you've been busy. How many pups do you have there, girl?" Kasey counted. "My goodness, eight, nine, ten? You must be one pooped pup."

Maggie charged out of the pool toward Scott, who entered the room carrying her bowl.

Scott put the bowl of food on the floor, then squatted next to Kasey. "Are they the cutest little things you've ever seen?"

"They're adorable. And so many. The brown one is huge. He looks like someone snuck him in from an older litter."

"Yeah. She usually has a couple chocolates. This

time they were all black with the exception of those two. One brown and one yellow. The yellow pup is the runt. She's my favorite."

"Ohhhh, she's cute, too."

Scott scooped up the tiny yellow lab and handed her to Kasey. The puppy snuggled against her chest.

"Their eyes just opened about a week ago." Scott picked up another puppy.

The yellow lab licked at Kasey's nose. "Puppy breath. There's just nothing better than puppy breath. I have got to get my camera."

"You can take pictures later. They won't be going far for a while. Let me show you the boats."

"Okay." She kissed the puppy on the nose. It reached its tiny paws toward her face. Kasey nuzzled it one last time, then followed Scott out to the dock.

Kasey felt a tug of regret. "That makes me miss our black lab, Dutch. I left him back at the other farm. Everyone thought he was too old to uproot. He'll get way more attention there from familiar folks, too. It was the right thing to do, but it was hard. I miss him."

"I bet." Scott took her hand and helped her step onto the floating dock. "Steady there."

"Two boats," she said, looking from the big pontoon boat to the bright, glitter-bottomed boat.

"Yep."

"That one has quite a bit of bling on it, doesn't it," she teased.

"The fish love it."

"You'd think it would scare them away."

"They like shiny stuff." He leaned back against one of the dock posts. "Do you like to fish?"

"I've got my fair share of fishing stories, and I have to admit I do like shiny stuff."

"Ahhhh. There's nothing like fishing early in the morning as the sun just peeks over the horizon. So peaceful, you can hear the fish wake up."

"Sounds nice." She looked out over the water. Trees hung over the edges of the river, lush and green. "It's pretty down here."

"I grew up on this river. I never tire of it." He glanced at his watch. "We'd better get back up to the house. Folks should be here soon."

"Okay."

They hiked back up the steep incline to the house. People were already in the kitchen, making themselves at home.

Scott opened the screen door.

"Hey." Scott cuffed a guy on the shoulder, then hugged the woman next to him.

"That your famous marinade?" the man asked.

"You better believe it. Y'all would run me out on a rail if I didn't produce the best steak in town, as promised." Scott turned away from them, then looped a black apron over his head and tied the strings behind him.

He faced them and everyone laughed.

Best Mooin' Marinade was embroidered on the front of the apron in bright red. Beneath it was a caricature of Scott with a chef's hat, grill fork, and a sheriff's badge, chasing cows.

"You like?" he asked.

Scott reached for Kasey and pulled her in to the group. "This is Kasey. She just moved in over on Nickel Creek."

"The house they've been renovating for like a year?" a tall, lanky brown-haired man asked.

Kasey extended her hand and shook his. "Yep. That's the one."

He gave her a firm handshake. "I'm Dusty. I did the tile work over there."

She brightened. "You're kidding."

"Bathroom and kitchen," he said, satisfaction in his eyes.

"It's lovely. It's so nice to meet you."

He smiled and tilted his head toward the woman who stood by his side. "This is my bride, Angie."

"Nice to meet you, Dusty and Angie."

"Angie made this apron for me," Scott said. "She's quite talented with that embroidery machine."

"Did you design it, too?" Kasey asked.

Angie nodded.

"Beautiful needlework. I love the detail."

She blushed. "Thanks."

"I did some work over there on Nickel Creek, too," said the shorter of the two men. "I hauled all the debris from the demolition away. They gutted that place."

"Chaz was telling me about it. I never saw the house before it was done. My husband surprised me with it."

"How romantic," Angie said, elbowing Dusty. "Why don't you ever think of sweet stuff like that?"

Ignoring his wife's comment, he shifted his attention back to Kasey. "Aw, man. You should have seen it. What a mess. We hauled junk for three days before they could even start the demolition. We all thought the guy was nuts. I couldn't believe it when I came back to do the tile work. That place is a miracle makeover."

"I wish I had pictures of it before the renovation," Kasey said, feeling more comfortable with them already.

"Is your husband coming over later?" Dusty asked.

Kasey took in a sharp breath. She'd been fine up to that point.

Scott jumped in. "Remember that accident over the summer? The pickup truck in the Nottoway and the missing child? That was Kasey's husband and son."

A chill ran through Kasey.

Angie put her arm around Kasey's shoulder.

"Sorry. We didn't know. We're glad you're here. You'll love this town. The people are wonderful."

Kasey gave her a wan smile. "I can see that. Thanks." Her eyes grew moist. "It's still kind of hard."

"I'm sure," Angie said. "Don't worry about tears. We understand. Most of us were out there helping look for your little angel."

Everyone in the small group nodded.

"You know, Kasey," Dusty said, his tone upbeat, "I would bet money that Chaz has pictures of that place from before y'all bought it. If he doesn't, Garrett Malloy will. He did most of the renovation work. Let's ask Chaz when he gets here."

"That'd be great," Kasey said, relieved at the change in subject.

"Kasey is a professional photographer," Scott said.

With that Kasey reached for her camera bag and lifted it out of the case. "Be forewarned. I was telling Scott: it's an occupational hazard. Does anyone mind if I take pictures?"

"No, no, we don't mind." Everyone shook their heads and smiled.

Before Kasey could snap her first photo, Chaz and his wife walked in, followed by Scott's duck hunting buddy, Jeff, and the dispatcher from the police station, Allison.

"Hey, everyone," Chaz said in his booming voice. He grabbed a beer from a tub of ice, tossed a diet soda to his wife, and handed a beer to Allison. Then he noticed Kasey. "Hey-ey-ey, I see you've met the new girl in town."

Kasey waved from across the room.

"How did you and Scott meet?" Chaz's wife asked.

Kasey and Scott shared a look, then laughed.

Kasey put up her hands. "I'm not talking."

Everyone looked curious.

"I sprung her from jail after Deputy Dan arrested her," Scott said, and paused for a reaction.

The room got quiet.

Allison almost choked on a swallow of beer. "Oh, no. You're not the one he accused of stealing Scott's car, then threw you in the slammer?"

Kasey nodded and put both of her hands in the air. "Guilty."

"Man. We've been riding him all week about that. That man gets in more fixes."

"All right," Scott said. "Now let's be fair. Everything worked out, and we got to meet our new neighbor. How about a toast to our new friend Kasey?"

Everyone raised their glasses and cheered.

Allison waved from across the room, capturing Kasey's attention. "You know, you look so familiar. I just can't place you. Have we met?"

"I don't think so. I haven't been here long," Kasey said.

"And you're a photographer?" Allison asked.

"Yes."

Allison's brows pulled together. "Really? Like at the Walmart?"

Kasey smiled, trying not to snicker. "No. Not exactly. I shoot advertisements and calendars, commercial photography. Celebrities, cars, that kind of stuff."

Allison squealed in a pitch so high that the people around her leaned away. She snapped her fingers. "Oh. My. *God!*" She bounced as she spoke. "I know who you are. You're the Kasey Phillips that was on tour with Cody Tuggle. I can't believe it. I just love him. You were dating him?"

Chapter Twenty-Four

Kasey felt the color drain from her face. "No. No. No. You can't believe everything you read. I was shooting his tour. It was a job. That's it."

"But you're like friends, right?"

"Yeah." Her mood lifted a little. "Yeah, I'd call him a friend."

"I keep hoping he'll come to the Carolina Crossroads. I'm dying to see him in concert."

"I photographed the tour for a book that will be coming out later this year," Kasey said. "I'll get you a copy."

"Oh. My. *Gosh!* Like, he is so freakin' hot, and I read in that newspaper—which one was it?—I don't remember, but I did see y'all on the cover together. You looked pretty cozy. I am so jealous."

A momentary look of discomfort crossed Scott's face.

Kasey said, "Strictly business. He's a nice guy. We were running to the car and dodging paparazzi. That's it."

Allison winked at her. "Oh. Okay."

"I'm serious." Kasey could tell there was no changing Allison's opinion. To her that gossip rag was gospel. Kasey started to say something else, but figured there was no point.

Thankfully, Chaz shifted the conversation and the group headed out to the patio.

Scott's outdoor kitchen was as nice as the one indoors. A propane grill took up at least five feet of one end of the deck. Scott plopped the steaks on the sizzling grate of the stainless steel monstrosity, and then everyone split into teams to throw horseshoes.

Kasey had never played, and she didn't have beginner's luck. Her new friends were getting a good laugh over of her lack of skill. That was fun for a little while, but she decided she'd do better taking pictures than playing. She took some candid shots. When Scott halted the games so he could flip the steaks, she got everyone together for a group picture. She set the timer on the camera and joined the group for the photo.

Chaz's wife was fluffy and had an outdated

hairstyle. Her cheeks plumped from the smile that never left her face. She was the kind of person you instantly liked. "I just love photographs, Kasey. I hope you won't mind getting me copies of a few of these pictures to remember this nice day."

"My pleasure. I love to scrapbook. I'd be happy to put something together for you."

"I'm a scrapbooker, too! We should get together sometime."

"I'd like that. And I want to thank you personally for the delicious cake you baked for me. I really enjoyed it. That was such a sweet gesture."

"I am glad you liked it, and I'm glad you're here. It will be nice to have some new young folks around this old town."

Scott clanged a dinner bell from the porch. "Okay troops, soup's on."

Everyone lined up around a long oak table and piled their plates high. Once they took their seats, they bowed their heads for a prayer that Chaz led before they dug into the bounty. Kasey eyes misted as Chaz said the prayer and everyone held hands. She felt so much comfort and love with this quirky group of folks that seemed to accept her as one of their own. No questions asked. Well, except for Deputy Dan, but she figured he'd show up with an apology one day and she'd have to accept it.

After dinner, they all moved inside since the sun sank lower and the air grew chilly. Folks departed, few by few, until Kasey and Scott were left alone.

"I had the best day. Thank you so much for inviting me."

"You were the best part of it."

Kasey swallowed hard, searching for a response. "You have a beautiful home and terrific friends," she said. "And you're right: you do make the best steak around."

"Thanks." Scott hesitated as if he wanted to say something but couldn't decide whether he should. He put some leftovers in the refrigerator, then leveled his gaze on her. "So, I have to ask. Did you really date Cody Tuggle?"

"No. That was just a gossip rag lie. You can't believe anything they print in those things."

"Good. I don't think I could compete with a country star."

The comment caught her off guard. As nice as he was, that wasn't something that she could even imagine. "Well, I'm no prize," she said quietly. "I've got more baggage than the airlines and I doubt this old heart will ever be the same after what I've been through."

He nodded once. "I didn't mean it. Actually, yes . . . I did mean it like that." He let out a loud breath and then shook his head. "I'm sorry. I know it's lousy timing. But you're nice. I like you." He shifted awkwardly. "You know, I was married once."

"You mentioned an ex-wife. You don't seem the marrying kind, though."

"You saying I'm ugly?"

"No," she responded—almost too quickly. "You just seem very well settled into your bachelor life."

"It is pretty sweet." He smiled easily. "But I miss having someone in my life."

"What was your wife like?"

"A little like you. A city girl. Ruth and I met in college. She was from Atlanta." He shook his head and frowned a bit. "Man, I loved that girl." He walked into the living room.

"What happened?" she asked as she followed.

"I guess the country sounds more charming than it is." Scott sat on the couch and motioned for Kasey to join him. "She was lonely, hated the quiet and being so far from shopping and fancy restaurants. She couldn't stand being so far away from folks, and she didn't like the fact that there wasn't much privacy in a small town."

Kasey sat next to Scott.

"She spent most of her time begging me to transfer to a bigger town. Ruth hung in there for almost two years. She was miserable and . . . well, before we knew it, we both were. I wasn't going to live in the city. I'm not the type, and she couldn't live here."

"Different worlds. Sometimes it works, sometimes it doesn't. Sorry that happened to you."

"Yeah, me too. But hey, we get through what we have to, don't we?"

"Yep."

He put his arm up on the back of the couch. "How are *you* liking the country life so far, Miss City Girl?"

"Loving it. So far, so good."

"No regrets?"

"Not one."

"It's only been a week," he reminded her.

"Hey, give me a break. I can handle the country. I did live on a farm out in the country in Pungo, remember?"

"That's pretty close to Virginia Beach, though. You could go to the mall without much trouble, or to a nice restaurant." He brushed her hair behind her shoulder. "But I hope you're right. It will be nice to have you as a neighbor."

"Thanks."

"What are you doing on Wednesday?" Scott asked.

"I'll probably get some of my stuff put away. I don't know. Why?"

"It's my day off. I'm going fishing. Why don't you join me?"

"It's kind of cold, and isn't it supposed to rain?"

"Nothing more peaceful than sitting on the dock listening to the rain splatter."

"Could make for a bad hair day."

"You could wear a hat," he said.

A man with an answer for everything.

She started to turn him down, but why? "What should I bring?" she asked with a smile.

"Just that smile. Rain or shine. We get started at seven."

"In the morning?" She rolled her eyes. "I'm still hugging a pillow at that time of the day. I'll bring coffee."

"Sounds good. I think you'll have fun. If you don't catch a fish, maybe you'll at least catch a good picture or two."

"How could I say no?"

He nodded. "You're my kind of gal."

He leaned in and kissed her softly on the mouth. When they parted, she opened her eyes and blinked.

"Holy crap." The moment froze in her brain. She blinked, so stunned she stated the obvious: "You just kissed me." She touched her lips, still warm from his soft, moist kiss.

He held her close. "Not sure where that came from. I just couldn't resist."

"It's okay," she whispered. "I think it's okay. It was kind of nice."

"Well, this is certainly a little awkward now, isn't it?"

"Yeah." Conflicting emotion made her dizzy.

"Ready to head home?" he asked.

"I think I should."

"All-righty then. Let's go."

"Should we finish cleaning up first?"

"No. I'm not sure I can trust myself with you bent over my dishwasher."

That lightened the moment. "You're being silly. But okay."

The drive home was a little quiet. She was thankful it wasn't that far.

As Scott neared her driveway, they saw another car parked next to Kasey's Porsche. "Looks like you have company."

Kasey stiffened.

"Do you know who that is?" Scott asked.

"Yes, but I don't know why he's here," Kasey said. "He works for my grandmother. He already stopped by this morning. I wonder why he's back. I hope something hasn't happened to her."

"You weren't expecting him?"

"Nope."

Scott stopped the car and she got out.

"I wondered where you were." Jeremy's voice sounded full of possessive desperation.

"What's wrong?" Kasey approached him, embarrassed.

"I forgot to give you some mail that came to the estate. When I came back, your car was here but you weren't answering the door. I thought something was wrong."

"I have my cell. You should've called. How long have you been here?"

"Hours."

Scott stepped next to Kasey. "If you were so worried, why didn't you call the police?"

Jeremy shuffled his feet and shot Scott an angry look.

"I gotta go. Your mail is on the porch." He stomped off.

Kasey stood dumbfounded as Jeremy got into the car and pulled out of the driveway. She and Scott looked at each other. "That was the oddest thing."

"I won't disagree with that." Scott stepped over to where Jeremy had been standing next to the car and scooped up a handful of bright yellow wrappers, twisting one in his fingers. "He must've been here a while."

"Kojak had suckers, Jeremy has butterscotches."

"Does he always pop up unexpectedly like that?"

"No. I don't know what got into him. I guess he's a little protective of me sometimes."

Chapter Twenty-Five

The next morning, Kasey woke to the phone ringing. Not her cell, but the house phone. She ran into the living room to answer it. She fumbled with the cordless phone as she tried to answer. Every time the phone rang, her nerves twitched—wishing, hoping for good news.

"Hi, Kasey. It's Von."

"I was asleep. What time is it?" She walked into the kitchen and checked the clock on the stove.

"It's early. I've got some news."

She stopped in her tracks. "News? You mean . . ."

"About Jake."

Her heart beat double-time. "Is it good?"

"It's not bad," Von said.

Thank God!

"A man has come forward. He thinks he's seen Jake. More than once."

"I knew it. He's alive." She sat on the floor, pressing the phone close to her ear. "Thank you." She'd dreamed of this call for so long. Her heart swelled with hope.

"Now hang on. I don't want you to be devastated if the child this man's seen isn't Jake."

"It has to be him."

Von sighed.

Not get my hopes up. Is he crazy?

"Where is he?" she asked. "Let's go get him."

"Not so fast. The report was taken near Raleigh."

Kasey looked to heaven and tried to not hyperventilate as Von filled her in on what they knew. "When can we get him?"

"It's not that simple, and it's not a guarantee, Kasey. They are talking to the guy now, and following up on the report. We should know more in a couple of days. Maybe sooner, but—"

"A couple of days? I'm not waiting here.

Waiting. Wondering. It's all I've done for months. Let me grab a pen and paper. Where do I need to go?"

"How did I know you'd say that?"

"Because Riley told you I would."

"She was right," Von said. "Again."

Kasey heard Riley in the background telling him, "Told you so."

Von cleared his throat. "She's already packed. We're coming to pick you up."

Kasey's heart raced. Good thing they were coming to get her. She was in no shape to drive. "Thank you. I'll be ready."

"Hey, before you hang up, I wanted you to know that the lead came from someone that recognized the picture from Tuggle's concert."

"Hurry." Kasey hung up and then raced around the house to get dressed and packed. That all took less than seven minutes. It was going to be a long hour-and-a-half until they got here. She put her overnight bag next to the front door, then sprawled on the couch and closed her eyes, letting the tears fall.

Tears of hope.

Relief.

"Please let this be him, Nick. I need Jake home with me. I miss you both . . . so much."

She got up, paced the room, then straightened the kitchen. It would still be over an hour before Von and Riley arrived.

She dialed Grem's number, knowing she would want to hear the good news.

Jeremy answered on the first ring. "Jeremy, it's me." Kasey tried to control her excitement.

"Hey, girl. How are you?"

"Great. Is Grem around?"

"She's napping. What's up?"

"I wanted you both on the phone so I could tell you at the same time. I've got news. I'm getting ready to go to Raleigh. There's a lead on Jake."

"Wh—You're kidding!"

Her excitement rose again. "No. I can't believe it. Someone called the police department there. They've seen Jake."

"You're sure?"

"The police have reviewed the tapes. The likeness is enough that they've called to have me confirm. They're investigating. Jeremy, this could be it. Jake could be coming home."

"What else do they know?"

"I'm not sure yet. Von and Riley are picking me up and we're headed down there."

"I would've taken you," he said. "You're not mad at me for stopping by yesterday, are you?"

"No. No. That's not it. I'd have gone by myself, but Von insisted. It's killing me, sitting here waiting on them. I could've been there by the time they get here."

"What can I do? I can come now if you want."

"No. Just give Grem my message. You can toss

any prayers you've got stacked up around there my way, too. Do you know what it would mean to . . ." Kasey tried to hold back her emotions, but they were like an undertow—sweeping her off her feet and tugging her under.

"I know," Jeremy said. "I know how much you love Jake. Good luck, and keep me posted."

Kasey dialed Scott next and asked for a rain date on the fishing trip. Then she called Cody.

"It worked," she said after he answered the phone. "It really worked, Cody."

"What? Jake?"

"Yes!"

"They've found him?"

"Not yet, but a man came forward. He saw the picture of Jake at your concert in Raleigh and couldn't get it out of his head. His daughter went to your concert down in Louisiana and mentioned it to her dad. When he told her he'd seen a child that looked like Jake, his daughter made him go to the police. Oh, Cody. This could be it."

"I hope so. What can I do to help?"

"Nothing, but I'll let you know if that changes," she said. "I can't thank you enough."

"Stop that. No *thank you* is needed. Let's just hope this brings the little guy home. I'm prayin' for you, girl."

"Von and Riley are on their way. They should be here shortly. We're heading to Raleigh."

"Will you call me tomorrow to let me know how it goes? Or as soon as you know? Or text me. I'll be dying, wondering what's going on."

"Absolutely. Thank you again. Thank you, thank you, thank you."

"Take care. I'll be waiting to hear."

Just as Kasey hung up, she heard a car door.

"Man, they got here fast." She picked up her bag, ran to the door, swung it open and stepped forward.

Scott stood in the doorway.

"Scott?" She stepped back. "I thought you were Riley and Von."

"I don't think they could get here that fast."

He pulled Kasey into his arms. She relaxed into his warm hug.

"I figured it would be the longest wait ever. I thought you might need a friend."

"You're right. It feels crazy sitting here waiting when I could be halfway to Raleigh by now."

"You know these things take time, right?"

She stepped back from him. "Time? I've been waiting since last August, trying to find Jake. I know what time is. It's torture. I've waited so long."

"I know, but these leads aren't always a beeline to the suspect."

She nodded and took a breath. "I know, but if that's him on the tape and he's alive . . . and . . ."

He pulled her back into his arms and held her. "What time did they call?"

"I'm not even sure. Not long before I called you."

He picked up the handset of her phone and searched back through the list of last calls. "Looks like he called an hour ago. You've still got a good thirty-minute wait."

Flopping into a nearby chair, she felt like an impatient six-year-old.

"Do you mind?" Scott gestured toward the kitchen.

"No. There's not much in there. Make yourself at home."

Scott disappeared into the kitchen. The microwave beeped as he punched the buttons. He came back into the room carrying a mug of tea for her.

"Nothing for you?" she asked.

He shook his head. "No. The tea is decaf. It said 'soothing' on the tin. Hope it helps."

That was thoughtful.

She lifted the mug to her lips, took a sip, then set it on the side table.

Scott sat on the arm of the chair. "Turn your back to me."

She did. He placed his hands on either side of her neck, and massaged her shoulders. "That feels *so* good."

"Your neck is in knots. Close your eyes. Relax into my hands."

Her body went warm as he pushed into her muscles, kneading at the tension in her neck and upper back. He placed his hands on her neckline, then over her ears, massaging her head with his fingers.

A tear ran down her cheek. "You never told me you were a massage guru," Kasey said, as she rested in Scott's hands, her tension seeping away.

"Holding out on you." His hands soothed the stress in her weary muscles.

"I like it."

Once Kasey relaxed the time seemed to pass more quickly. But her nerves twisted again when she heard Von and Riley pull into the driveway and honk the horn.

"This is it." Kasey clenched her fists and let out a deep breath.

"Don't forget your new neighbors and friends," Scott said. "We're here for you, no matter what you need. We want to help. Don't be shy about asking." He kissed her forehead.

"I knew I did the right thing moving here. Thank you for coming over."

"I'll lock up. Go." Scott urged her toward the door.

"Thanks." She kissed him on the cheek and ran outside, leaving the door wide open behind her. She jumped into the back of the SUV, hugged Riley, and waved to Scott as they drove off.

• • •

The ride to the police station in North Carolina was painfully slow.

When Von finally took the exit from I-85, Kasey's stomach began to spin. "I might be sick."

Riley hugged her close. "It's okay. You're going to be fine."

After speeding down the interstate, it felt as if they were slowly coasting along the town roads. Von braked after a few miles and turned in front of a small brick building.

Kasey sat forward. "There's no way this is the Raleigh police station."

Von looked over his shoulder and released his seatbelt. "We're in Leighsboro. Just outside of Raleigh. The guy saw the alert at the Raleigh concert, but he saw Jake here in his hometown."

Kasey looked doubtful, then it struck her.

Lala had tied her answer to an "L," a Lee to be more specific, could this be the answer? Finally? She'd owe Lala an apology if Jake was here.

"My house is bigger than this police station," she said as they walked to the front entrance.

Von opened the door and held it for them. "Size isn't everything."

"I'm not responding to that." Kasey shared a nervous laugh with Riley.

"I will." Riley reached up and patted Von's cheek. "Honey, you have nothing to worry about."

They stepped inside and lined up in front of a row of four desks.

Von asked the officer at the first desk to see the police chief.

A huge man walked toward them with his hand extended. "Chief Phipps." He had a voice that commanded authority, despite his apparently young age. "You got here quick."

"Perry Von, my wife Riley, and this is Kasey Phillips."

The chief led them to a private conference room at the back of the station. A buzz-cut ex-marine-looking kind of guy, he pulled out one of the chairs and invited them to have a seat around the table. "Let me bring y'all up to date," he said.

Everyone leaned in closer.

Kasey reached for Riley's hand and squeezed it. *Please let it be Jake.*

Chapter Twenty-Six

"The gentleman who came forward is Billy Goodwin. He's fifty-eight, laid off from the mill when it closed this past fall. Worked there over thirty years. Currently employed at Walmart as a part-time greeter. That's where he saw the child that resembles your son." Chief Phipps's eyes met Kasey's.

Was there hope in his glance?

"Reliable guy, well-known in the community." Chief Phipps pushed the top page of the report to the side. "Mr. Goodwin stated that he saw the picture of your son at a Cody Tuggle concert in Raleigh the first week of January."

Kasey nodded. "Yes?"

I was there.

The image of Jake, over seven stories high on that backdrop, was burned into her memory.

Phipps continued, "He'd seen a child who looked familiar while working his shift at Walmart. But he didn't make the connection until his daughter mentioned the same plea for help and the picture of the child she'd seen at the concert she attended in Louisiana. She suggested he come forward. Which, as you know, he has."

Kasey swallowed and forced herself to take a breath.

"We've secured security tapes from two of the visits Mr. Goodwin remembered." Chief Phipps turned two black-and-white glossy prints toward Kasey. Kasey's hand shook as she focused on the picture. The image was grainy and from a distance, but it was Jake.

"Jake!" She swallowed hard. "My baby."

She looked at Riley and grabbed her arm.

"He's got Bubba Bear with him. Look at the way he has it hiked under his arm with his thumb in his belt loop. Only he would do that. He's okay. He looks okay, right?"

Riley nodded. "He does. He looks good."

Von agreed. "It's him. The bear. Yep." He turned back to the chief. He pointed to the pictures. "Do you have a lead on the woman he's with?"

"No, not yet," the chief said.

Von opened his leather portfolio, then handed him a drawing. "This is a sketch of the woman suspected to have sent photos of the crash to Kasey from Nashville a few months ago. I can't tell from the picture if it's the same person."

The chief nodded and looked. "Me, either. The woman's image isn't clear in that picture. Billy Goodwin says he's seen Jake on three occasions. When Goodwin's daughter called after the Cody Tuggle concert, and went on and on about the missing child, that's when it clicked for him. She'll show up again."

Kasey held her shaking fingers to her lips.

"Can I get you some water?" Chief Phipps asked her.

"Yes. Yes, please." Kasey's tongue felt thick, and she was having difficulty swallowing. "I feel like I can't breathe."

Chief Phipps leaned out the door and asked an underling for water, then came back in and sat at the table.

Riley pushed Kasey's hair back over her shoulder and rubbed her back. "Calm down. Inhale through your nose. That's it. It's going to be okay."

Kasey took in a shaky breath.

"That's good," Riley said.

Following two raps on the door, another officer entered with a bottle of water and some paper cups. Riley poured a cup for Kasey.

"It's Jake," she said. "What do we do?" Her hand shook as she lifted the cup of water to her lips.

"We're working to identify the woman," Phipps explained. "When she comes back into the store we'll know for sure, but we're hoping we can run her down before then."

"Can we talk to Billy Goodwin?" Von asked.

"Yes. That's fine. He said he'd cooperate any way he can." Chief Phipps pulled a pen from his shirt pocket, copied Goodwin's number on a slip of paper, and handed it to Von. "Here you go."

"Is that it?" asked Kasey. "This is all we can do? Wait?"

Chief Phipps exchanged a glance with Von. "For now."

Von shook the chief's hand. "You've got my numbers and the hotline's. Keep us posted. Thank you so much."

He led Kasey and Riley out of the station.

"My son is alive, probably somewhere nearby, and we just have to wait?" cried Kasey.

"We're getting closer. Don't flip out on me now." Von fastened his seatbelt and started the truck. "We'll get a room and stay for a couple days. Maybe we can speed things along. I'll give Mr. Goodwin a call and set something up. It's not that big of a town."

The Walmart was near the interstate. There were a couple of hotels and a strip mall there, too. Von pulled into the Hampton Inn parking lot and went inside to register.

"I can't believe it," Kasey said.

"He's alive." Riley turned to her. "We'll find him."

"His hair was long. Did you see how long his hair was in the back?"

"First thing I noticed, too," Riley said. "Nick was always fastidious about Jake's hair being short."

"So he wouldn't look like a girl," Kasey finished the thought as the memories of arguments between she and Nick about Jake's hair came to mind. Such a stupid thing to fight about.

Von came out a few minutes later. "I got connecting rooms. We're right around the corner here," Von said as he pulled the vehicle around to the side of the building and parked.

They piled out of the truck and wheeled the bags to their rooms. Riley propped open the door between them. She and Kasey sprawled across the king-sized bed in one room.

Von set up his laptop in the other and called Billy Goodwin. He hung up the phone and stepped into the doorway between the two rooms. "Hey, girls, Billy Goodwin will be here around five-thirty. He's going to stop by on his way to work."

Kasey lifted her head from the pillow and looked at the clock. It was just after lunchtime. "What do we do until then?"

"Rest?"

"At least you didn't say wait. I'm about over that word," said Kasey.

Von pulled his keys from his pocket. "I'm going to take a ride. Can I get y'all some lunch first?"

"I'm not hungry," Kasey said. She turned the pillow over and scrunched it under her chin. "I'm going to try to sleep so five-thirty gets here quicker."

Riley said, "I'm not hungry either. Too excited, I guess. Bring something when you come back, just in case."

"Sounds good. I'll call if I hear anything, but I don't expect news for a while. I'll be back in a couple of hours." Von closed the door behind him as he left.

Riley got up and twisted the privacy lock, then lay back down with Kasey.

A knock at the door woke Riley—Von's knock. She jumped up to let him in. Von gave her a peck on the cheek as he breezed by her and placed a bag of takeout on the small table. "I didn't know what to get. It's sort of a buffet."

Kasey walked into the room, bleary-eyed.

Von handed her a large drink. "Diet?"

"Thank you." Kasey accepted the cup and took a long sip. "You're the best."

"I know. She tells me all the time." He smiled and tugged Riley to him. "What do I get for bringing you a regular Coke?"

Riley raised her brow suggestively. "We'll discuss that when there isn't so much going on."

"Thanks for that," Kasey said, rolling her eyes. "What time is it?"

"Almost five," Von said.

"I slept hard." Kasey scrubbed her fingers through her hair and tugged her bangs into submission. "By the time we finish eating, it should be time for Billy Goodwin to show up."

Von arranged Chinese takeout containers on the table, along with two cups of egg drop soup. "I know you girls love that egg drop soup. Looks like snot to me, but anything that looks that gross has to be good for you."

"Thank you, sweetie," Riley said as she grabbed a container of soup and handed the other to Kasey. "You've put a real scrumptious light on it. I bet the Food Network will be hunting you down to write blurbs for them."

"I call 'em like I see 'em," Von said, looking innocent.

When the knock came at the door, they all stopped in mid-bite. Von wiped his hands on a napkin, strode to the door, and opened it.

"You must be Billy Goodwin."

The round-faced man extended his hand. "Yes, sir." His smile showed perfect teeth, and his blue eyes almost danced. "Hope you don't mind I came early."

"Not at all. Come on in. Thanks so much for coming to talk to us." Von gestured for Billy to come into the room. "This is my wife, Riley, and our dearest friend, Kasey. She's Jake's mom."

Billy walked over to Kasey. She stood and extended her hand, but he opened his big arms wide. "I bet you could use a hug instead."

"Thank you," Kasey said. "I've been looking for Jake since the end of August. I knew in my heart he was alive. I never gave up, but I can't believe we're finally getting close to finding him. Thanks to you, Mr. Goodwin."

"Billy," he said with a smile. "Call me Billy. Everybody does."

"Thank you, Billy," Kasey cried—tears of joy, fear, hope and frustration.

They all sat down at the table.

Von flipped to a clean page on his notepad. "Do you mind talking us through everything? I know you've already done all of this with the police. But it might help. If you don't mind."

"No problem. Are you kidding? Anything to help." Billy started from the beginning and told his story. It lined up with what Chief Phipps had already shared, but with a few questions from Von, they got some additional details.

"You say you saw him a few times?" Von tapped his pen on the pad.

"About once a week, I think. He looked familiar. But it wasn't until my daughter was tellin' me how it broke her heart when Cody Tuggle made that announcement at the end of his concert that it occurred to me where I'd seen him." Billy turned to Kasey. "I went to the concert here in Raleigh. Anyway, I remembered the bear. One time when they came in, I greeted them and offered them a cart, and the little guy was standing there hugging that bear." Billy laughed. He had a hearty laugh, the kind you can feel across a room.

"He was hanging on to that ragged bear for dear life. I asked him what his bear's name was. He buried his face in it and giggled. When I asked him how old he was, he showed me on his fingers. I guess he's three or four. Not sure."

Kasey laughed. "I know. He has trouble negotiating all those tiny fingers. He's four now."

Billy nodded. "Cute kid. I had a bear like that when I was young. I guess that's why I remembered him. Mine was named Brown Bear. It was a pitiful-lookin' thing, but my mom hung on to it for years. She probably still has it."

"He loves that bear," Kasey said, her voice quiet and steady. "Calls him Bubba Bear."

"Cute," Billy said. "He looked fine. I mean, I

didn't think he looked dirty or mistreated or anything. Trust me, I see some bad stuff come through there sometimes. Nothing stood out as unusual."

Kasey dabbed her tears with a tissue. "Thank you."

Von continued taking notes. "And they were in every week?"

"Yeah. I can't be sure, but I think I saw them when I was working my afternoon shifts, so it would have been either Tuesdays or Thursdays. It's been about a week since I last saw them."

Kasey handed Billy the photo album she'd brought along. "Do you mind taking a look at these other pictures to see if you still think it's him?"

Billy slid the album in front of him. "Yeah. Yeah, that looks like him."

Kasey relaxed. Her lips quivered as she smiled.

Von stood. "I don't have any other questions. I know you have to get to work. Thanks for giving us your time, and more than that, thanks for going to the police with this information." Von shook his hand.

"I told the police chief I'd call him if I see them come in again," Billy said, then turned to Kasey. "I'll do everything I can to help."

Von handed him a card. "Here's my direct number. If you think of anything else, just give me a call."

Von walked Billy out to his car. When he came back, Kasey asked, "What do we do now?"

"Wait."

Kasey grunted. "I would hate your job. It has to be the worst job in the world. Is it always like this? Every time you get one answer it leads to two more questions."

"That's pretty much it, but when the puzzle comes together, it's worth it."

"Well, it's killing me," Kasey said. "I'm going to call Scott and fill him in."

Kasey dialed Scott, who answered on the first ring. She gave him the update and he gave her just the pep talk she needed. She was glad she'd called him. When she hung up the phone, Von called out to her: "Hey, Kasey. I'm going to take a ride. You want to go?"

Kasey jumped to her feet and appeared in the doorway. "Absolutely. Anything is better than sitting here."

"Where are we going to go in this little town?" asked Riley.

Von shrugged. "We'll just cruise around. Who knows, we might stumble onto another clue."

"In that case," Riley said, picking up her purse, "I'd like to go, too. If there's any chance in a million that it might help us bring home Jake faster, I'm in."

They piled into the SUV, and Von cruised the

streets. It was a small town, with a typical main street and a grid of numbered and named streets. Several of the storefronts on Main Street were empty. The economy was tough on these small towns and family-owned shops.

They drove through neighborhoods, not really sure what they were looking for. After they'd driven every street in the grid around the town's center, Von headed back toward the interstate. Traffic got heavier as they neared the strip mall. Von turned into the parking lot of the small shopping center.

"What are we doing?" Riley asked.

"Surveillance," Von said. "There's a pizza joint, an ice cream store, and a grocery store. All places someone with a kid might go." He pulled his money from the front pocket of his jeans and peeled off a twenty. "Why don't y'all get us some milkshakes?"

Riley snagged the cash from his hands. "You don't have to ask me twice. Chocolate for you, right?"

"You know it." He pushed his seat back from the steering wheel and got comfortable.

Riley and Kasey came back with the milkshakes.

When Kasey got into the backseat, she leaned forward and said to Von, "Okay. This might not be the *worst* job in the world. I could get used to sitting around drinking milkshakes for a living."

They watched for a while. Not long after the lights in the parking lot came on, Von's cell phone rang.

Seven-thirty.

"Yeah, Von here."

Kasey and Riley strained to listen.

Von nodded. "Yeah. Okay . . . When? . . . Right." Von tucked the phone between his cheek and neck and turned the key in the engine. "What color? . . . Thanks. We're on our way." He let the phone drop from his chin to his lap as he threw one arm over the back of the passenger seat and whirled the SUV out of the parking spot.

"What?" Kasey and Riley asked in unison.

Von sped back out to the main road.

"What's going on?" Riley fumbled for her seatbelt, steadying herself by grabbing for the dash as Von squealed around the next corner.

"She just left the Walmart." Von's jaw tensed, his attention laser-focused on the road.

"Who?" asked Riley.

Kasey reached over the seat and grabbed Riley's arm. "With Jake? The woman and Jake." She slapped the seat like a jockey urging a racehorse. "Go!"

Von got to the main highway and turned right.

"Where are you going?" Kasey yelled. "Walmart is the other way."

Von weaved in and out of traffic. "Keep your eyes open for a black Nissan sedan."

Chapter Twenty-Seven

Von navigated through three traffic lights on green and hit the accelerator to catch up to the cars ahead of them on an open stretch of road.

"Be careful, honey," Riley said.

They came up behind the first vehicle. A white Volkswagen. Von maneuvered around it and floored the accelerator to catch up to the next cars: two SUVs, and the last a battered blue pickup truck. The road ahead was dark. No taillights in sight. Von smacked the steering wheel and swerved to the side of the road. "Damn."

"What the hell was that all about?" Riley hung on to the door and console. "Why are we stopping?"

Von squealed tires back onto the road in the other direction, then slowed to the speed limit.

"When Billy Goodwin came back from his break, he saw the woman leaving Walmart with Jake. He got the car description and a partial plate number." Von's lips pulled into a tight line. "I thought we might catch up to them. He said they went left out of the parking lot."

"Could we have beaten her to the light?" Kasey asked.

"Possibly. I'm still looking. Keep your eyes peeled."

Kasey leaned against the window. Her breath fogged the glass as she focused on each passing car.

"He called the police. They should be at the Walmart by now. We'll go see what they've got."

When Von pulled into the Walmart parking lot, four police cruisers were already there, blue lights still flashing. Billy Goodwin stood out front. Von, Kasey and Riley bailed out of the truck and headed toward the crowd. Billy walked over to meet Von. He looked upset.

"I'm sorry. When I came off break, there she was. She'd just checked out—pushing her cart out the automatic doors. I dialed the police and then ran to the lot. I saw her get in the car, but by the time I got close, she was driving off. I'm so sorry." Billy looked defeated. "So close."

Chief Phipps strode over and patted Billy Goodwin on his shoulder. "It's okay. It's not your fault. You did the right thing." The chief turned his attention to Von and Kasey. "He did get us a partial tag and the make of the car. We're working that now."

"That's good, right?" Kasey rubbed her hands up and down her arms, trying to chase away the chill.

"Yes." The police chief nodded. "I've also got two men upstairs reviewing the security tapes. They've closed that register. We're trying to match the sequence at the register and tape. With any luck she used a debit or credit card."

"Please. Please. Please." Kasey paced back and forth, clenching her jaw to stifle the sob in her throat.

Riley put her arms around Kasey while the officer updated Von. "I've already called to get a warrant for the information off the card, if she used one."

"Good. We don't want to waste any time." Von crossed his arms. "Did she see Billy running toward her?"

"I don't think so. Sounds like he was a few steps behind her. She didn't seem to be spooked, from what I gather from the other cashiers. I talked to the employee working the lot collecting carts. He seemed clueless as to what was going on, if that's any indicator."

"That's good."

The police chief nodded.

A young officer walked up to Chief Phipps. "Bingo, sir."

Kasey tensed. Riley hugged her close.

"She used a credit card. Here's her name." He handed the chief the information.

"Libby Braddock." Chief Phipps's gaze settled on Kasey. "Ring any bells?"

Kasey and Riley shook their heads. "Never heard of her," Kasey said.

"Stay right here." Chief Phipps stepped away.

He called in to Dispatch on his radio and spoke to someone else on his cell phone.

Kasey squatted to stop the dizziness that consumed her and to steady her breathing.

Von shook his keys toward Riley. "Here. Why don't you take Kasey back to the room?"

Kasey jumped to her feet. "I'm good. I'm fine. No. I want to be here."

Von started to say something, but stuffed his keys back in his pocket instead.

Two police cars drove out of the lot. Chief Phipps hurried over to Von. "Good news. She doesn't have a record, and we have the address. We're heading out there now. Y'all can ride with me."

Von rode shotgun. Kasey and Riley jumped into the backseat of the cruiser.

Kasey shivered. Even her teeth chattered. The neighborhood was well-lit. They'd been on this street earlier today.

So close.

Judging by the size of the yards and the large trees that lined the streets, it appeared to be an older, well-established neighborhood. The homes weren't cookie-cutter replicas of one another. They turned a corner and slowed to a stop behind the other police cars that lined the curb, one behind the other.

The house was small, but under the light of the

moon and the streetlights, it looked very well-maintained. Garden lights lined the flowerbeds. A flag with a snowflake pictured on it hung from the front porch. A swing set took up most of the side yard.

Jake loves to swing.

"I didn't expect the house to look like this," Riley said.

"I know. Normal," Kasey said. "But thank goodness. I had visions of something terrifying."

Riley nodded. "I know. I'm surprised, too."

"Nothing surprises me anymore," Chief Phipps said as he watched his men approach the front door. One peeled away and went around back. Chief Phipps stayed in the car, but he had one hand on the door handle.

An officer rapped on the front door with the end of his flashlight.

No answer.

A neighbor wearing a bathrobe stepped out onto her porch and leaned over the railing to see what was going on.

The chief opened the car door. "Wait here." He grabbed his hat from the dashboard, then walked toward the woman.

"Excuse me. Ma'am?" Chief Phipps said.

The woman on the porch spun around, clutching her chest. "Lord, son. You could scare an old woman to death."

He smiled. *Serves her right, being nosy like that.* "Sorry about that. I'm Chief Phipps."

"My goodness." She tugged her robe tighter, then ran her hand through her hair, fluffing it. "I voted for you in the last election. Ex-military man and all. I knew you'd keep us safe. What's going on over at Libby's place?"

"You know the woman that lives in that house?"

"Yes. Libby Braddock. Dear woman. Nothing has happened to her, has it?"

"No, nothing like that."

"Thank goodness. Widowed and all. That would be terrible."

"Has she been here today?"

"Yes. She's not there now. She just left about an hour ago. Seemed in a hurry. Her and her nephew. She said it was some kind of family emergency."

"I didn't catch your name, ma'am," Phipps said.

"Doris Moon. Call me Doris, please."

"Thanks, Doris. Her nephew? How old is he?" Phipps pulled a notepad from his pocket.

The old woman shrugged. "Four, I think."

"Do you know his name?"

"Of course. I babysit when she has doctor appointments and such. That little Jake is the sweetest child."

Phipps scribbled JAKE across the page. "Know where they were going?"

"No. She asked me to pick up her mail and paper. Said she'd be back in a couple weeks." The old woman studied him. "She was in a hurry. I didn't want to pry," she explained.

Probably a first.

"I understand. Does she hold a job?" Phipps asked.

"No. I don't like to talk about people, but I think she's on some kind of disability. I've noticed her checks when I get the mail sometimes."

Phipps laughed to himself. This nosy neighbor was probably the queen of gossip. "The child. You said Jake, right?"

She nodded.

"Is he in good health?"

"He's fine. So many questions. Are you sure something hasn't happened to them?"

"Just following some leads, ma'am." She didn't look convinced, but he had a few more questions, and she seemed to have a lot of answers. "How long has the boy been staying with her? Do you remember when she first brought him here?"

"No." She shook her head, and then her eyes lit up. "Yes I do. It was right around Sally Mae's birthday. We met at Shoney's for lunch. That was . . . well, wait." She held up her finger and headed to the door. The screen door slammed behind her. "I have it on my calendar."

She stopped and opened the door. "Come on in."

He followed her inside. She waddled into the kitchen and took a calendar down from the tack on the wall. "Can I get you some lemonade? Coffee?"

"Nothing, thank you."

"Oh. Here it is." She folded the calendar back and laid it on the table. "Yes . . . that would have been September seventh." She ran a finger around the entry on the calendar. "See."

"Yes. Thank you." He jotted down the information. "Why is he staying with her? Did she say?"

"Awful custody battle. Her poor brother. Divorce is tough on a man with children, you know." She reshuffled the calendar and tacked it back on the wall. "He travels a lot, and the mother is just an awful person. She left him. No warning."

"Thank you." Phipps turned to the door. "I'll just let myself out."

When the chief walked out of the neighbor's house he gave Von a nod, and Von met him in the street. They walked, talking as they joined the other officers in front of the house.

Kasey and Riley clung to one another.

A moment later, Von jogged back to the car.

"Well?" Kasey asked.

Von leaned into the open passenger door.

Riley scooted to the edge of the bench seat. "What's going on?"

Von blew out a breath. "She's not here. They left about an hour ago. The neighbor says it was a family emergency."

"Where? Let's go get them," Kasey said, her

voice filled with frustration. "Why are we still here?"

"She doesn't know where they went. But Kasey, the neighbor said the little boy's name is Jake. He's been here since September. It's him. It's got to be him."

"Oh, Kasey," Riley whispered.

Kasey tried to force her confused emotions to cooperate. A million questions floated through her head, but none of them made it to her lips. She covered her face with her hands.

"She said he's healthy," Von told them. "He's fine."

"It's him. It's really him?" Riley asked.

"He's safe. He's alive, and she said he's okay? I've prayed for this moment." Kasey wiped tears from her face. "I want my son back. Why did she take him?" Sobbing, she choked on the words.

Riley shook her head. "There are some nut-job people in this world."

"I don't want my son with a nut-job!" Kasey squeezed her eyes tight.

"I didn't mean that," Riley said. "I'm sorry."

While Von updated Kasey and Riley, Phipps went back to ask Doris Moon about a few more details.

"Sorry to bother you again, Mrs. Moon—I mean, Doris. Do you have a key to Ms. Braddock's house?"

"Why, yes, I do have a key. We have each other's. You know, just in case."

"Would you mind letting us in? I can get a warrant if you're uncomfortable giving me access without one."

She hesitated, but only for a moment. "I suppose it wouldn't be a problem—if I went with you."

"Thank you."

The woman slipped her feet into a pair of bright green gardening clogs that were on the floor next to the front door, then led the way next door. Her steps were short and swift, leaving a trail in the dewy grass. She slipped the key into the door and opened it, stepping aside to let them in.

Four police officers spread out into different rooms of the tidy house. Especially tidy for a house with a four-year-old boy living in it. Doris stayed by the door as the officers opened drawers and checked trashcans for any hint as to where the woman had gone. Phipps hit the caller ID list on the telephone and wrote the last ten numbers on his notepad. The last call was from UNKNOWN CALLER. He hit *69 to see if the number would replay. No luck. No address left behind, and no notes next to the phone.

The policemen filed out of the house and it wasn't long before Phipps's cruiser was the only one left. Phipps helped Doris secure the house, and walked her home before joining the others in his car.

"I'm sorry." Phipps put his arm on the back of the seat and turned to Kasey. "I know this has got to be hard for you. We're on your side. We'll follow every lead to find your son. I promise."

"I hope you won't mind keeping me in the loop every step of the way," Von said.

"Not at all. I can definitely do that." Phipps looked at his list. "I've already put an APB out on the car. I don't think she knows she was made at the Walmart, so if she was naïve enough to use that credit card once, hopefully she'll use it again." He looked up from his notes and turned toward Kasey. "Von already updated you on what the neighbor said?"

Kasey nodded.

"We'll find them." Phipps radioed the dispatcher and asked her to schedule a drive-by check of the Braddock house for the next week. "Mrs. Moon said she'll call and let me know when they come back, but we'll keep an eye on things, too."

Phipps started the car and took his disappointed passengers back to the Walmart.

Silence reigned during the drive from the Walmart back to the hotel. Von went to get ice and sodas from the vending machine. Kasey and Riley went back to their room.

"More waiting." Kasey got into bed and crawled under the covers, fully clothed.

Von came back in the room and flipped on the

television and his laptop. Riley closed the door between the rooms and crawled into bed next to Kasey.

"I wish there was more I could do," Riley said. She lay there, wide-awake, wishing and praying that this nightmare would end.

After Kasey fell asleep, Riley got up and tiptoed into the other room. Von hunched over his computer, reading something on the screen. She stepped behind him and rubbed his shoulders. "What do we do now?" she asked.

He reached up and patted her hand. He lifted her palm to his lips, kissed it, then squeezed her hand closed. "Love you."

"I love you, too." She leaned forward, put her chin on his shoulder, and looked at the website he had displayed on the screen. "What are you doing?"

"Grasping at straws, mostly. Just trying to think a step ahead of her."

She took several steps toward the other room, then turned back to him. "Von? We are going to find him sooner or later, right?"

He nodded. "Oh, yeah. Sooner, I hope."

Chapter Twenty-Eight

The next morning, Von met the chief at the precinct for an update, and then did his own drive-by of the Braddock house. Nothing had changed. With nothing else to do in the small town but wait, they decided it was best to head back to the house on Nickel Creek. The ride back was quiet except for the chatter of the all-news station Von had on the radio. Kasey stared out the window.

Riley nudged Kasey's arm. "Are you going to answer your phone?" Riley leaned forward in her seat.

"No," Kasey said without turning around.

"Want me to get it?" Riley grabbed Kasey's phone.

Kasey shrugged and looked outside.

"Hello, Kasey Phillips's phone," Riley said. "Hey . . . No. We're on our way back to the house . . . I know." Riley prodded Kasey and mouthed, "It's Scott."

Kasey shook her head, and waved off the call. She didn't have anything to say to anyone right now.

Riley let Scott know what had transpired since Kasey had last spoken to him and promised to keep him up to date.

"He's a nice guy," Riley said, tucking Kasey's phone back in her handbag.

Kasey nodded, vaguely distracted by the thought that one woman stood between her and her son. She was relieved when the Nickel Creek Road street sign came into view an hour later. They pulled into the driveway and went into the house.

"Y'all don't have to stay," Kasey said. "I'll be fine. I'm just going to go to bed and wait for news."

"I'm not leaving you here alone," Riley said. "You need your friends right now."

"I *need* my son." Kasey took a deep breath. "I'm sorry. That wasn't fair. I appreciate everything y'all are doing for me. I just feel . . . sad . . . *and* mad today."

"It's okay."

Kasey dropped her purse on the end table. "The guest room is made up. Make yourselves at home. I'm going to bed."

"Don't worry about us," Riley said.

Later that afternoon, Von sat in a rocking chair on the porch, drinking a beer, when Scott drove up. Scott pushed his sunglasses on top of his head as he walked up to the porch.

"Kasey's inside," Von said with a nod.

Scott didn't go to the door. Instead, he sat in the other rocker. "Mind talking through all the updates with me?"

"Not at all." Von put his empty bottle on the ground next to the chair and leaned forward, elbows on his knees. He went through the whole scenario, step-by-step.

"Libby Braddock was tipped off," Scott said.

"She had to be."

Scott's jaw tensed. "Do you think it was someone from the store who knew her?"

Von rubbed his morning stubble. "I really don't think so, although that seems most likely."

Scott rocked back in the chair. "Who else knew?"

"No one. Well, that's not true. Kasey talked to you, Cody Tuggle, and to her grandmother. That's it. Riley and I came here as soon as we heard, and that leaves just the local folks in Leighsboro. It's a small town. I'm sure half the population is related. News could've gotten around pretty fast." Von paused, remembering Scott was a small-town guy. "No offense, man."

"None taken." Scott shook his head. "No mother should have to go through this."

"Especially Kasey. She's a terrific mom." Von lowered his head and picked at his fingernail. "It's been hard for her. Losing Nick, then not knowing if Jake was even alive. At least now we know he's alive."

"I'd like to work on this with you. Let me know what I can do. I've got resources."

"Good deal. Maybe between the two of us we can figure this out."

"I'm going to call in a favor over in Southampton County," Scott said. "I want to go back through the evidence from the crash site. Maybe they overlooked something."

"Good idea. Will they cooperate?"

"Oh, yeah. I went to school with most of those guys."

"Let's stay connected," said Von.

Scott stood and extended his hand. "We will."

They shook hands, then Scott went inside.

"I didn't hear you drive up," Kasey said when Scott walked into the kitchen.

"You look beat," Scott said. He gave her a hug and nodded to Riley.

"Want a cup?" Riley lifted her porcelain teacup to her lips.

"I'm *not* a tea kind of guy." Scott held up his pinky. "Not me."

Kasey couldn't help but snicker.

Riley went to the fridge. "How about one of these?" She grabbed a beer and held it out.

"I *am* off duty." He smiled, accepted the beer, then turned to Kasey. "You hanging in there?"

"It's torture to sit here waiting. What am I supposed to do?" She chewed the inside of her cheek, holding back tears.

"You could pray," Scott said in a soft comforting tone. "I added Jake to the prayer list at church. Hope you don't mind."

Kasey looked into his eyes. "That was really nice."

"I didn't know if you were a church-goer, but most of us go to the same church around here. I take my mom every Sunday. Wish I could say I thought of the idea of putting Jake on the prayer list, but it was her idea."

"Thank you." His thoughtfulness surprised her over and over again.

"If you ever care to join us, just let me know. That's not why I came, though. I was wondering, what's on your calendar for the next couple of days?" Scott twisted off the cap of the beer bottle and took a sip.

"Waiting. Lots of it, if I have to guess." Kasey clapped her hands over her mouth. "I'm sorry. I don't mean to complain. I'm just a mixed bag of emotions today. Ignore me."

"It's okay," Scott said. "We all understand, but it does take time to vet this stuff out."

"You and Von both already gave me that lecture."

"Managing expectations," he corrected her.

"Whatever. I should be relieved that we're getting so close and we have proof that Jake's alive—and I am. But I never gave up hope that he was alive. I've known that all along. The other part of me is so mad I want hunt down that woman myself, kick her ass, and take my child back. Then I'd ask questions, or maybe not. I just want Jake back."

Scott flipped the beer cap in the air and caught it with one hand. "Kasey, you can drive yourself crazy like that."

"Short trip," she said.

"Or get arrested for real," Riley added.

"I'd get off on temporary insanity, that's for sure."

"Don't talk like that," Riley said. "We're going to find him, and things are going to be back to normal before you know it."

"I'm not sure I even know what normal is anymore," Kasey said. "Don't take this the wrong way, Riley, but I wish you and Von would go home. Y'all don't have to babysit me. I'm sad. I'm mad. I'm downright pissed-off about all of this, but I'm fine. I'm not fragile."

"I'm always just a phone call away, too. You know that, right?" Scott said, glancing from Kasey to Riley.

"I know. You're great. Thanks," Kasey said.

Scott nodded. "Don't let the anger eat you up. The woman has no record, and the neighbor said Libby adores Jake. Be thankful for that. Cling to it."

Kasey bowed her head into her hands and groaned. "I know it's good news. It could be so much worse." She lifted her head. "It's *been* worse. All these months, waiting, worrying. How am I ever going to get through this?"

"I have an idea about that," Scott said. "I was

thinking we could do a little investigative work together. I was talking to Von about it a minute ago."

"What kind of investigative work?" Kasey asked.

"We can go back through the evidence collected at the scene of the crash," Scott said.

"They searched all that stuff," Riley said. "They didn't get any leads from it."

"I know. Maybe Kasey and I will see something they missed. It might trigger an idea or connection, now that we know a little more. It couldn't hurt." Scott shrugged. "It might be a long shot, but any shot is better than no shot at all."

"Can we do that?" asked Kasey.

Scott nodded. "I can arrange it."

Kasey smiled. "How did I get so lucky to meet you, and have such great friends?" She grabbed Riley's hand, and then Scott's. "Y'all are the best."

"I don't know how you got so lucky to find Riley and Von, but be thankful you drive a finicky foreign car with electrical problems." He laughed. "Or you can thank Deputy Dan."

"Funny." She rolled her eyes. "I haven't forgiven him yet."

Riley put her teacup in the dishwasher. "Well, if y'all are going to be working on that angle, and you're sure you're okay, Von and I will get out of your hair—but just until the next lead."

"I'm fine. I'll call if anything changes," Kasey promised.

Riley hugged her. "I'll go talk to the boss."

"It'll take a day or two to get access to the evidence. Can I call in that rain check for tomorrow morning?"

"Rain check?"

"Our fishing date," he said.

She wrinkled her nose. "I don't think so. I'm not very good company right now."

"Come on. We'll do some fishing, relax, pass the day away. You need to be well and strong for Jake. The fresh air will be good for you."

Kasey wasn't interested.

"Tell you what. If you feel up to it in the morning, just show up. The invitation is open."

Chapter Twenty-Nine

Kasey twisted beneath the covers, then kicked them off. She repositioned her pillow, but less than twenty minutes later, she grew chilly and grabbed for the comforter.

The trip to North Carolina replayed in her head. They'd been so close to finding Jake. What could they have done differently? If she'd left for Leighsboro sooner, would the events have played out differently?

Tired of tossing and turning in bed, she went out

to the couch and tried to sleep there. She tugged the handmade afghan Riley had given her as a housewarming gift over her legs. But there was no getting to sleep. The sun began to brighten the sky. She pushed the afghan aside and turned on the television. The meteorologist forecasted the day's weather as sunny and bright, warm for this time of year. A day to be outside, he said.

She switched off the television and went into the kitchen to make a pot of coffee. She'd need the caffeine to get through the day. Too impatient to wait for the coffee to finish brewing, she poured a cup mid-way through the brewing process and swirled in a sugar cube and extra creamer. It was supposed to be a pretty day. Cardinals whistled as they flitted in the trees and vines in the back yard.

Maybe a day on the water wasn't such a bad idea after all. Sitting around the house wouldn't make the wait any more bearable, and Scott was easy to be with. She sure couldn't take rehashing this stuff over and over again.

She finished her coffee and went inside to change into jeans and a long sleeve t-shirt. The last time she'd been fishing, it had been with Nick and Jake. Jake caught a sunfish that was way too little to eat. Not even enough meat for a fish stick. She laughed at the memory. It had taken a lot of talking to get Jake to let that fish go, especially once he realized they'd be eating the fish that his daddy caught. Jake had always wanted to be just like Nick.

With her keys in hand, she locked up the house, jumped in her car and headed to Scott's house, making it there without one wrong turn. Maybe she was learning her way around the little town already. She must have paid better attention to the roads than she thought.

She parked on the street in front of Scott's house to not block him in. The neighborhood was quiet. *I hope he's awake.*

She looped her camera case over her shoulder then walked up the steep driveway to the side porch door. She stood there for a long moment, pondering her decision to come. It was early, but Scott had said he liked to get on the water just after sunrise. After wiping her sweaty palms on her jeans, she tapped on the screen door. She waited a two-count, and then turned to leave, regretting the trip over.

Scott opened the door. "I thought I heard something."

"Oh. Yeah. I didn't wake you, did I?"

"No. I'm up, dressed. Come on in."

She paused in the doorway. "Is the invitation still open? I mean, you said last night that you might go—"

"Yes, I was just getting ready to head down to the boathouse," Scott said. "I'm glad you came. Did you bring a jacket? It's cooler on the water."

"No," Kasey said, feeling stupid. "I didn't think about that."

A hooded sweatshirt hung on the hook next to the door. "Here, take this along just in case."

"Thanks." Kasey lifted a thermos. "I did bring coffee, though."

"Ahh, you *do* have your priorities straight." He smiled. "That was thoughtful. I'm ready. Are you?" He started to lead the way, then turned back. "Are you crying?"

She dropped her hands to her sides. "I'm sorry. I'm so tired. I feel wired, and I'm just a bundle of raw emotions. I shouldn't have come."

He put his hands on her shoulders, then hugged her to him. "It's okay. You have every right to be a basket case. It's exactly why you should call on your friends."

She cried into his shirt, then backed away. "The time is dragging by, and today is probably going to be even worse than yesterday. I just didn't know what to do with myself. I'm sorry." She sniffed and wiped her face with her sleeve.

"It's okay. I talked to my friend last night. We can look at the evidence from the crash site tomorrow. He'll have it all worked out for us, so we've got that to look forward to."

"You barely know me and you've done so much." Kasey cleared her throat and nervously ran her hand through her hair.

"I know. That's how we heroes roll." He dipped

a little to look her in the eye. "Not even a little smile at that?"

She smiled and let out a sigh.

He wiped a tear from her cheek. "Let's make the best of today. They say water relaxes you."

"It better be a huge-ass river then, because I'm about as far from relaxed as you can get."

Scott smiled. "I think it's big enough. Come on." He pulled the door behind him and guided her toward the dock. They stopped in the boathouse to pick up the gear. Scott selected fishing poles from a rack while Kasey watched Maggie's family frolic in the kiddy pool. The puppies snarled and yapped, still clumsy. They rolled over each other as they wrestled. Maggie split up a couple of sibling fights and nudged the puppies underneath her.

"She's such a good mother," Kasey said as she watched them, her back to Scott.

Scott pulled down another rod, and then went to the refrigerator to get some bait. "She should be. It's her fourth litter."

He closed the refrigerator and, when he turned, he saw Kasey's shoulders rising and falling. He put down his stuff, walked to her side, and wrapped his arms around her.

"I was a good mother," she said softly.

"I'm sure you're a wonderful mother, Kasey." He put his hand behind her head and rocked her in his arms. "Shhh, it's okay." He rested his chin on the top of her head. "You're going to have Jake back soon. We're getting close."

She nodded against his chest. "I know."

He looked into her eyes. "Repeat after me. Jake is coming home."

"Jake is coming home." Her words were tight, her voice raspy from crying.

"I know it in my heart." He tapped her chest. "And in my mind." He tapped on her forehead.

"I know it in my heart and mind," she repeated.

"I'll pray for his safe return, and know that God will bring him home."

"I pray for his safe return. God will bring him home," she said, squeaking out the last few words, her voice trembling.

"And in the meantime, Scott is really hot and such a great guy. How could I go wrong?"

She laughed and punched him in the gut playfully.

He feigned injury and let out a hearty laugh. "Can't blame a guy for trying. You okay?"

She nodded. "Yeah. For now." She shook her head. "You're not funny."

"Yes, I am. Come on, admit it. And by the way, tears don't scare me away. So just let them fall. They make your eyes sparkle pretty, anyway."

And one did fall, right down her cheek to her lips.

"Let's go." He tugged on her sleeve. "The fish are waiting on us."

Chapter Thirty

Scott loaded the fishing gear, then steadied Kasey as she crossed from the dock into the glittery boat and settled into the red-and-white leather seat.

"Am I going to be scared? You aren't going to go real fast, are you?"

"This isn't a speedboat. It's a fishing boat."

"It's got a huge motor." She cast him a suspicious glance.

"Relax, that's just for tournament speed. We're just going to chill. Today is all about relaxing." He tossed her a hat and she tugged it down on her head.

She leaned back and prepared for the ride. He used the quiet trolling motor until they got out to open water, then he started the big engine. As they paraded slowly along the river, the birds seemed to chirp a hello as they cruised by, and the ripples the boat splashed against the shoreline sounded like applause.

"I'm going to take you to my favorite cove." He steered the boat toward the center of the river that widened, then snaked off down small tributaries left and right. In some places, Spanish moss hung soft and gray from the winter trees. A moment later, they slowed. He shut down the noisy motor, letting the boat drift along, as they floated into the prettiest cove Kasey had ever seen. Scott put on a ball cap with a fishing logo on it and started shuffling through the gear.

"This is pretty secluded," she said looking around.

"It's my favorite fishing hole. I've never shared this location with anyone." He held out his pinky. "Pinky swear that it's our secret."

"Or what?" she challenged.

"Or I'll call Deputy Dan."

She wrapped her pinky around his and winked. "Your secret is safe with me. Heck, I can barely get to your house. I know I couldn't find my way down a river to a clump of trees." That splash along the shore had made her wonder. "There aren't gators out here are there?"

"Uh, no. No gators."

She relaxed a little.

"Turtles, muskrats, birds, fish—that's about all you'll see out here. No snakes this time of year to speak of."

"Good. I wouldn't want to be gator bait."

"No, that wouldn't be good. But speaking of bait, let's get these hooks baited and cast a few."

"I'm going to need a refresher course," she said as she picked through dozens of lures and tackle. She picked up one of the rubber worms. It reminded her of the day Nick proposed. She'd been pregnant with Jake then.

Scott rigged shiny spoons and bright jigs on their lines, then threaded worms on the hooks. He handed her a rod and demonstrated a cast. She watched in earnest, but when she tried her first cast, the lure clanked in the boat right next to her feet. "I'm rusty."

"Try again."

She did, but with the same results.

"You're not rusty. You suck." Scott tugged on his ball cap. "Here, let me help you out." He stepped up behind her, held his hands over hers on the rod, and guided her through the motions. "See. Nice and easy. Up and back, and then release when you have it right about . . . here."

"Oh. It's way easier with you helping me."

"There's more to fishing than just getting in the boat."

"Let me try."

"Sure. Just reel it in by pushing this button and then spinning this." He stepped back and let her cast. "Perfect. You're a natural." Scott tugged his hat and reeled in his own line to recast.

Kasey smiled, feeling suddenly hopeful that she could be good at this sport. Once she had the lure reeled back in, she went through the motions and tried a cast. "Crap."

"You doing all right back there?" Scott spun around.

"Well . . ." She bit her bottom lip and looked skyward. "Unless there are any treefish, I don't

302

think I'm going to catch much." She tugged on the line, but it didn't budge.

"You're snagged."

"Yep. A little more decoration for my lure. Like camouflage."

"Happens to the best of us." He stepped over and took the pole from her. He worked the rod back and forth and, by some miracle or maybe years of practice, he was able to tug the bright gear out of the tree.

She cheered and clapped as the limb-bedazzled line splashed in the water.

Scott squinted. "I don't want to sound like a pill. But I think you probably just scared all the fish out of my favorite fishing hole with all that noise."

She clamped her hands over her mouth. "Oh. Sorry. I knew that. You're supposed to be quiet when you're fishing, huh?"

"Yep." He didn't look mad, but she figured he wasn't thrilled about relocating. He moved toward the trolling motor, started it, and began inching through the water.

"Sorry."

"No problem. I hadn't caught anything anyway. It was time to move."

"I'll be quiet in the next spot."

"Somehow, I doubt that."

Kasey didn't catch a single fish, but Scott caught at least half a dozen.

She enjoyed the day even though she didn't catch anything. Scott didn't make her bait her own hook and, luckily for her, he was a master at untangling her line. She'd snagged it in at least four trees.

"Ready to head back?" he asked.

"Sure. If you are." She removed her hat and fluffed her bangs. "Scott?"

"Yeah."

"Thank you for being supportive, and thanks for today, too."

He nodded. "I love being the hero."

"It fits you well," she teased. "But seriously, thanks for believing me."

"I wouldn't doubt a mother's intuition." He stepped away from the motor and sat next to her. "A mother's bond, her connection to her child. It's real."

Kasey knew exactly what he meant. "Thanks for sharing your secret fishing hole. I wouldn't have made it through the day alone."

"Wanna drive?"

"I bet I'm a better boat driver than a fisherman."

"Well, that's not saying much." Scott started the motor, and Kasey moved into the driver's seat. She maneuvered according to his directions, guiding the boat back down the river to his dock.

The closer she got to the dock, the more panicky she became. "You better take over so I don't wreck us," she called to him.

"You're doing fine."

"I don't know how to stop." She looked around. "There's not a brake on this thing."

Scott came to her side, leaned over her, and took the controls. He eased back on the throttle. He was so close to her she felt his breath whisper against her neck. When the boat neared the dock, he killed the motor and let it drift the rest of the way. He stood and leaped from the boat to the dock, then wrapped a line around one of the pilings.

Comfortable on the small boat now, Kasey chose not to wait for Scott's assistance to disembark. She leaped from the boat, but missed the dock completely.

She screamed as she hit the water with a splash. Maggie came running out of the boathouse barking. Scott stood wide-eyed for a moment as she flailed, reaching for the pilings, pushing her bangs out of her face and spitting water.

She could tell he was stifling a laugh. "It's not funny."

"Got a little cocky, didn't ya?"

"Shut up and help me out." She held on to the dock with one hand and reached the other toward him. He took her hand. She tried to pull him in the frigid water with her.

He gave her a warning look. "You want help or not?"

"Uncle." She blinked her big brown eyes, trying to look as innocent as possible.

He helped her out of the water and took her right into his arms. Water splashed against him, getting him almost as wet as she was. "You were going to pull me into the water, weren't you?"

She giggled but shook her head, furrowing her brow as if the idea had never entered her mind.

He hitched her up and cradled her in his arms, his nose to hers. "Really now. I think you better confess."

"Never."

He leaned in and caught her lip. Not once but twice, and then his mouth opened, warm and gentle against hers. Her lashes batted against his cheeks, then she kissed him back, relaxing into his arms. He set her on her feet, but their kiss didn't abate. They melted into one another. Tender kisses turned hungry, and the chill in the air was of no concern. Feeling safe, Kasey let herself become lost in his kisses. In his arms, there was hope. He kissed her again. Slowly and gently, without hurry.

Chapter Thirty-One

Scott opened his eyes, looking into Kasey's. "You're beautiful."

"I can't believe I just did that."

"It's not against the law." He kissed her forehead.

"Thank goodness. I wouldn't want to go to jail again. They don't feed you very well in there." She shivered.

"You're cold." He held her close again.

"I feel kind of funny."

"Don't. It felt right to me." He held her gaze.

She closed her eyes.

"It was just a kiss."

But it was more than that. Her heart still pounded from his touch.

"Come on." He took her hand. "Do you still want to cook up our catch of the day?"

"I think I want to go home," she said. "Would you mind?"

Scott put a warm palm to her cheek. "I didn't mean to rush you."

She pushed her wet hair over her shoulder. "No. It's not your fault. It's me. I just wasn't expecting it."

He laughed. "That's because it wasn't planned. Come on, let's release these little guys." He dumped the fish back into the water, and they floated, stunned for a second, then wriggled away.

She stood there dripping wet, watching the fish swim away. Freedom.

He handed Kasey her camera bag then hooked his arm around her waist, and guided her to the boathouse. After he'd wiped down the rods and put them back in the rack, he walked over to the corner of the boathouse and scooped up the little yellow puppy. It wiggled in his arms as he walked to Kasey.

"Here. She needs some love."

"They are so playful." She snuggled the puppy. "She is the cutest one. She's feisty, too."

"Like someone else I know."

"I'll take that as a compliment." She put the puppy down.

The yellow lab sat and looked up at Kasey, her head tilted.

"Look. She even poses for me." Kasey took out her camera and snapped a digital photo. "She is just too sweet. Have you named her?"

"No, Maggie said there were too many for her to name."

"What's your name, my little friend?" Kasey picked up the puppy and took her back to the pool with the others. Kasey took another picture, then called over her shoulder to Scott. "She's a camera ham. How about naming her Shutterbug?"

He walked up behind her and rested his hand on her hip.

"What do you think about being called Shutterbug?" he asked the puppy, who sank back on her haunches, then leaped, barking.

"I think she likes it." The puppy climbed the side of the slippery pool, trying to get back to Kasey. Her little paws hung over the edge, her feet just climbing in place.

"Shutterbug it is." Kasey snapped another picture.

"Let's head on up to the house," Scott said as he walked toward the door. Then he stopped and went back and got the puppy. "Come on Shutterbug, why don't you come up to the house with us for a while?" Scott handed the puppy to Kasey.

"Maggie won't mind?"

"Are you kidding? Consider it a favor. They're ready to be weaned, anyway. I'll take her back down to her momma in a little while."

"Come on, Shutterbug." Kasey hitched the puppy up into her arms.

Scott patted the dog's head. "There's nothing like puppy breath to make you feel good."

"Maybe I need the whole litter," she teased.

"Hey, whatever it takes. A whole river. A whole puddle of puppies. Whatever will help, I'll make it happen."

They climbed the stairs from the boathouse to the back yard, then followed the sidewalk to the deck.

"You can park your butt right in the middle of the pool with Maggie if it will make you feel better."

Scott opened the sliding glass door, went inside and flipped on the lights in the kitchen. Kasey put Shutterbug down so the puppy could explore.

"Let's get you dry before you go home," he said.

"I'll be okay."

"But the leather interior of your car may not. Come on. It won't take long to toss your clothes in the dryer and be done with it. I'll get you some sweats to put on."

She looked reluctant, but she shrugged and nodded.

"Great." He disappeared down the hall, and came back with a brown sweatshirt with SHERIFF written across the front, and a pair of sweat pants. "They'll be huge on you, but they're dry."

"Thanks. These will be fine." She changed in the bathroom and came out with her pile of wet clothes. "Where's the dryer?" she asked as she stepped back into the kitchen.

He smiled at the sight of her bare feet. Her bright pink painted toenails looked like Skittles. He tried to ignore the distraction. "Right here off the kitchen." He pointed the way. "There's a laundry room and door out to the deck that way."

He was waiting by the counter when she walked back into the kitchen. "Here. Hope you like marshmallows." He handed her a steaming mug of hot chocolate.

"Of course." She took a sip and came up with a frothy marshmallow moustache. "The best part." She ran her tongue across her top lip.

Scott grabbed a roll of paper towels and Shutterbug. "You never know when they are going to leak."

Kasey gave him a funny look. "Oh, you mean the puppy."

"Let's go sit in the living room while your clothes dry."

Scott sat on the couch and let Shutterbug run wild across the hard wood floor. She had trouble keeping all four feet under her. Each time she slipped, she'd turn, snarl and yap—not realizing she was causing herself to slip.

Kasey sat on the floor and drummed her fingernails on the hardwood. Shutterbug turned and raced toward her.

Being with Scott was less awkward with the distraction of Shutterbug.

Scott stretched out on the couch on his stomach and reached out his arm, sweeping his hand across the floor. Shutterbug ran between him and Kasey until the dryer beeped, sending her scurrying under the end table, whimpering.

"Ohhhh. That was pitiful," she said.

Scott laughed. He had a great laugh. Deep and real.

"Not so ferocious now, are you?" he said to the cowering puppy.

Kasey crawled over and coaxed Shutterbug out from under the table.

"Ooops." Scott tossed the roll of paper towels to

Kasey. "Looks like we scared the pee out of her."

"It was an accident." Kasey wiped up the mess. Shutterbug followed her into the kitchen where Kasey tossed the paper towels into the trash and washed her hands, then took her clothes from the dryer.

Kasey nearly tripped over Shutterbug when she turned around. "Watch out, girl." Kasey walked through the living room to the bathroom. When she closed the door, Shutterbug whimpered from the other side.

"You're breaking her heart," Scott yelled.

"I hear her," Kasey called, then screamed and ran from the bathroom with her jeans and bra on, her shirt held up to cover her.

Chapter Thirty-Two

"What's the matter? Are you hurt?" Scott said.

Kasey slammed into him just outside the bathroom door. "Look. I heard something. And then—" She was frantic, looking behind her, then back to Scott, not making any sense. "And it clanked, and I looked. A giant—there's a snapping turtle in your tub!"

"Oh. That. You scared the heck out of me."

"I'm serious. Go look."

"That's Turtle Mike."

"Who? What? You knew there was an animal in

the bathroom, and you just let me go in there? He could have bitten my toes off."

"Turtle Mike isn't dangerous. He's not a snapper—just a big old box turtle. He wouldn't hurt a fly. Okay, he *would* eat a fly, but he won't hurt *you*."

"What's it . . . he . . . whatever . . . doing in your bathroom?"

"He lives there. My nephew found him last summer. He loves that turtle."

"How do you bathe?"

"I have a shower in the other bathroom, but frankly I shower more often at the station or the gym. Tubs are for girls . . . and turtles."

"All-righty then. I guess that makes perfect sense. *If* you're a guy." She let out a breath. "Scared the heck out of me."

"Sorry. I don't even think much about him anymore except to feed him each day. He's usually pretty quiet."

"Yeah, well he scared about four years off my life." Kasey turned her back to Scott and pulled her shirt over her head. "It's never a dull moment with you, is it?"

Shutterbug ran up behind Scott.

"That's a compliment, right?" Scott picked up Shutterbug and shoved the puppy into Kasey's arms. "Forgive us?"

"Don't you blame that thing on Shutterbug. She's traumatized, too."

"Sorry." Scott closed the bathroom door. "You can use the other bathroom from now on. Will you stay?"

She didn't say no, but he could see the wheels turning. "We want you to stay." He took Shutterbug from her and held the puppy next to his cheek. They both panted. "Please?"

"We already let the dinner swim away," she said.

"I can cook something else. It'll give me a chance to impress you with my culinary skills again." Shutterbug licked Kasey's nose.

"How can you say no to that?" he asked.

"This is moving kind of fast." She ran her hand through her hair. "I just don't want to mess up our friendship by starting something I can't finish. I—"

"Don't. Let's just take it a day at a time. No promises. Our focus is just getting through each day, and finding Jake."

She patted Shutterbug on the head.

"That's it, Kasey. I promise."

He stooped a little to get eye-to-eye with her and smiled. "And Shutterbug. We have to keep Shutterbug happy, too."

She smiled a little smile.

He put his arm around her shoulders, and they walked back into the living room.

Kasey gave him a sidelong glance as they sat down. "We couldn't disappoint Shutterbug, and I

314

am anxious to see if you can cook something else besides steaks on the grill."

"Oh, you'll be impressed."

She raised a brow. "Impress away."

Shutterbug barked.

"Shutterbug has her doubts," Kasey said.

"I think she's just hungry. Let's take her back to Maggie and feed them. Then I'll work my magic on something wonderful for you."

Kasey looked worried.

She has to feel the attraction. I sure as hell can't deny it. "Dinner." He rolled his eyes. "I mean dinner."

Scott made a salad and stuffed pork chops for dinner. Kasey wiped her mouth and sat back from the table after eating every bite. "I'm going to tell you right now, I am *never* cooking for you. I'm a bad cook on my own, but compared to you . . . Well, there is no comparison."

"It can't be that bad."

"Trust me. You don't want to find out."

Scott cleared the dishes and stacked them in the dishwasher. Then he and Kasey went back into the living room where Scott channel-surfed until he found a movie they could watch.

"I probably ought to head home," she said.

"Why don't you stay here? Or I can drive you home, then come back and pick you up in the morning to go to the police department in

315

Southampton County. You haven't slept. You don't need to be behind the wheel."

"No. Don't be silly. You don't have to do that."

Scott cocked a brow. "We're adults, and I do have a guest room."

She sat up. "The guest room?"

"Sure."

She relaxed back into his arms. "Okay. I *am* kind of comfy. Can I borrow the sweats to sleep in?"

"Anything you want."

She fell asleep in his arms, still in her clothes, within the hour. He finished watching the movie and then turned off the television.

Kasey didn't stir. She had to be exhausted. He wrapped his arms around her and snuggled his chin into the nook of her shoulder. That's where they stayed, there on the couch, all night.

Scott held Kasey in his arms. The sun hadn't been up long, but his body clock had tripped about fifteen minutes ago.

Kasey stirred.

"Good morning," whispered Scott, then kissed her hair. "Did you sleep well?"

She twisted to look up at him. "I did. Thank you."

"How are you feeling today? Fresh air and good sleep make you feel a little stronger?"

She nodded. "Yeah. Thanks."

"Repeat after me," he said. "Jake is coming home. I know it in my heart and mind."

She repeated each word and took his hand in hers.

He rubbed his thumb over the top of her hand. "We pray for his safe return and know that God will bring him home."

"We pray for his safe return and know that God will bring him home," she said, followed by a deep breath. "And with you here to help me, how could I go wrong?"

"I wasn't going to say that," he teased.

"But I mean it. Thanks, Scott."

He squeezed her tight. "Are you ready for some coffee?"

"Don't move. I can't cook, but I make a mean cup of coffee." She stood and stretched her arms over her head. "Last night is the first whole night's sleep I've had in a while. Thanks for yesterday."

"I had a nice day, too." He swatted at her butt with a throw pillow as she headed out of the room.

She went into the kitchen, then leaned back into the room. "Where's the coffee?"

"In the cabinet right above the coffeepot."

"Got it," she said. "Don't move."

He plopped back on the couch, waiting.

A few minutes later Kasey walked in carrying a mug in each hand. "Here you go."

He took a sip of the coffee. "You're right. Perfect."

"What time are we going to the station?" she asked.

"I told them we'd be there around eight-thirty."

"Good. We've got some time. I'm going to run down to the boathouse and see the puppies while you shower and get ready. Is that okay?"

"Sure. And hey, while you're down there, will you feed Maggie and put a bowl of the soft food out for the puppies?"

Kasey grabbed his jacket from the hook next to the door. "You got it."

At the station, Kasey and Scott followed their escort to a big room with only a table in it, and six large boxes of files and evidence from the case.

"Goodness gracious. Where do we start?" Kasey looked at the numbered boxes stacked on the floor.

"Systematic approach. Let's start with number one," Scott said. "You review the log, and I'll look over the items. Then we'll switch."

Kasey opened the box. The summary sheet was long, with the bagged evidence neatly lined up in the box. Scott reviewed the contents of each bag, placing a cardboard divider in its place to insure they maintained the logged order.

After three tedious hours, they'd reviewed the content of two boxes. Even though the items were catalogued, going through them was still a mind-numbing exercise. The original investigative team had spent weeks examining the evidence, piece-by-piece, cataloging and tagging every little snippet they'd collected before Hurricane Ernesto hit.

Scott ordered lunch in so they wouldn't have to stop the review. They continued to work through the junk. That's what most of it was: Trash, wrappers, coins, cigarette butts, even a miniature American flag, but nothing that yielded any ah-ha moments.

Kasey put the last plastic bag back in box three. "That's it," she said.

"I'd hoped maybe something would trigger a thought or an idea, or make the connection to Libby Braddock. It was worth a try." Scott rubbed his hand across the back of his neck. "I'm sorry to have gotten your hopes up."

She wrapped her hands around his arm. "Don't say that. Anything that might help is worth it. Thank you."

They signed the return forms to check the boxes in with the clerk at the evidence desk. They'd made a copy of the logs for Scott to take with him. He signed for those, too.

Scott pulled in front of his house and put the car in park. Kasey jumped out, ran to her car and pulled out into the street in front of him so he could follow her home. He'd insisted.

When they got to her house, she walked to his truck. "Are you going to come in?"

"I didn't want to crowd you. Thought you might need some time to yourself."

She shook her head. "No, I'd like you to come in."

He shut off the engine and followed her to the door.

"Looks like you had a delivery." He nodded toward a large box on the porch.

"I wonder what that is? I'm not expecting anything." She stooped down to read the return address. She shrugged. "I have no idea."

Scott lifted the box with a grunt. "Whatever it is, it's heavy."

She unlocked the door, and he followed her inside. "Just set it over there in the living room. Let's see what it is."

He placed the box on the floor and Kasey came out of the kitchen with a pair of scissors. She sliced through the tape and opened the box. There was a light blue envelope with her name printed on the front, on top of a stack of books.

"These are the Cody Tuggle tour books." The cover of the coffee-table–size picture book was glossy. She ran her hand across the familiar picture. "I had no idea they were sending me a whole box of them." She flipped one open and thumbed through the pages. "Gosh, it looks great."

She handed him a copy.

"You took all these pictures?"

"Sure did." She moved next to him and pointed to a photograph. "I was on the catwalk over the audience when I took that one. It was amazing. I could feel the heat, their energy. I've never felt anything like it before."

"You sure didn't seem like such a daredevil yesterday!"

She laughed. "It was pretty cool. When I get in the zone behind that lens I'm much braver."

"Talented, too." He turned the pages, glancing at picture after picture of Cody, the band and fans. He flipped back to the first pages. "Hey, this one is autographed for you."

"Let me see." She took the book and read the inscription. "That was so sweet."

"Sounds like a pretty friendly note from a client," Scott said. Even a little jealous, though he had no right to be.

"We spent a lot of time together on tour. It was right after the accident. He's a good friend."

"What's that mean in the note about seeing you in Texas?"

"I didn't tell you about the cookbook? We're doing a barbecue coffee-table book. I'm going to shoot his team cooking at an annual BBQ cook-off this fall."

"So you're going to Texas?"

"Yep. We signed a contract for it a few months ago."

Why do I always fall for the city girls? "So, when do you jet-set off?"

"That's not until Labor Day weekend."

"I sure can't compete with a guy like that," Scott said, tossing the book on the coffee table. He regretted his words as soon as they came out of his mouth.

"This isn't a competition, and I'm no prize. And even if I were available, I already told you, Cody is just a friend."

"You're right. I was out of line," Scott said. "How about I make you some tea while you go through that stuff."

"That sounds good." Kasey sat on the floor and flipped through the book.

Scott filled a mug with water and microwaved it for Kasey's tea, then started opening drawers, looking for a spoon. Just after he closed the drawer next to the stove, he paused and re-opened it. Amidst the batteries, stamps, paperclips and sticky notes in the junk drawer, there were a dozen butterscotch candies and a couple of empty wrappers. He picked up one of the candies and held it in his hand, then stuffed it into his pocket. He opened the next drawer and retrieved a spoon just as the microwave signaled. He dropped the tea bag into the hot water, stirred in a teaspoon of sugar, then grabbed his beer and went back into the living room.

Kasey had pushed the box of books to the corner

of the room. She sat on the couch, going through yesterday's mail.

"Here you go," he said, handing her the mug. "What are you going to do tomorrow? Any plans?"

Kasey placed the hot mug on the table beside her. "I was just thinking about that. Busy is the best thing I can do, besides pray; so I think I'm going to drive to Virginia Beach and visit my grandmother. I'm way overdue."

"That sounds like a good idea."

"I'll have my cell. You'll call me if you hear anything, right?"

"You can count on it," he said. "I'm heading home. I've got a busy day tomorrow."

"Thanks for everything." She walked him to the door and gave him a hug, then watched as he left. *Am I wishing you would stay?*

The phone rang, shattering the moment. She ran to answer it before the call went to voice mail.

"Did you get the box? The book is awesome," Cody said.

"I did. I know. I was just looking at it."

"It's going to be a hit, but enough about that. I wanted to see how you're doing."

"Some days are better than others. We're still looking—and waiting."

"The wait won't be as long as it has been."

"Thanks to you."

"That's what friends do: help each other," Cody said. "Speaking of which. I have a favor to ask."

"Sure. Anything. What's up?"

"I told you about Lou, remember?"

"Yep. You saw her?"

"It was like old times. The chemistry, everything."

"Cody, that's great."

"I know. We're going to give things a try. Thanks so much for the lecture. I never would have tried to contact her if it hadn't been for you."

"I'm so excited for you."

"Lou and I've already wasted too much time. So here's the favor part."

"Ask already, would ya?"

"I'm flying in to see her. Would you mind if she meets me at your place?"

"Here?"

"Yeah. I can land at the Greensville-Emporia strip. It's secluded out there. No paparazzi or people waiting for flights. No one to start rumors. I promise we won't impose long. I'd like you to meet her."

"I'd love that. When?"

"It's short notice." Cody cleared his throat. "If it's not a good time, just say no. Tomorrow, if you can swing it. If not, don't sweat it. I can have her wait for me there at the airport. I just thought it would be nicer this way."

"I'm glad you thought of me. No problem at all. It's the least I could do for you. Do you need me to pick you up at the airport?" Kasey's mood lifted. It would be good to see him again.

"I'll call you and let you know when we have an ETA."

"Y'all are welcome to stay here overnight if you need to, depending on how the schedule works out."

"That would be great. You won't tell anyone about us coming into town, will you?"

"No way. I've seen first-hand what the press does with news about you. I won't tell a soul."

Chapter Thirty-Three

The next morning Kasey got up early to get ready for the drive to Virginia Beach. Flat gray clouds sprawled across the sky. The forty-percent chance of scattered showers looked more like the chance of a dark, stormy day. But she didn't let that stop her from moving forward.

She put on a pair of khaki's and a black top. Then, she took off the black shirt and tossed it on the bed. She went back into the closet, picked out a hot pink sweater and slipped it on. Pleased with the switch, she turned and looked at herself in the mirror. *The brighter the better. Anything to help keep my mood in check.*

She leaned closer to the mirror and put on some plum crazy lip color, smacked her lips, and then hit the road.

Positive thoughts. Only positive thoughts.

Instead of calling ahead to set up time with her grandmother, she decided she'd just take things at her own pace.

Heading east on Route 58, she had an idea as she neared Main Street. She flipped her blinker on and turned right. Parallel parking had never been her forte, but that's all they did in this part of town. She cruised to the end of the block until she found an opening with two spots in front of the bakery—she could negotiate her tiny car to the curb there, for sure. Floral & Hardy was a short walk up the block.

This was her first time in the flower shop, though the name had stuck with her since the day she met Chaz Huckaby. His shop was right across the street.

"Can I help you?" asked the young man behind the counter.

"Yes. By the way, I love the name of your shop."

"Thanks. I'm Ted Hardy. You must be new around here."

"I am. I need an arrangement. Do you have any pre-made?" she asked.

The young man hurried around the counter and led her to the glass front refrigerators on the other side of the store. "Heavens, yes. What's the occasion?"

"Not an occasion. I wanted to put something graveside." She shook her bangs away from her eyes. "My husband."

He slumped and put his hand on her arm. "I'm sorry. Has it been long?"

"Not even a year."

"Oh, my golly. I have just the thing." He slapped the refrigerator door shut. "You don't want something fresh. The deer will just gobble it up or it will wilt and look like crap in a few days. Follow me."

He whisked behind the counter. "Come on, you can come back here. I was just finishing this."

She stepped behind the counter and into the back room. It looked like a ribbon-and-flower truck had blown up in there. Snippets of leaves and flowers, ribbon, and lace littered the table.

Ted turned around and held up a gorgeous arrangement. "Tah-*dah!* What do you think?"

"It's perfect." Almost burgundy–colored roses, gold mums and white carnations fanned out among tons of greenery. "Very masculine. I love it."

"It needs a ribbon. What color? No, wait. What was your husband like?" His mouth pursed, as he seemed to size her up, then he gave her a knowing look. "Outdoorsy fellow. Handsome, too, I bet."

"Yes. That's Nick. Very outdoorsy. Farmer, hunter, the whole thing."

Ted lifted his shoulders and grinned. "I have something perfect."

He turned his back to her. All she could see were his arms flying and scissors snipping. When he spun around, he'd woven a camouflage ribbon through the arrangement and tied a beautiful bow at the bottom.

Kasey's jaw dropped. "It *is* perfect. Better than I ever could have imagined."

"Right here," he said, tapping a finger to his cheek.

She ran to his side and kissed him on the cheek.

"That's what Teddy here lives for. People squealing over flowers."

"Thanks," Kasey said.

She paid Teddy, then carried the arrangement to the car. She nestled it in the floorboard so it wouldn't get smooshed during the ride. The smell from the bakery made her stomach growl. No wonder. She hadn't eaten since . . . well, she wasn't sure.

She got back out of the car. The smell almost made her mouth water as she opened the door and went inside.

"Good morning, young lady," a portly man in a white t-shirt and work pants covered by a brightly colored apron waved her to the counter.

Kasey surveyed the baked goods in the case. "What do you recommend?"

He gave her a toothy grin. "I'm known for my cinnamon rolls and bear claws. Just took the bear claws out of the oven. They're still warm."

"That must be what smells so good. Give me two."

"You must be hungry."

"One for me, one for a friend."

"You're my kind of friend," he winked.

Kasey drove around the block and parked in front of the police station. She walked back to Scott's office. "How are you?"

"What a nice surprise." Scott pushed a stack of paperwork to the side.

"Are you busy?"

"Not too busy for you. I was just filling out paperwork to assign some security to the Indian Pow-Wow Festival next month."

"Sounds interesting."

"It is."

"Do you have an Indian name?"

He laughed. "No. Maybe I could be Fish-While-She-Talks? What do you think?"

"I think you're real funny. How about Bear Claw?"

"I like it. Sounds manly." He pretended to swipe the air with a claw.

"Hold up, tough guy. I meant this kind." She held up the waxy white bakery bag. "I brought you a bear claw. It's not a doughnut, but I figured it was close enough."

"You sure are in a good mood this morning." Scott leaned back in his chair.

"Feeling feisty. Ready to face the world today," Kasey said.

"Good," he smiled. "Where are you off to so early?"

"Heading to see Grem, so I better get going."

"Thanks for stopping by—and for the bad joke and good treat."

"Anytime." Suddenly feeling a little nervous, she grasped the leather strap of her purse as if it was a lifeline. "I appreciate everything you're doing—have done—for me."

"You'd be there for me, too." He got up and came around the desk. "I'll walk you to the door."

They walked outside, and he stood at the curb. "Drive safe," he called after her.

There wasn't much traffic on Route 58 this morning. Fields of just-harvested cotton lined the sides of the road. The white fibers that remained on the plants glistened like fresh snow. Nick used to tease that he could t-shirt the world with the waste cotton left over after harvest. He'd probably been right.

Kasey slowed down as she passed the accident site, but didn't stop.

A first.

There was nothing there for her anymore.

An hour later, she neared the little church in Pungo—her first stop. It had been too long since she'd been there. And until now, just too painful to return. Nick had gone to the church when he was a boy. She, Nick and Jake had attended there as a family—a Sunday ritual that ended with a late breakfast at the Farmer's Diner of pancakes and fresh eggs from the chickens the owner raised on his farm.

The last time Kasey had been here was the day Nick had been laid to rest.

She pulled into the parking lot, gravel crunching under her tires. The old building looked as serene as it always had, the cemetery grounds as well groomed as the finest golf courses.

She hadn't made a departure from the grace of God, but it was easy to feel betrayed, to place the blame of the anger and sorrow there. After all, Nick was a good man. How could it have been his time? How could something this heart-breaking be part of a grander plan—God's plan?

But now, she knew she was only cheating herself by being angry and staying away from church.

When Scott had mentioned the prayer list, her heart had melted. The warmth of that love, of faith, flowed through her. She pulled her keys from the ignition and sat with them in her lap, in no hurry.

Their wedding took place only a few short weeks after Nick's goofy proposal with the rubber fishing worm, and the church had been booked by another couple well in advance of that day. They hadn't wanted to wait, so they opted to be married at the farm.

It was hard to believe that was four years ago since they married.

So much had happened since then.

She got out of the car and walked up the steps to the tall doors of the church. Finding them unlocked, she ducked inside, and scanned the wide-open space of empty pews. So quiet. She tugged her cell phone out of her purse and turned it off. Although she was the only one in the sanctuary, she didn't feel alone.

Kasey inched her way down the center aisle, her hand gliding across the smooth wood back of each pew as she moved forward. With each step, she relived the Sunday mornings she, Nick and Jake had slipped into the third row on the left. Same place each week. Jake was always such a good baby, never a whimper out of him no matter how long the sermon ran.

She slid into the cool wooden pew, their pew, and took a hymnal from the rack. The corners of the book were fuzzy from the hands of so many over the years who held it, sang the same songs.

She closed her eyes, and for the first time in a long time, cleared her mind and opened her heart.

A sunbeam came through the arched stained glass window, shimmering along the top of the pew in front of her. She reached out and let it dance across her hand, then tipped her hand up and then grasped the light, holding the rainbow.

After some quiet reflection, she went out the side door, and got the flower arrangement from her car. Nick was buried not too far from the church, near a huge oak. Strong, like he had been. The tree limbs rustled in the breeze. Everything had been lush and green last summer, yet looked different this time of year. As she walked through the small cemetery, she read the headstones of generations of past church members. Some young, some old, some recently passed, some gone so long that she could barely read the engraving on the worn stone anymore.

The marble-arched headstone read:

NICHOLAS JACOB ROLLY ~ Beloved Husband ~ Father ~ Friend.

Von had arranged all of it, even decided on the inscription. It had been something she couldn't do, probably couldn't do it now either. Kasey placed the flowers at the base of the headstone, then knelt, skimming her fingers over the word *Beloved*. Her heart swelled.

"Oh, Nick. I still miss you every day. Is talking to you here any different than talking to you like I do every day? I wish I knew that you heard me, that you knew."

She hugged herself. "Jake's been missing since the accident. Everyone believed he was dead, but I knew he was alive. I felt it. You knew, too, didn't you? Oh Nick. I've needed you so much. You two are the best things in my life."

She sat in the grass. "We're so close to bringing Jake home."

The sun broke through the clouds, and Kasey tipped her face to the warmth.

"Coming here has been impossible," Kasey said. "Too final. Even now it tears my heart to face that you're gone. I'll always love you."

She bit her bottom lip. "I messed up. I should have put my faith in God to bring Jake back, but instead I've been cursing him for taking you away. For taking Jake, too. I've been so angry and sad. Selfish. You would've never been that way. You always knew what to do."

She pulled a tissue from her pocket, then wiped her nose. "You kept me balanced—made me a better person. Oh, Nick. Help me get it together.

"The house is perfect. You thought of everything. Everything we ever dreamed of right down to the darkroom and the cubbyholes in my workspace, the color of Jake's room, you knew it would be perfect.

"I want to be ready, to be the best mom to our son. He's coming home soon. I'm going to bring him home and make the surprise house the home you wanted it to be."

Closing her eyes, she sniffled, and then prayed for the strength, the help, the way, to make things right.

She stood. Feeling better, stronger.

"You're always in my heart." She looked heavenward.

Her legs felt like rubber bands as she walked back to her car.

Inside the car, she stretched to look in the rearview mirror. She dabbed away the makeup the tears had smeared under her eyes. She felt a renewed strength and focus.

Even a visit to Grem didn't seem too ominous a task now.

Chapter Thirty-Four

Scott sat at his desk going over paperwork. His cell phone rang and he answered without looking at the caller ID, hoping it was Kasey. "Scott Calvin here."

"Scott? It's Von."

"Hey, man. What's up?" Scott signed a report and put a stack of papers back on top of his inbox.

"We just got a hit on Libby Braddock's credit card. She just checked in at the Holiday Inn Express there in Emporia."

"You're kidding." Scott scribbled the information on a pad by his phone. "We're on it." Scott didn't even say goodbye. He hung up, grabbed his keys and ran for his car.

Not wasting a moment, he keyed the mic on his two-way radio and called out orders to Dispatch.

"I need you to call the front desk of the Holiday Inn Express on Main. I need the room number for a guest who just checked in. Libby Braddock. She's under suspicion for kidnapping. I'll be there in three minutes. Have Dan Taylor back me up. No lights."

"Ten-four," said the dispatcher, and then she repeated back the request.

Scott hit his lights and sounded the siren to get through the light at Main and Route 58, then turned them off again. He couldn't take a chance on spooking Libby Braddock. Arriving at the hotel, Scott identified the black Nissan that they had been looking for, parked right in front. The tag matched the plate they had on report.

He blocked the car with his, then jumped out of the cruiser.

The manager of the hotel ran out to meet him. "Angie just called. That lady is in room 118. Follow me."

"Was she alone?"

"I didn't see anyone with her."

Scott nodded and followed the manager back into the building.

"She just checked in," the manager said.

Just past the elevators, the manager pointed across the hall to the room. Scott approached the door with his hand on his gun. He knocked on the door. "Libby Braddock. It's the police," he announced.

An older dark-haired woman answered the door. "Is something wrong?" she asked, holding on to the edge of the door.

"Libby Braddock?"

"Yes."

Scott flashed his badge, pushed the door open and walked inside.

"What's going on?" She backed against the wall and watched as Scott scanned the room and checked the bathroom.

"Where's the boy?" he asked.

She looked dumbstruck, but recovered quickly. "I'm traveling alone."

"I know you left Leighsboro, North Carolina four days ago with Jake. Where is he now?"

She pressed her lips so tight the skin whitened around her mouth.

"I'm going to ask you again. Where's the boy?"

She looked away, fidgeting.

"Fine. We can discuss his whereabouts down at the station." Scott cuffed her and escorted her to his car.

"My purse. My stuff." Panic rose in her voice.

"We'll take care of that."

Deputy Dan hustled through the lobby as Scott walked through with Libby Braddock. Scott transferred her into the deputy's care and went back to impound her possessions as evidence. He called Von as he carried Libby Braddock's one suitcase and the paper bag containing her purse to the car. "We've got her. But Jake's not with her."

Scott heard Von's fist hit something, probably the desk. He felt the same way.

A bitter edge filled Von's voice. "Damn it. How is she one step ahead of us every single time?"

"I don't know. She's not saying anything yet. Hasn't even admitted to knowing Jake. I'll keep you posted."

"Do you want me to call Kasey?" Von asked.

"No. I'll call her."

"I'm on my way."

"See you in a couple hours." Scott pulled onto the main road and dialed Kasey's cell phone. His call went directly to voice mail. "Kasey. It's Scott. I've got a lead. Call me."

He tossed the phone in the seat, his heart racing. *I've got to get Jake back to Kasey.*

Chapter Thirty-Five

By the time Kasey got to Grandma Emily's, it was mid-day.

"Knock-knock," Kasey called as she let herself in the front door. She put her purse on the table in the foyer.

Jeremy came out of the kitchen, drying his hands on a dishtowel.

"Hey. I tried to call you earlier." He met her

halfway down the hall and gave her a hug. "I was just getting ready to take your grandmother her lunch. Open-faced turkey sandwich. Want one?"

"Sounds great. I'm starved," she said, rubbing her stomach. "I must've been on my way when you called."

"I called your cell, too. Went straight to voice mail."

"Really? That doesn't—" Realization struck, and she nodded. "I must have forgotten to turn it back on after—Let me go do that."

Kasey went back to the foyer, got her phone and turned it on. The voice mail signal chimed. "Did you leave me a message?"

"Nope. I better get this lunch finished before the old woman barks."

Kasey typed in her password to retrieve the message as she followed him. "It smells so good in here."

Jeremy stirred the turkey gravy and popped thick slices of bread in the toaster.

"Two messages. Aren't I popular?" She pressed the button to listen to the first one.

Jeremy put a slice of toast on each plate. He took a knife from the magnetic cutlery strip, and began slicing the turkey, but then noticed the look on Kasey's face. "What?"

"The first message was from Von." She raised her hand to her heart and swallowed hard. "They've tracked down the woman who has Jake." She fumbled for the buttons on the phone to listen to the next message.

"What?" Jeremy asked. "Damn!" He'd sliced his forefinger wide open. Jeremy whipped around to the sink and ran his hand under the water. "Who? A woman?"

Kasey ran to his side. "Are you okay?" She reached for his hand and had a look. "Ouch, that's deep. You might need a stitch." She backed away and put her finger up as the next message played.

"That was Scott. I've got to get home."

"The sheriff?" He wrapped a paper towel around his finger. "Wait! Do you need me to come with you?"

Kasey ran to the door. "No. Tell Grem I'll call later."

She raced to her car, and spun tires as she sped down the driveway. In her rearview mirror, she saw Jeremy, watching from the door.

She gunned the engine and whipped around the corner. Her phone slid from the seat to the floorboard before she could catch it. She shook her bangs back and glanced to heaven.

"Nick. This is it. I know it!"

Chapter Thirty-Six

Libby Braddock sat alone in a small, windowless interrogation room while Scott filed the response to the APB and updated the system with her arrest. He called Von to apprise him of the situation.

"Yes!" Von shouted triumphantly. "Not a step ahead of us this time, was she? I'm almost there."

"I'm going in to question her now. I'll see you shortly."

Scott left his office and stopped in the small room adjacent to the interrogation room. From here, he could see her through the one-way glass. Middle-aged, the woman was colorless. No makeup, except for the dark pencil on her eyebrows. Nothing special about her—average height, weight, and build. No light dancing in her eyes, clothes in shades of gray. Not the image of someone you'd picture loving a child. She looked broken, tired, but then maybe a four-year-old could do that to a woman her age.

He crossed his arms and shifted his weight. She didn't show any emotion at all. No nerves, no remorse, nothing written on her face. Usually he could tell by a suspect's body language how the interrogation would go, but she didn't give him any clues. He checked his watch.

Scott opened a drawer and took out a small digital recorder. He carried it into the room where Libby Braddock sat, looking straight ahead with her hands folded in her lap.

The fluorescent lights made the greenish-colored cement walls look like washed-out khaki, about the same color as Libby Braddock's face. Scott closed the door behind him and set the recorder on the table between himself and the woman.

She raised her eyes to meet his.

"Ms. Braddock." His voice was deep, authoritative. "You know why you're here?"

She raised a heavily-penciled brow, but that was the only sign that she'd heard him.

"You've been read your rights?" he asked. He knew the answer, but it was always a good spot to start for the tape. "What would you like to tell me?" He steepled his fingers, then tapped his thumbs together.

"I haven't done anything wrong."

He lifted his chin. "We responded to an all points bulletin on you. Your name, your car. You fit the description."

She shook her head.

"APB's don't get put out without a reason. Why do you think there was one out on you?"

"I couldn't guess."

"I think you could." Scott leaned over his notes. "You live in Leighsboro, North Carolina. Correct?"

"Yes."

"Why are you here in Emporia?"

"Passing through."

"You know someone who lives here?"

"No."

"Where were you headed?"

She rolled her thin lips in, bearing down. Then she just shook her head.

The chair screeched under Scott's weight as he moved toward the table and leaned forward—an intentionally intimidating posture. He rubbed his hands together. "Let me explain something to you. This is serious. You could go to jail."

She licked her lips and turned her gaze to the cement block wall.

He leaned back and waited, allowing the silence to stretch. She didn't bite.

"The charge is kidnapping."

She jerked her head in his direction.

"Yeah. Kidnapping. We know you had a child with you when you left Leighsboro four nights ago. We have witnesses."

Her arms tensed. She clenched her hands into fists, and pressed them in her lap.

"Was that your child, Ms. Braddock?"

She didn't move a muscle. She didn't even blink.

"Ms. Braddock, let me put this another way. Are you a mother?"

"I've never had a child of my own, if that's what you mean." Her voice was tight.

Her look was as cold as an arctic morning. It unnerved him. "So, the child that was staying with you. He's not your child, is he?"

She looked to the wall, silent.

"How could you take another woman's child?"

No reaction.

Scott skipped the compassionate stuff. It didn't seem to be reaching her anyway. "Kidnapping is a federal offense. You go to prison for that. This isn't a slap on the wrist we're talking about."

She spun toward him. "I didn't take anyone's child."

"Really? Then tell me about how you came to be taking care of the boy."

She bowed her head and picked at the cuticle on her thumb. It was already torn and scabbed. "I'm not a kidnapper. I'm a Christian. I'd never do something awful like that."

"That's not the way I see it. I *believe* you kidnapped that boy. Somehow, four nights ago, you found out the authorities were on to you. That's why you left Leighsboro—just in the time. That's what I think. Who told you that you'd been made, Libby?"

Scott tapped his fingers on the table in a slow rhythm.

She stiffened with each tap and cowered, closing her eyes.

"Hey. Are you listening to me? This is serious."

"Stop it," she whispered. "I wouldn't do that. I would never hurt anyone."

"But you did. Why did you take that child? Did you see the accident?"

She looked at him—eyes wide, jaw slack.

Was that surprise on her face?

"Accident? I don't know what you're talking about," she said, shaking her head, brows knit. "What accident?"

She appeared genuinely bewildered.

"The accident that happened last August," Scott said. "The boy was in the truck at the time of the accident. Were you there?"

She shook her head. "I don't know what you're talking about."

"Don't lie to me, Ms. Braddock. A good Christian doesn't lie."

"I'm not."

"A good Christian, or lying?" He knew that would get her goat. "What did you do with the boy? Where is he?"

"Quit calling him boy." Her voice sounded shrill, and her gaze held his. "He has a name. His name is Jake."

"Fine. Where's Jake?"

Libby's hands trembled in her lap.

Scott's nostrils flared. He leaned in closer to her. "What kind of woman takes a child from his mother?"

"Stop." She covered her face with her hands. "I

love Jake. He's a good boy." Tears shimmered in her eyes.

"Where is he, Ms. Braddock?"

She took a deep breath. "I did the right thing."

Scott stood and prayed he'd keep his cool. "What do you mean?" His words were slow and controlled. "What does 'the right thing' mean?"

He moved to the other side of her.

Her chest heaved with each breath she took.

"I'm going to ask you again. Where is Jake?"

"I'll tell you where." She sat taller in her chair. "He's with his father. Where he belongs."

Scott blew out a breath, as if he'd been sucker punched. He tried to swallow, struggling to keep his composure.

"He's with his father?" Scott's insides sank.

"It's where his father would want him to be."

"What did you do to him, Ms. Braddock?"

She shook her head.

"I did the right thing," she whispered again. "I love him."

Bile rose in Scott's throat. He winced.

Had she harmed Jake once she'd learned they were on to her?

There was a double-rap on the door, and Deputy Taylor poked his head in. "Sheriff?"

Scott slapped the table as he walked around it and headed out to the hall. As soon as the door clicked closed behind him, Scott kicked the metal file cabinet three times. "Damn it."

"What'd she say?" the deputy said.

Scott shook his head. He couldn't repeat Libby Braddock's words. "What do you have?"

Dan handed him a small photo album. "I just finished inspecting her bags. You need to take a look at this."

"What's in it?" Scott flipped open the small book. Pictures of Jake filled the album. It was sort of a brag book like the one a grandmother might carry around in her purse.

"Flip to the very back," Dan said.

Scott turned to the last page—to a picture of a woman and a man.

The woman was Kasey. Next to her stood a man he recognized—the guy he'd recently met at her house.

Jeremy.

Kasey wore a wedding gown, Jeremy, a black suit. If Scott didn't know better, he would have thought it was their wedding picture.

Von rushed down the hall toward them. "Hey. I got here as quick as I could," he said, out of breath. "What do we know?"

Scott turned the picture to Von. "Ever seen this?"

Von looked surprised.

Scott said, "I thought that guy was the chauffeur or nurse or something—for her grandmother."

Von nodded. "He is. But he's like a family member. That picture is from Kasey and Nick's wedding. Where'd you get this?"

Dan spoke up. "It was in Libby Braddock's suitcase."

"I wonder how *she* got it." Von looked from one of the two men to the other.

Scott leaned against the filing cabinet. "That guy showed up at Kasey's one day, unannounced. I was with her. It was during her first week there."

"At the new place?" Von asked.

"Yeah. She seemed surprised to see him." Scott rubbed his chin. "I had a bad feeling about him. And those butterscotch candies he's always eating. What's that all about?"

Von laughed. "I don't know, but he's always got a pocketful. Sugar addict? Ex-smoker, maybe?"

"It might be a coincidence, but when I was at Kasey's the other day, I was looking for a spoon and there were a bunch of those candies in one of the drawers."

"Interesting." Von crossed his arms. "Could be a coincidence."

"He's got something to do with this," Scott said.

"Kasey will never believe it. She thinks that guy walks on water. You better have a rock-solid case."

Scott rolled his eyes. "I hear you."

Von snapped his fingers. "You know, the neighbor said Libby Braddock was keeping her nephew. Did you ask her about that?" Von rubbed his upper lip. "Do you think she's Jeremy's sister?"

"She could be." Scott motioned for Von to follow him, leaving Dan standing in the hallway. Scott led Von into the room next to the interrogation room.

"She has the same color hair as Jeremy," Von said, shrugging, "but then half the world has brown hair. I guess she could be his sister." He held up the sketch artist's picture. "This is not Libby Braddock, though. A different woman sent Kasey the pictures from Nashville."

"Partners?"

"Maybe," Von said.

"I'll ask her about it." Scott took the sketch from Von. "I have to tell you what she said." Scott rolled his shoulders. "She said Jake is with his dad."

Von whistled and stepped back. "That can't be what she means. Not with Nick."

"I know. I sure hope not." Scott scrubbed his hands on his face. "That was before we made this connection to Jeremy. How about observing— listening—while I go back in and see if I can get more out of her."

Von clapped Scott's shoulder.

Scott stood in front of the door of the interrogation room. He flexed and unflexed his hands, then opened the door and went inside.

"Let's try this again." He sat in the chair across from Libby Braddock. He slid the sketch artist's rendering in front of her. "Know her?"

Her eyes widened. "Yes."

"Who is she? What's she got to do with this?"

Anger flashed in her eyes. "She's my half-sister. And I have no idea what she's got to do with anything. We haven't spoken in over ten years. She's nothing but bad news, that one. She travels around like a gypsy, pretending to tell the future." Her face pinched as if she smelled something rotten.

Scott pulled the picture in front of him, and turned it over. "The police spoke to your neighbor the night you left town. She said you've been caring for your nephew."

She nodded.

"How long has he been with you?"

"Since the end of the summer." Her face had softened, and so did her tone. "He's a good boy. An angel."

The word "angel" twisted in Scott's gut. "Why is he staying with you? Why isn't he with his mother?"

"I had to help him."

"Who? Jake?"

"No. Well, yes. Him too, but that woman . . . I told my brother that woman was out of his league. He was so smitten with her. When he told me they were married, I couldn't even believe it."

"What's your brother's name?"

"I don't know why he wanted to marry that rich girl. He was a servant to them. He slaved away for her and that wicked grandmother of hers, too. I told him it wouldn't last. I warned him."

"What happened?"

"She left him, and then she wouldn't let him see his little boy. I had to help him."

Scott pulled the photo album out of his back pocket. "Is this your brother?"

Her lips pressed together. "Yes. That's Jeremy. Stupid fool. He still wants that woman back." She reached for the book. "That's my personal property."

He moved the book out of her reach. "Not while you're in my custody."

"So you see, I didn't kidnap anyone. I was helping my brother. He was so upset the day he brought Jake to my house. Desperate. He was crying. I'd never seen Jeremy cry. Never."

Scott let her keep talking, welcoming the flood of information.

"The little boy was filthy and had scrapes on his arms and cheek."

Her eyes softened. "It was the first time I'd ever even met my nephew. He was scared. When I held Jake in my arms that day, he cried."

Her breathing became heavy. "That woman is a terrible mother. She'd do anything to keep Jake from Jeremy. It's not fair. I had to help him. He has rights."

"Where is Jake now?"

"I can't tell you."

"Libby, your brother lied to you."

She shook her head. "No. He wouldn't do that. You're the one lying. You're trying to take him away from Jeremy."

"No, Libby, listen to me. Kasey wasn't married to your brother. She was married to Nick Rolly. You said it yourself: your half-sister is trouble. She's involved here, too."

"I have the picture. You saw it." She blinked. "You're trying to confuse me."

"Nick Rolly died in a car accident in August. We found Jake's car seat at the scene, but not Jake. I think it's because Jeremy took him that day. I think Jeremy was desperate, and he took Jake to you looking for help. Think about it."

"I don't understand how . . ."

"I'm telling you the truth. He lied to you, and that little boy is not his child."

"That can't be true," her voice wobbled and her face paled. "You're confusing me."

"Is Jake alive, Libby?"

"Yes. He's fine. I love Jake. I'd never hurt him." She clutched the side of the table, steadying herself.

"Where is he?"

She started breathing heavily, then she mumbled.

"What did you say?" Scott asked.

"I'm dizzy." She shook her head. "Something's wrong." Her hand trembled like that of a junkie needing a fix.

"Libby. Stay with me." Scott left his seat and crouched in front of her. "You hear me? Breathe in through your nose and out through your mouth."

She followed Scott's instructions.

Once her breathing slowed, he returned to the chair across from her. The color came back to her face.

"Do you need medical assistance?"

"Can I have some water?"

"Sure." Scott left the room.

Von met him in the hall. "Thank God. He's alive. Now we just need to find out where he is. What the hell is Jeremy up to? I don't really know the guy, but he's always been there for Kasey."

Scott pulled a paper cup from the side of the water cooler and filled it. "Wish me luck," he said, then went back in.

Scott handed Libby the cup. The water rippled as she lifted the cup to her lips, her hand trembling.

"Thank you." She set the cup on the table in front of her.

Scott rubbed the back of his neck, then straightened. "Let's start over. How do you know Kasey Phillips? She's never heard of you."

"Of course not. She doesn't care about our family, just her own."

"Even if that's the case, you can't take a child from his mother and get away with it. It's illegal."

"Jeremy has rights."

"Even if they were married, matters of custody are for a court to decide. Not you."

She rested her head on the table.

"I know this is exhausting, but if you're a Christian, I know you want to do the right thing."

"Of course."

"I want to show you something. I'll be right back." Scott walked out of the room, went to his desk, and got the case files from the accident and Jake's disappearance. He walked back in and started reading facts to Libby.

Logic outweighed the story she'd been told by Jeremy. Scott saw the expression on her face change with each fact. He licked a finger and turned to another page, chronicling the last several months of the investigation.

Thirty minutes later, Libby had the whole string of events laid out for her.

Her jaw went slack. She kept muttering, "I can't believe it." Her gaze darted, unsettled, as if she was looking for a way out.

Control was finally shifting.

Only one thing could save her now—the truth.

Scott spoke slowly, careful to choose the right words. "Libby, Kasey is a wonderful mother. She lost her husband. She loves Jake. Please help us reunite them."

"What about Jeremy?"

"Libby, you better worry about yourself right now and doing the right thing."

She zoned out for a long moment, then turned to Scott. "The address is written inside the cover of a paperback book I was reading. It's in my car."

"Who is he with now?" Scott asked. "Is he safe?"

"Oh yes. I'd never have taken him there if I didn't think so. They've been friends of our family for years—they have four kids of their own. I was supposed to go pick him up next weekend. Jeremy was going to visit Jake there."

"Thank you, Libby."

"I am so sorry." She lowered her head. "I had no idea. You've got to believe me."

"I do." Scott walked out and locked the door behind him. Von shadowed him down the hall while Scott gave orders to move Libby to a holding cell. He and Von located the keys to Libby Braddock's vehicle, and ran to the cruiser to go back to the hotel and search the car.

Chapter Thirty-Seven

Kasey rushed to the processing desk at the station. "Is Scott around?" she asked one of the officers.

"He just left."

Her shoulders drooped. "How long ago?"

"Ten minutes, maybe?"

She dropped her hands to her sides. "Did he leave a message for me? Kasey Phillips."

The officer shuffled some papers and checked a rack of cubbyholes. "No. I don't see anything up here for you."

Kasey tried Scott's cell phone but it went to voice mail; she left him a message then scribbled a note on a slip of paper and handed it to the gal at the desk. "Can you see that he gets this if he comes back?"

"Sure."

Kasey thanked her and left for Scott's house.

Not five minutes later, Von and Scott returned to the station.

A young officer sat at the front desk. "You just missed a visitor. She left a note."

"She?" Scott reached for the piece of paper. "We just missed Kasey," he said to Von. "She's at my place."

"Go get her," Von said. "I'll work with the deputy to get the rest of the address from Libby, and coordinate how we can get Jake home."

Scott nodded. "Great. I have my phone. Call me if you need me. I'll bring her up to date and meet you back here."

"Good luck. She's not going to want to believe that Jeremy betrayed her. He's like family to her. Go easy."

Chapter Thirty-Eight

Kasey's cell phone rang just as she pulled next to the curb in front of Scott's house. She answered and Scott was already talking before she could say hello.

"Got your message," Scott said. "Where are you?" His voice sounded tight, his words clipped.

"I'm sitting in my car right in front of your house. Is everything okay?"

"There's a key to the side door, on top of the bird feeder. I've got news."

"Your voice sounds funny." Her stomach swirled with dread. "The news. It's not bad is it?"

"No. Not bad. I promise. I'll explain when I get there."

"When—" But he'd already hung up. She found the key easily and went to the side door. It took a minute to get the key in the right way, but finally it slipped in the lock and she opened the door.

Inside the house, the room was dark. She patted the wall looking for a light switch, but something brushed against her as she did. She instantly thought of Turtle Mike, but then whatever it was grabbed her wrist, pulling her away from the open door. The fear of imminent danger pulsed through her veins, gripping her so tight she couldn't make a noise.

Kasey scrambled to keep her balance, tugging hard. She slapped and kicked and was able to free her arm, but the door slammed behind her, trapping her inside.

In the darkness of the room, she felt something pass in front of her face, but her eyes hadn't adjusted and it was too dark to see. A strong hand clamped around her arm. She bent forward and bit down until the intruder screamed, but he didn't let go. Instead, cool metal settled on her temple.

Her body went rigid. Afraid to move, her temple pulsed under the pressure of the barrel.

She heard a slap on the wall next to her, and the lights came on.

"Kasey?"

"Jeremy?"

They stared at each other for a stunned moment, then she breathed a sigh of relief and stepped away from the gun. "You scared me to death. I thought I was a goner. What are you doing here?"

His jaw moved, but he didn't respond.

"Jeremy. Why are you here?" She stepped toward him. "Why do you have a gun? What's going on?"

He stepped back. "This isn't . . ." Jeremy's voice drifted. Sweat dampened his forehead. "You shouldn't be here."

"Why are *you* here?"

"It's not how it seems." All the color had drained from his face. "He's got to pay for this."

"Who's got to pay? Scott?" She blinked, shaking her head. "You don't think Scott had something to do with Jake's disappearance?"

Jeremy straightened.

"That can't be. He's helping me find Jake."

He scratched his head with the barrel of the gun. "He's not helping you. He just wants you."

"Wait. This doesn't make sense. Did Scott . . . ?" She took a step back. *Scott had said he was there at the accident site. Could I be so wrong about him?* "Do you think Scott did something to Jake?"

"I'm here to make everything right," Jeremy said. "Don't worry. I'm going to take care of Calvin and then I'm going to take you to Jake."

"You found Jake?"

"Yes. I'd do anything for you and Jake. You know that."

"Of course, you're like family. Let's go," Kasey said and turned to the door.

Jeremy waved the gun and it went off, scaring them both.

"Careful with that thing. Just put it down."

"Wait! I have to stop Scott first."

"Why? Is Jake with Scott?"

Jeremy shook his head.

"Then take me to Jake. I just want my baby." Kasey's voice became loud and impatient. "Quit standing there. Let's go. We can let the police take care of Scott."

"But he is the police."

"Von will know what to do. Come on."

The side door swung open and Scott steadied his gun on Jeremy. "Hold it right there."

Kasey stepped between them. "How could you? I thought you were my friend."

"Kasey, get out of the way."

She didn't budge. "He told me you took Jake."

Scott scoffed and looked at Kasey. "And you believe that? Kasey, Jeremy was behind your son's disappearance. Nick's death, too." He nodded to Jeremy. "Isn't that right?"

Kasey turned to Jeremy.

"I'd have been a good Dad to Jake. Before Nick. You know. I would've married you and taken care of Jake. Raised him like my own. Like Nick did. I'd have been there for you. Nick's gone. But I'm not. You know I love, Jake. Right?"

Jeremy raised his gun towards Scott.

Scott steadied his aim. "Don't do anything stupid."

"Go sit down, Kasey." Jeremy's hand shook.

She stepped out of range. "What's going on? Who is taking me to Jake?"

"Sit!" Jeremy yelled. *"Now!"*

She dropped to the floor right where she was.

"No!" He shouted, then waved the gun at her. "In there." He motioned her toward the living room.

She got up and walked backward, afraid to turn her back on him.

His voice rose. "This isn't how I planned it."

She backed into the living room. "Planned what? Jeremy. Tell me you didn't take Jake."

He rocked from side to side. "He's going to tell you, but it's not how it looks." Jeremy blew out several small breaths in a row, then cocked the hammer.

"Whoa!" She took a step back. "No. Wait. You don't want to do this. We're like family, and whatever you think Scott has done . . . You killing him isn't going to be better for anyone."

"Drop it," Scott ordered.

"Don't. Both of y'all, stop!" Kasey screamed.

"Family," Jeremy said, nodding his head, and then he began to cry. "Jake should've been mine."

"He's not your child. You know that."

"He wasn't Nick's but you let him be. I've always loved you, Kasey. Nick had already taken you from me. Then he . . . he wanted to take you away." His hand shook.

"Put the gun down," Scott commanded.

"Whatever you did, it can't be as bad as you think." She glanced at the end table. There wasn't much on it—a magazine, an old horseshoe and a coaster. She dipped and wrapped her fingers around the rusty antique horseshoe. It was heavy in her hand.

Jeremy wiped the sweat from his eyes. "I never meant to hurt you. I love you." His eyes turned dark. He raised the gun towards his own head. It shook in his hand. "The pictures. I sent them."

"Kasey, let me handle this," Scott said. She raised a hand and gave Scott a begging look. He nodded.

"A woman sent the pictures." Kasey paused, trying to regain control of her emotions and voice. *Smooth and soothing—stay calm and he will.*

"Me." Pain twisted in Jeremy's face. "I set that up. You said you wanted to know Jake was alive. I wanted you to . . ." He wiped his face with his sleeve—the gun flailed. "You needed to feel hope. I wanted you to have hope. I never meant this to go so wrong. All I ever wanted was to be in your life."

She squeezed the horseshoe, praying she wouldn't drop it.

He leveled his gaze on Kasey. "I didn't want him to move you away. I only meant to scare him."

A loud clunk came from down the hall. Jeremy spun toward the noise. Kasey hurled the horseshoe. It flew across the room like a Frisbee. She dove behind the couch and crouched low to the floor.

Jeremy turned just as the horseshoe made contact with his face. He yowled, and a string of expletives followed.

Kasey peered over the couch. Blood dripped down his arms. She must've hit him square in the nose. Even with his hands to his face, there was a lot of blood already.

Jeremy stumbled toward her, and the gun went off again.

Chapter Thirty-Nine

Jeremy spun to face Scott. Blood gushed from his nose and mouth, but the gun remained steady in his grip.

"Drop the gun," Scott said as he stepped closer. He reached up and keyed the mic at his collar. "This is Calvin. I need EMTs on the scene, and backup."

Jeremy wavered. He looked over his shoulder at Kasey. She saw the confusion on his face. The darkness in his eyes. He swallowed and turned back to Scott.

Her heart pounded in her throat. "No, Jeremy. Drop it." Her feet wouldn't move. She sank back against the wall, her mouth and eyes wide. "Don't do it."

Jeremy spun her way.

"No!" Kasey held her hands out defensively. "Please. Listen to me."

The gun dropped to the floor.

Jeremy ran his sleeve across his face. Blood stained his skin and clothes, and droplets splattered on the floor.

"Kick it my way," Scott said.

Jeremy kicked his foot forward, but the blood from his sleeve impaired his vision and he missed, staggering backwards.

Scott scooped up the gun, then restrained Jeremy with his handcuffs. He Mirandized him, then jerked him tight against him. Scott's jaw pulsed. "Is Jake still in Tappahannock?"

Jeremy nodded and hung his head.

"He'd better be safe. Don't make me regret not killing you while I have the chance." He shoved Jeremy into a kitchen chair.

Kasey clung to the doorjamb. "He's going to bleed to death."

"If he's lucky." Scott went to the sink, pumped anti-bacterial cleanser into his hands and washed the blood from them.

Two EMTs rushed into the house. Scott motioned them to Jeremy and they started tending to his injuries.

Scott walked over to Kasey as he dried his hands. "Are you okay?"

She lunged into his arms. "I was so scared."

He kissed the top of her head. "Scared the hell out of me, too."

"Thank goodness you showed up when you did."

"You were doing pretty well without me."

"Thank God for Turtle Mike."

"You must've been sandbagging the day we played horseshoes here."

"Lucky shot." She laid her head against his chest.

The EMTs cleaned the gash on Jeremy's face. His nose was broken. They moved him to a gurney and fastened a strap across his body. Two officers showed up just as the EMTs rolled the gurney toward the door. Scott updated the officers with all the details. "Get him out of here." Scott's directive set the officers in motion.

He moved to Kasey's side, tipped her chin and looked her in the eyes. He cleared his throat. "That's what I was going to tell you earlier. About Jeremy."

"Where's Jake?"

"I tried to tell you," said Jeremy through the gauze. "Jake's safe."

"I've been in a living hell for months." She hurled the words like stones.

Scott put his hand on her arm. "I'll be able to prove Jeremy killed Nick with the slug he fired in here. I'm sure it'll match those we found at the scene. We have Libby Braddock at the station. She's Jeremy's sister."

"His sister?" Her breathing grew louder. "No, Jeremy. How could you?" She lunged past the EMT and pounded Jeremy's chest with her fists. "How did—"

"Whoa, *whoa!*" Scott grabbed her around the waist. "He'll get his punishment, don't you worry."

Her feet kicked at nothing. "Why?" she screamed.

"It was an accident." Jeremy choked out the words.

"An accident? He was in his truck, for God's sake."

His gaze locked on hers, intense, desperate. "I meant to scare him. He was going to move you away. I couldn't lose you."

"Lose me? What the hell are you talking about?"

"I didn't want you to move here."

"You knew?" She pounded the air. "You knew about the house. You lied. And Jake? What about Jake?"

Jeremy turned his head. "I'm sorry. I saved him, but then I didn't know what to do."

"All this time? Where is he? Tell me!"

Scott turned her toward him. "Shhh. It's over. We're going to get Jake."

Von opened the door, then held it wide as the medics wheeled Jeremy past.

Jeremy struggled against the restraints, shouting, "I tried to fix it."

Von rushed to Kasey's side. "Thank goodness you weren't hurt. I was at the station waiting on Scott when the call came in. You're okay, right?"

She nodded, then her cell phone rang.

"That's mine," she said.

"I'll answer it." Von grabbed the ringing phone from the counter. "Hello. Kasey Phillips's cell."

He listened and nodded. "So let me get this straight. You're in the air, headed for the Greensville-Emporia airport . . . Here?"

Cody's deep voice reverberated from the phone and across the room. Kasey could almost make out his words.

"I'm putting you on speaker." Von punched the speakerphone button on the cell and laid it on the counter. He leaned over the phone. "This couldn't be better timing. Where are you exactly? We just got a lead on Jake. I think you can help."

"Hang on. Let me check with the pilot," Cody said, then his voice became muffled.

"The pilot says we're like forty miles from the airport. We can change course. Where do you need us to go?"

"Tappahannock Airport. I don't know the code. I can get it, though."

Cody talked to the pilot and came back on the line. "He's already got it dialed in from the navigation system. We're on our way."

Kasey looked confused. "What's going on?"

Scott put his arm around her and hugged her close. "Jake's coming home."

She clung to Scott's arm.

Von continued: "Cody, the police in Tappahannock are supposed to be picking up Jake right about now. I'm waiting on confirmation. I'll let them know to meet you at the airport and release him to you. Can I call you back on this number?"

"Yeah. It should work, but if I don't hear from you I'll call back."

"I'll update you with information and timing as I get it."

"You got it," Cody said.

Von ended the call and handed the phone to Kasey. "We better go back to the station. We're going to have to fax a release form."

"Jake's really coming home this time? I'm almost afraid to believe it."

"Come on." Scott guided Kasey to the car. She was unsteady, so he swept her up and carried her. He pulled out onto the street with Von right behind him.

Von called home as he drove. "Hey, baby."

"What's going on? Did something happen?" Riley asked.

"I'll fill you in on everything when you get here, but the bottom line is Jake's coming home."

"Tonight? Von, this is amazing."

"Yep. Cody Tuggle called from his plane. He was on his way to see Kasey. They've rerouted. Now he's flying to Tappahannock to bring Jake home. We're going to meet them at the Greensville-Emporia airport."

"Not the little airport on the way to Kasey's new place?"

"That's the one."

"I didn't know planes actually landed there. I'm heading that way."

"I knew you would. I love you, Riley. Drive careful. I can't take any more excitement today."

"I will. I promise."

Von ended the call, then redialed the Tappahannock police to coordinate the transfer at the airport and confirm what forms needed to be filed to make it all happen.

Von and Scott pulled into the station at the same time. Von's cell phone rang as they walked inside.

He swept the phone from his hip to his ear, nodding and yessing. "Great . . . Yes . . . I'm going to dial you back from a landline."

Von grabbed Kasey's hand. "The Tappahannock police are at the address. They're going in." Von ended the call and turned his attention to Scott. "You got a speakerphone in your office?"

"Come on." Scott led the way. He spun the desk phone around. Von dialed the number. The phone on the other end rang once. "Hankins."

"It's Perry Von. I've got Sheriff Scott Calvin and Jake's mother, Kasey Phillips, on speaker-phone."

Kasey hung on to Scott's forearm and Von's shoulder as they all leaned over the phone, waiting.

"Stand by," Hankins said. Radio communications and the muffled sounds of movement came from the other end of the line before Hankins came back on the line. "We've got the boy."

Kasey collapsed, sobbing.

"Is he okay?" Von asked.

"He looks fine." Hankins's voice relaxed. "We'll head to the airport. Get those papers faxed over to us in the meantime."

"Already in the works," Von confirmed. Scott gave him a nod.

"I'll call you when we get to the airport," Hankins said.

Kasey hugged Scott, then turned and hugged Von.

Scott and Von high-fived over her head.

A young clerk stepped into the doorway of Scott's office. "Pardon me," she said, holding up the fax. "They said these were urgent."

"Excellent." Scott snatched the papers and filled out the form, then turned to Kasey. "I need you to sign right here."

She signed the paper, not that the scribble looked anything like her signature. Her hands trembled so much she could barely hold the pen.

Scott handed the papers back to the clerk. "Fax these back right now."

"I'm on it, sir." The clerk rushed out of the room.

Von picked up the handset and dialed Cody's number. "I just got off the phone with the police. They have Jake. He's fine."

"Hallelujah," Cody shouted. "Yeah! Let me see how long we have before we land."

While Von waited, the clerk came back in and handed Scott a note. Scott read it and handed it to Von.

Von nodded. "Hey, Cody. I need the tail numbers on the plane for our paperwork." Von scribbled some numbers on a pad of paper. "About fifteen more minutes before you land in Tappahannock? The police will be there waiting for you. They'll release Jake to you."

"Perfect," Cody said. "How's Kasey hanging in there?"

"She's afraid to believe it."

"Tell her not to worry. I won't let anything happen to her baby."

Von believed him. "We'll all be waiting for you here at the Greensville-Emporia airport. Let me know when you take off."

"You got it," Cody said. "Let Kasey know that Lou is going to meet us at the airport."

Von hung up and clipped the phone on his belt.

"Who is Lou?" he asked Kasey.

"That's Cody's girlfriend."

Scott looked surprised. "He has a girlfriend?"

She nodded. "An old flame. They just recently reconnected. I'd forgotten they were coming to stay with me tonight."

Von interjected. "Cody asked me to let you know that she's going to meet him at the airport."

"You never mentioned they were coming," Scott said to Kasey.

"Yeah, it was short notice," she said. "Guys. This isn't a dream, is it? My baby is coming home." She held her stomach. "I feel sick."

"You're going to be fine." Scott stroked her back. "Just breathe."

"How long is the flight from Tappahannock?" Her stomach twisted into a knot.

Scott looked to Von who shrugged. "No idea."

"We'll ask when Cody calls back."

A half-hour later, the call they'd been waiting for came in. Von answered, then handed the phone to Kasey.

"Hello?" she said.

"Mommy?"

She knelt to the floor with both hands on the phone. "Jake? Is that you, honey?"

"Hi, Mommy. We're flying an airplane."

"I know, baby. Don't be scared. Cody will take good care of you. He's mommy's friend."

"He's nice. I miss you, Mommy."

She gulped back tears. "I miss you too, sweetheart. Cody's bringing you home to me."

Kasey heard Jake's voice drift from the phone. "Mommy's crying."

Cody's voice came over the line. "Hey, Kasey. I thought you'd rather hear his voice than mine."

"Thank you. I can't believe it." Kasey sucked in

a breath and let it out. "How does he look? Did he ask for me?"

"He looks fine, acts fine. Running around like boys do. Says he misses his mommy. Look, we're cleared for immediate takeoff, so I'm going to get this little guy buckled in. The pilot just filed his flight plan and says that we should land in Greensville-Emporia in about twenty-five minutes."

"The longest twenty-five minutes of my life. Thank you." She turned to Von and Scott. "They're on their way."

"Riley is too," said Von.

She rubbed her hands together. "Feel my hands." She pressed them to Scott's cheeks.

"Holy cow. You're freezing." Scott closed his office door and took a jacket from a hanger on the back. "Here, put this on."

She slipped it on and pushed her hands in the pockets. "Thanks. That's better." She shivered. "I'm so nervous. Can we go there and wait? I can't sit here. I just can't."

Kasey got into the car with Scott, and Von followed them to the airport.

Except for one truck, the airport parking lot was empty. They went inside to wait. A few minutes later, a tall brunette walked in.

She walked straight to Kasey. "Hi. Are you Kasey Phillips?"

Kasey nodded.

"I'm Lou. Cody called. I'm so glad I'm here for this special day."

She was pretty in a girl-next-door kind of way. "Thank you. It's nice to meet you. I can't believe his timing."

"How are you holding up?"

"Look at my hands." Kasey held out one of her trembling hands. "Even my knees are wobbling."

"I can't even imagine what you're going through." Lou sat on the bench across from Von and introduced herself. He filled her in on the details. Kasey got up, walked over to the wall of windows and stared out. Her eyes played tricks on her, making her think there were lights in the night sky where there were none.

Kasey spun around to the sound of her name. Riley ran through the small terminal lobby toward her and then hugged Kasey tightly. "I can't believe it. Finally."

"I know. I can hardly breathe. Thanks for coming."

"Nothing could keep me away. How much longer?"

Kasey looked at her watch again. "About seven minutes."

Scott's two-way radio squawked. He turned his back and leaned in to listen to it.

"I don't know how he understands what they're saying on that thing." Kasey shrugged. "This doesn't feel real. I feel like I'm dreaming."

"The nightmare is almost over. You're getting Jake back. It's nothing but good from here on."

Scott rushed over to her side. "I've got to get to the station. There's a problem. I'm sorry. I'll be back as soon as I can."

"Okay." Kasey called after him as he hurried away, "Be careful." But Scott was already hauling ass out the glass doors. She watched as he hit the blue lights on his cruiser and pulled out on Route 58.

Riley tapped Kasey's shoulder. "That's got to be them." She pointed out the window.

Von and Lou joined them.

They all grabbed hands—Von, Riley, Kasey and Lou—and watched the jet touch down and taxi toward the terminal. Kasey gripped Riley's hand and Lou's arm, steadying herself just in case her legs buckled. Her heart pounded harder as the jet engines got closer. She watched the plane come within jogging distance in what seemed like slow motion.

Kasey looked to Von. "Can we go outside and wait?"

"I don't think there's anyone here that's going to stop you," Von said.

They put on their coats as they hurried outside. Kasey could see the pilot flipping switches. The engines shut down and it was silent. Not even a cricket chirped. The door on the plane pushed forward, then the stairs folded down.

Kasey held her breath, her hands clasped in prayer.

Cody appeared in the doorway. Kasey's stomach plummeted. And then there was Jake. Right there in the doorway of the plane.

In one sweep, Cody lifted Jake to his hip and started down the steep stairs, just like Nick would've carried him. Jake looked so small in the arms of Cody Tuggle.

Kasey broke into a run toward them.

Jake's eyes lit up when he saw her. "Mommy!" He reached for her.

"Oh, my . . ." Kasey whisked her son from Cody's arms and clung to him. "How's my boy?" She brushed his bangs away from his eyes, then pulled him close again.

"Let him breathe," Cody said with a laugh. "He's in good shape. Aren't you?" He scrubbed his hand through Jake's hair.

"Mommy. I was missing you. We flew the plane fast and there were lights. It was like lightning bugs—lots of them, and it was pretty."

"I love you, Jake." She knelt in front of him. With her arms still around him, she looked up at Cody. "Thank you. Thank you so much."

He nodded, then Lou walked up and kissed him on the cheek.

Jake clung to his mother's hand. "Mommy. I missed you and Daddy."

"I missed you too, sweetie. I missed you every

day." She kissed Jake on both cheeks and on his forehead.

His lip quivered. "Why are you crying, Mommy?"

"Mommy's happy." Kasey tweaked his nose. "I'm so happy to see you. These are good tears, I promise," she choked out between sobs of relief. "I love you."

Jake reached out and put his hands on Kasey's cheeks. "Don't cry, Mommy."

He brushed at her tears with his sleeve. "I didn't mean to make you sad."

"I'm not sad, honey."

Jake lowered his head. "Daddy can't come home, Mommy."

"I know." Kasey hadn't even considered how she'd tell him about his dad.

"Jeremy and me swam, and Daddy went to the angels." Tears filled Jakes eyes and his lip poked out. "Mommy? Uncle Jeremy's not Daddy, is he? Miss Libby thinks Uncle Jeremy is Daddy."

"No, baby. He's not. She was mixed up." She held him close. "You're home now. No one will ever separate us again. I promise."

"I'm a big boy. I'll take care of you."

"I know you will. You are my little man." She hugged him and kissed his cheek. "Mommy missed you so much."

They walked into the small terminal and sat at a Formica-topped table. Kasey moved her chair close to Jake, facing him. "Were you afraid?"

"Miss Libby is nice. She's old, but she likes swings. Jeremy said you were busy, but you missed me. I was a good boy."

"I'm sure you were, my little angel."

Scott strode in looking tense and serious, but a grin spread across his face when he saw Kasey sitting with Jake.

"Success," he said as he joined the small, special group of friends around Kasey. "Thank you." Scott shook Cody's hand. "Right place, right time. Couldn't have worked out better."

"Happy to be a part of it." Cody gave Jake a wink.

Jake's face contorted as he tried to mimic Cody.

"Thank you," Kasey met the gaze of each of her friends—Riley, Scott, Von, Cody and Lou. "All of you. Thank you for believing in me when everyone else thought I was crazy. I don't know what I'd have done without your help. I never would have found Jake without each and every one of you."

She felt a raw but healing ache in her chest.

"Never doubt a mother's love," Scott said.

Cody nodded and the two men exchanged a knowing glance.

Chapter Forty

"You've grown," Kasey said as she carried Jake to Von's SUV. He was really too big to be carried, but she couldn't bear to let go of him.

"I'm big," he said.

They rode with Von and Riley back to her house. Scott followed in his police car, and Lou and Cody followed behind him in Lou's car.

Jake was asleep before they pulled into the driveway.

Von carried him in. "Where do you want me to put him?"

Kasey pressed her lips together. "I don't want him to wake up in a strange place. He can sleep through anything. Just put him on the couch. He'll be fine."

Von laid him on the couch, then joined the others in the kitchen.

A rush of adrenaline coursed through her as they rehashed the chain of events. Everyone else seemed hyped up, too.

Cody got up from the table and walked behind Kasey's chair. He put his arms around her and gave her a squeeze. "Girl, I know you've got to be emotionally beat. When you come down off this rush, you'll crash for a week."

"I'm sure you're tired too. Want me to show you the guest room?"

"No, no. We aren't staying here."

"I don't mind."

"I know, but I've made arrangements up the road for us to stay at the B&B tonight. We'll stop by tomorrow to say goodbye. You need to be with Jake, not entertaining us."

She jumped from her chair and put her arms around him. "Cody, this never would've happened if you hadn't made that announcement in Raleigh."

He hugged her and put his cheek to her hair. He pulled back slightly. "I told you there was value in a country music network."

"You were right."

"People helping people, it's what country folks do," Cody said.

Scott nodded. "Couldn't be more true."

"You've done so much for me," Kasey said to Cody.

"It didn't work out so bad for me either. You know that song went gold."

"'*A Mother's Love*'? I didn't know. Congratulations."

"I was thinking I owed *you* a big thank you." He gave her a wink. "Two, really. If it hadn't been for you and our talks on tour, I never would have looked up Lou again."

"I'll never be able to thank you enough," Kasey said.

"I guess we'll be friends forever then, won't we?"

"I sure hope so. And Lou, you have a great guy here. I wish you both so much happiness."

Lou hugged Kasey. "I feel like I already know you. We'll come back. I promise."

Kasey walked them out to their car. After they drove away, she stood there staring at the sky. Among the stars, in the heavens, she knew Nick was with her. "Nick, our baby is home. Thank you for watching over us."

She went inside. Riley, Von and Scott had all moved into the living room. She sat on the couch with her arm across Jake's ankles. He looked so sweet sleeping there, without a worry in the world. He seemed to have no understanding of the drama that had been going on for all these months, and she was thankful for that.

A tear ran down her cheek. "I still can't believe he's home."

Riley snuggled against Von in the loveseat. "I don't think I've felt this happy in a long time. We are so blessed."

Scott leaned forward in the oversized leather chair. "Kasey, I need to tell you something."

"What?"

"When I got called away from the airport, it was about Jeremy." Scott let out a long breath, then leaned in closer to her. "While he was being treated at the hospital, he . . . he took his own life."

Kasey opened her mouth, then shut it. She froze. "I'm not even sure how I feel about that." She blinked. "He was like family. None of it makes sense. Part of me wants to say he deserved to die, but that's wrong and I know that. I wouldn't wish that on him, or on his family." She shook her head. "I guess we won't be getting a lot of answers then."

"I know." Scott leaned toward her and rested his cheek on the top of her head. "A lot of emotions tangled up.

"Y'all are going to stay the night, aren't you?" Scott asked Von.

"Yeah. Thought I'd head back in the morning, and I think you're staying another day, aren't you, honey?" Von patted Riley's leg. She nodded.

Scott stood. "Good deal. I'm going to head on out, but I'll stop in and check on things tomorrow, if that's okay with you."

"I'd like that." Kasey got up from the couch and looked back down at Jake.

Scott gave her shoulders a squeeze. "Happy endings. Good stuff."

The next morning Jake woke up before Kasey. She'd snuggled up on the couch with him, unwilling to let even a room separate them.

"Mommy! We're at the surprise house."

"Jake?" His shouting scared her to a sitting position. She relaxed a bit when she saw the smile

on his face. "Yes. We're at the surprise house."
She'd almost forgotten the whole surprise regarding
the house.

Jake's little mouth formed an O. "Me and Daddy
made it."

"I know. I love it."

Von came out from the guest room in a jog, with
Riley at his heels. "Everything okay?"

"Yeah." Kasey smooched Jake's tiny fingers.
"We're good. Sorry we woke you up."

Von bent over and opened his arms to Jake.
"Where's my buddy?"

Jake giggled and ran toward Von, full-speed.
Von caught him and airplaned him around.
"Vrrrrroooooom."

Jake laughed so hard he hiccupped.

Von set him down and Riley slapped Von on
the butt. "No horsing around in the house, boys.
Anyone hungry?"

Von and Jake both raised their hands. "Me.
Me," they yelled.

"I gotcha covered." Riley disappeared into the
kitchen.

Soon the smell of bacon wafted into the living
room.

Kasey called to Riley, "Need my help?"

Riley leaned into the living room with a
dishtowel over one shoulder and a spatula in her
hand. "You're kidding, right? I know how you
cook. You stay right where you are."

Kasey twirled her hair and flopped back on the couch. "Works for me."

Ten minutes later, Riley banged a spoon against a plate and yelled into the living room, "Breakfast's ready. Come and get it."

Kasey and Von each grabbed one of Jake's hands and ran into the kitchen, swinging Jake through the doorway.

"Awwwww." Kasey's head tilted as she spotted the plate of pancakes on the table. "Heart-shaped pancakes. Aren't you just a regular Martha Stewart?"

"It *is* Valentine's Day." Riley walked over to Von, slung the dishtowel around his neck and pulled him to her for a kiss. "Be mine?"

He hugged her tight. "Better believe it. You're my Sweet-tart, sweetheart."

Kasey sat at the table and took a bite of the pancakes. "These are tasty." She took a sip of coffee. "I can't believe I almost let Valentine's Day sneak by."

Riley twirled her fork in the air. "You've had a little bit going on, my friend."

Kasey wrinkled her nose at Jake. "Yeah. Good stuff."

Jake chomped on his pancakes. "My favorite." He took another bite and swung his feet. "Hey, Mommy?"

"Yes, sweetie?"

He tilted his head. His lips glistened from the sticky syrup. "Am I your valentine?"

"My very favorite valentine."

"Good." He grinned, then dug back into his pancakes.

Von finished his breakfast, then got ready to head home. Riley walked him out to the SUV while Kasey helped Jake up to the kitchen sink to wash the syrup from his hands.

"Hello," Scott yelled from the front door. "Kasey? Riley said you and Jake were in here."

"In the kitchen," she answered.

Jake jumped down and ran to greet Scott. "Hi."

"Good morning, Scott," Kasey said.

"Bet you slept good."

"Best night in a long, long time."

"I brought you something. Sort of a welcome home present for Jake."

"You didn't have to do that."

He lifted a shoulder. "I wanted to. I hope you don't mind. It's out in the car. Can y'all come outside?"

"Sure." She took Jake's hand and followed Scott out to the porch. Riley waved to Von as he backed out the driveway.

Scott put his hand up to stop Kasey and Jake. "Stay right there."

They stopped. Riley joined them. "What's going on?" she asked.

"Scott said he has a present for Jake."

Scott opened the passenger door of his truck, then leaned over, disappearing behind the open door.

"What's he doing?" Riley asked.

"Who knows?" Kasey stood on her tiptoes, trying to see.

A little golden puppy pranced out from around the truck, across the yard. A huge silk bow, with pink and red hearts on it, tripped her up about every fourth step. The pup paused, twisted, then nipped at the huge floppy bow.

"Mommy!" Jake ran across the yard and knelt in front of the puppy. He placed his hand flat on the puppy's back and stroked her. "He's soft. Does he have a name?"

"He's a she." Scott looked up and locked eyes with Kasey. "Her name is Shutterbug. She likes getting her picture taken."

"That's a funny name." Jake looked up at Scott. "My mommy loves clicking pictures."

"I've heard that about her."

The puppy flipped her long pink tongue out to kiss Jake. He laughed and fell back on the ground. There must have been syrup on his face, because Shutterbug licked Jake's face making him wiggle and twist away, which only encouraged Shutterbug.

"She's so funny," Jake said. "Mommy, come see her."

Scott gave an innocent look. "Shutterbug needs

a home, and I thought you might need someone, too. Is it a good match?"

"Mommy, can we keep her?"

Kasey smiled at Scott. "You don't play fair. You know she's my favorite one."

"You could say you'll love her and give her a good home."

Kasey bent down and picked up the puppy. "Oh, I do love her." She snuggled Shutterbug. "So sweet."

"She's adorable," Riley said.

Kasey squatted next to Jake. "I had to leave Dutch at the old house. He was too old to make the move, and he likes being a farm dog with his old friends. Do you think Shutterbug could live with us?"

"Yes, ma'am. I'll take good care of her. I promise."

Kasey turned to Scott. "How can I say no to that? Thank you. The puppy was a thoughtful gift."

"She's Jake's present. I have something for you, too," Scott said.

Just then, a car pulled into the driveway. Kasey recognized the vehicle. "That's Chaz."

Chaz got out of his truck and walked toward them. "I heard there was reason to celebrate today." He handed Kasey a foil-covered plate.

"You heard right," she said, grinning. Her cheeks hurt from smiling.

"Seems like every time I run into one of you, the other is around." Chaz gave them a knowing look, wagging his finger between Scott and Kasey. "That's good. Real good."

Jake glanced over. His eyebrows shot straight up when he recognized Chaz.

Chaz waved to him.

"Mr. Hucktabeeeeee," Jake yelled as he ran toward him. "Mommy knows about the secret."

"I know," Chaz said.

Jake put his hands on his hips. "Did you tell?"

"No. Not until we were supposed to."

"She likes it."

"We done good, didn't we?" Chaz said.

Jake tipped his head back, and then gave a giant nod. "Yeah!"

"I haven't seen you in a while," Chaz said to him. "I wasn't sure if you'd remember me."

"I've been on a trip," Jake said. "I'm home now."

Chaz nodded. "He seems fine," he whispered to Kasey. He held out his hand to Jake. "Put 'er there, partner."

Jake stuck his hand out and shook Chaz's hand.

"Good job," Chaz said.

Kasey had never seen her little man shake hands before. How sweet.

"Okay. I have to play with Shutterbug. She's lonely." Jake ran off, squealing as he ran in circles, enticing the puppy to chase him across the yard.

Chaz cuffed Scott's shoulder and gave Kasey a hug. "I'm not going to stay. I just wanted to deliver the treats and let you know how happy we are for you." Chaz hustled over to his truck, always in a hurry.

"He is the nicest man," Kasey said as she watched him leave and waved.

"Chaz is good people. We've got more than our fair share of nice people in this town."

"I'm beginning to see that."

"Speaking of nice," Scott said, "I'd like to invite you to brunch on Sunday."

"Brunch?"

"Yeah, I take Mom to brunch every Sunday after church. Mom thought it would be nice if I asked you to church with us. I don't want you to feel like you have to. I mean, I'd love it if you'd like to, but no pressure."

Kasey stood quietly for a moment, then looked over at Jake and back at Scott. "Church and brunch is perfect. Jake and I used to go to church every Sunday with Nick. I haven't been since. It's perfect timing. Yes. Thank you."

"Really?" His grin made the wrinkles on the sides of his eyes more pronounced. "Mom and I will pick y'all up at nine on Sunday."

Sunday morning, Scott walked into church with his mom on one arm and Kasey on the other. Jake ran alongside them, holding Kasey's hand.

"Mommy," Jake said in a loud whisper.

They slid into the fourth pew, and Kasey helped Jake up into the seat between her and Scott.

He leaned forward. "This is God's house," Jake said to Scott and Mrs. Calvin.

"That's right," Scott said.

Kasey handed Jake a hymnal and put a finger to her lips. It felt familiar for a moment, except that Nick wasn't here. Jake looked up, then twisted in the seat and climbed onto his knees.

"What are you looking for, sweetie?" Kasey asked. "Do you need to go to the bathroom?"

"No, ma'am. I went before we left." He scanned the church, craning his neck, then flopped back on the pew with his brows furrowed and lips puckered.

"What are you thinking?"

He folded his hands on the hymnal, then leaned forward to talk to Scott and Mrs. Calvin. "My daddy lives here with God. He's an angel." His eyes were wide, but his words slow and serious. "He might be sleeping because I think a lot of angels have to work at night."

Scott's mom mouthed, "He's so precious," to Kasey.

Kasey patted Jake's leg. "You are a smart boy."

Jake sat back in the seat. "I wanted to see Daddy."

Kasey brushed his bangs to the side. "Close your eyes. If you close your eyes and open your heart, you'll see Daddy. He's always right here."

She tapped his tiny chest. "In your heart. Looking after you."

Jake squeezed his eyes so tight that his cheeks bunched up and touched his thick black lashes. He held his hands together under his chin in prayer. Kasey watched him, wishing she could roll back time.

Jake's eyes flashed wide. He looked up at Kasey and grabbed her sleeve. "Mommy?"

"Yes?"

"Daddy says he loves us and he's glad we're here." Jake smiled and placed his hands in his lap. "He likes this church."

Kasey swallowed back tears. Scott passed her a handkerchief.

"I love you, Mommy." He raised his eyebrows. "Ten and five."

She took his hand in hers. "That's a bunch. I love you, too." Kasey put her finger to her lips and whispered, "Time to be quiet."

He nodded and sat still.

The sermon was about God giving us second chances when we ask for them—perfect for the day. The preacher's voice reverberated through the church, a kindness in his tone that felt like a warm blanket.

"Since those second chances take place in the parameters of the life we already have," he said, "second chances include baggage and ghosts of our past."

Kasey turned to Scott. He was looking at her. She smiled.

He reached over and held her hand.

After brunch, Scott dropped off his mother first.

"It was so nice to meet you," Kasey said to her, and gave her a hug.

"You're right down the street. If you need me to sit with Jake, don't you hesitate to ask. I'm old, but I love little boys." She put her hand on Scott's cheek. "I raised a pretty good one."

"You sure did." Kasey admired the tender relationship between Scott and his mom.

It was only a two-minute ride from her place to Kasey's house. Jake changed clothes and raced outside to play with Shutterbug. Kasey poured two glasses of tea, then she and Scott went outside to sit and watch them.

Jake ran over to her, looking serious. "Hey, Mommy? Do we have a ball to throw?"

"Hmmm. Let me see." Kasey pretended to match his serious look. "I *think* I saw one in the hall closet."

"Can I go look?"

"Sure." She watched him run into the house. "He knows this place better than I do."

A minute later Jake came out with the ball and a glossy white box with a big teal-blue bow on it. "Mommy, what's this present?"

"I forgot all about that. Bring it to Mommy."

She took the shiny wrapped gift from Jake and turned to Scott. "Cody gave me this when I left the tour. I never opened it." She shook the box. "I forgot all about it."

"Can I open it?" Jake asked.

"Sure. Here you go." She handed him the box.

He climbed up in one of the chairs and pulled on the ribbon, which captured his attention more than the idea of the gift. He jumped from the chair with the streamer, tempting Shutterbug to run after him.

"Can't get good help these days," Scott said, laughing.

Kasey peeled off the paper, crumpled it into a ball, then lifted the lid of the box. Inside was a note and a CD. "It's the original cut of '*A Mother's Love*'."

"He wrote that song about you and Jake, didn't he?"

"Yes. On the plane when we were on tour. In fact, I knew the melody well before I'd ever heard the song. He'd been working on it on the plane every night while I was reading. He played it live the last night I was on tour with them."

Her eyes met his. "That was in Raleigh. That's where Billy Goodwin saw the picture of Jake and heard about the kidnapping."

"Cody is a good friend." Scott smiled.

"He *is* a good friend. But it's not like our friendship," Kasey said. Her heart felt full.

He reached across the table, and she laid her head on his arm.

Scott stood. "Come walk with me."

She popped back up. "Okay."

He took her hand and led her to the side of the house.

"Mommy? Where you goin'? Can I come?"

"Sure. Bring Shutterbug," Scott said.

Jake and Shutterbug caught up just as the big oak tree came into view. The tree was similar to the one that Nick was buried under: strong and tall, with one long, low branch. Two fat ropes hung from the limb with a red, white, and blue wooden seat.

"You made the swing." She took both of Scott's hands in hers. "You are the most thoughtful man in the world."

"You like it?"

"It's like that one I saw in the magazine that day at your house. I love it."

"A swing! Cool!" Jake ran up and jumped in the seat. "Push me."

Scott pushed while Kasey smiled and clapped. Jake soared higher and higher. Fearless.

The swing slowed and Jake leapt to the ground. "That was fun."

Scott caught the seat mid-air and bent down beside it. "Come here, Jake's mom."

Kasey gave him a what-the-heck-are-you-doing look but stepped up to the swing.

He put his hands on the edge of the swing. "Someday. When the time is right." He tipped the seat of the swing up, the bottom facing her. Painted in bright red letters:

SOMEDAY . . .
Will you be my bride? Yes ___ Maybe ___

Kasey tilted her head. "Hedging your bets a little there, aren't you?"

"What?"

"Yes or maybe? I take it you won't take no for an answer."

"Whoops. Sorry. Turtle Mike and Maggie did the editing, they must have missed that." He put the seat back down and patted it, encouraging her to sit.

"Scott, you've been a true angel in my life."

"You are the angel." He leaned forward, brushing her lips. "I love you, Kasey Phillips. I want you and Jake to be a part of my life always, and in all ways."

The words poured like melted chocolate over her heart, sweet and warm. Tears trickled down her cheeks.

She missed Nick. Her heart broke every day without him, but there was a feeling when Scott said those words. A feeling of joy that her body recognized before she did.

She put her hand on top of his. "My head isn't

ready for this, but my heart feels it. Something. Someday . . . when I am . . ."

"I'll be here. Waiting."

"It might be a month. It might be five years. I can't make any promises. But I can't imagine sharing my heart with anyone but you. My life has been out of focus this past year. It's starting to become clear again, thanks to you."

This must be what joy feels like.

"Is that a maybe?" His mood seemed buoyant. He glanced over and smiled at Jake and Shutterbug, running through the yard.

"It's not a no. So much has happened, I've put off dealing with most of it. But if you can be patient with me . . ."

"I'm not going anywhere." He gently pressed his hand to her cheek, kissed the tip of her nose, then pulled her close. "We'll take it a day at a time."

Acknowledgments

Special thanks to the team of folks that helped me on the journey to bring this story to the finish line.

From beta readers and cover art input to copy and line edits, these folks are the best of the best. Thank you to Jerry Hampton, Tracy Mastaler, Barry Ergang, and so many other special friends including all the Facebook friends that gave feedback on the cover as we made final decisions.

To my family, thank you for believing in me and for spreading the word. Mom, thank you for your unwavering support through every up and down as I live this dream.

About the Author

Nancy Naigle writes love stories from the cross-roads of small town and suspense. *Out of Focus* is the second novel in her contemporary romance series set in Adams Grove. When she isn't writing, she enjoys antiquing, cooking, and spa days with her friends.

A native of Virginia, Nancy now calls North Carolina home.

Center Point Large Print
600 Brooks Road / PO Box 1
Thorndike, ME 04986-0001 USA

(207) 568-3717

US & Canada:
1 800 929-9108
www.centerpointlargeprint.com